AN ARTFUL MURDER

An absolutely gripping crime thriller

JUDI DAYKIN

DS Sara Hirst Book 4

Joffe Books, London
www.joffebooks.com

First published in Great Britain in 2022

Cover art by Dee Dee Book Covers

ISBN: 978-1-80405-400-0

Fear no more the heat o' the sun,
Nor the furious winter's rages;
Thou thy worldly task hast done,
Home art gone, and ta'en thy wages:
Golden lads and girls all must,
As chimney-sweepers, come to dust.

William Shakespeare, *Cymbeline*

AUTHOR'S NOTE

It has been my great delight to call Norfolk my home for the last forty years. As with all regions, we have our own way of doing and saying things here. The accent is lyrical and open, just like the countryside and skies. If you would like to pronounce some of the real place names in this book like a local, the following may help:

Happisburgh = Haze-bruh
Wymondham = Wind-am
Barnham = Barn-um
Norwich hides its 'w'

The universities and the SCVA are all real places. The habit of using part of the name or the capital letters of the places mentioned interchangeably is engrained with locals. For the sake of clarity this is what we mean:

UEA = University of East Anglia, sometimes just 'the university'
SCVA = Sainsbury Centre for the Visual Arts, sometimes just the Sainsbury Centre

CRU = Climatic Research Unit, sometimes said as
a single word, as in 'crew'
NUA = Norwich University of the Arts

The SCVA has a wonderful collection of both modern
art and ethnographic artefacts. The paintings and items mentioned in the story are all (usually) on display, apart from the
Alec Clifton Urn, which is fictional. I undertook my MA in
creative writing at the UEA and am proud to be an alumni
of such a famous course.

PROLOGUE

It was just after 6.30 p.m. on a miserable midwinter evening, and raining hard. The heavy clouds were obscuring any chance of moonlight. The wind drove the water into sheets, which swirled across the farmland in hammering waves. The road was greasy with diesel oil. There were no street lights on such a minor road this far out of the city. The driver had chosen well.

A small black car stood in the gateway to the field, invisible behind the untrimmed hedges on either side. From the driver's seat, it was possible to watch the headlights of the few vehicles that used this narrow lane as a rat run to escape the post-work traffic, but only if you knew what you were doing. At irregular intervals, commuters turned down the lane towards the one tiny village that lay a couple of miles past the car. Beyond that, a tangle of minor roads eventually led to Wymondham. The number of vehicles diminished as the driver waited patiently.

The evening had been carefully chosen, just like the location. The weather forecast had been checked and checked again. The route the cyclist took home had been divined by following and overtaking at different points. It had taken a great deal of planning. There would be only one chance.

Knowing the cyclist lived in the tiny village of Brampton, still with his parents, had been a bonus.

The driver snorted in disgust. The idiot was still living at home, spending all his income on racing bikes, stupid Lycra outfits and travelling to these triathlon events. Not for much longer.

The headlights of a late car swung in an arc at the top of the lane, hopefully overtaking the cyclist the driver was waiting for. It had to be the right rider — this was the same time he passed here every Tuesday night. The engine turned over comfortably. It idled in first gear the clutch depressed in anticipation.

The bike's front light zigzagged a little as the rider adjusted for the passing draft of the car and the buffeting of the wind. The waiting driver wound the window down, listening for the sound of the vehicle diminishing and the swish of bike tyres approaching. It was hard, though not impossible, to hear both through the miserable weather. Besides, the cyclist was loudly cursing the overtaking driver, shouting his anger into the wind.

Oh, yes. This was the right man. The voice was all too familiar.

Double-checking that they were alone in the lane, the time had finally come. As the bike's light flickered through the hedge, the driver engaged the clutch and depressed the accelerator hard. The car shot out of its hiding place. It clipped the front wheel of the bike, spinning it away towards the opposite hedge. Metal screeched on metal. The volume was shocking.

With a deep-throated scream, the cyclist smashed into the tangle of branches. The wind pounded rain into the driver's face through the open window as they drove on towards the village without waiting, rounding the next corner before flicking on the headlights.

Damn! The impact had been a fraction too early. The damage to the cyclist might not have been enough.

The driver swung the car around and accelerated back to the cyclist, who stood swaying in the middle of the lane.

Shaking his head and staggering, the rider held up his hand to flag the car down. Instead, headlights on full, the vehicle gathered speed.

This time there was no mistake. This impact sounded more shocking than the first, the crunch of bones piercing the squall.

The car halted a few yards further on. A glance in the rear-view mirror confirmed that the cyclist was lying motionless on the tarmac.

The driver wound up the window. Now the job was done.

CHAPTER 1

At the sound of a cake tin being opened, Detective Sergeant Sara Hirst leaned back in her chair and stretched her arms over her head. She didn't bother to silence her yawn. The mid-week blues and the rain outside had combined to make the morning dreary. Nothing had happened for the Serious Crimes Unit team to investigate for weeks. The last outing of note had been their participation in a county lines drug swoop, organised by the National Crime Agency and run across eleven counties. Despite this, she still thought that her move to the Norfolk Constabulary had been her best decision for years. Wild horses couldn't drag her back to her old job in the Met.

Of course, Sara kept her connections with her home city. Hard not to when her mother still lived and worked in Tower Hamlets. Jamaican-born Tegan ran a specialist hairdresser, which Sara regularly visited to keep her braids neat. It gave her an excuse to keep an eye on her mum.

'Might have known it was you.' She smiled at her colleague DC Mike Bowen. 'As if you don't get enough of Aggie's cakes at home.'

Bowen's hand paused in the tin. He and Sara had history when it came to banter. They hadn't always got on. During her first months in the team, she'd considered him an unreconstructed male chauvinist and had told him so. Although that was a long time ago, Sara still wasn't always sure he knew when she was teasing him, or vice versa.

Bowen narrowed his eyes. 'Keep it down, Sarge. No one is supposed to know.'

'Worst kept secret in the nick, mate.' Sara grinned. 'Everyone knows. What's the flavour today?'

'Carrot cake,' he said through a mouthful of crumbs. 'I'll put the coffee on.'

'Is it common knowledge, then?' Aggie, their civilian admin, asked while Bowen headed off to fetch water for the machine. She pulled the hand-knitted cardigan tightly around her generous waist. April was still too cold for Aggie's liking.

Sara carefully selected a piece of cake and placed it on a tissue on her desk. She'd eat it when the coffee was ready. 'Pretty much. It isn't a problem, surely?'

'Mike thought that the bosses might not like it.' Aggie fiddled with her computer mouse, her fingers twitching the central wheel so that her screen scrolled up and down. She sounded embarrassed. 'Besides, at our age.'

'Nobody else's business,' said Sara. 'As long as you two are happy.'

'I never expected to find a new chap.' Aggie looked down at her ample figure, then, letting go of the mouse, fiddled for a moment with her hair. 'I thought those days were over for me.'

'Did it worry you?'

'Maybe a little bit,' sighed Aggie. 'You just get used to being on your own. And baking is my only skill.'

'Hardly!' Sara thought of Aggie's facility with the internet and the police databases. 'Aggie, I don't think you're breaking any workplace rules. But why don't you ask someone in personnel, if it bothers you so much?'

Aggie hesitated. 'If we are — breaking the rules, I mean — then if we asked, it would be out in the open. I can't afford to lose my job, and Mike is still three years away from his pension.'

Bowen had divorced years ago and had been a bachelor ever since. Aggie was a widow with a grown-up son who lived somewhere in Manchester. Both were in their early fifties and single. Sara didn't see how that could cause an issue for the force, but there were some arcane rules that had never been rescinded, just like some old-fashioned laws.

She nodded in sympathy with Aggie. Life as a police officer could be complicated on a personal level. For Sara, it was more than a job. It wasn't just about the wages. She knew she was lucky, in as much as she already owned a home, a pretty terraced cottage in the coastal village of Happisburgh, left to her by her father in his will. Searching for her absent cockney dad had cost Sara in a lot of ways. Finding out that he had been a decent copper and a well-liked member of his adopted community in Norfolk had changed her attitude towards him. These days, she was proud of her mixed heritage, not to mention following in his footsteps career-wise. She was coming to love living in Norfolk as much as he had.

'What about your boyfriend?' Aggie was moving into mother hen mode. Sara recognised the vibe. She got it from her mother too. *If I'm happy in love, you have to be happy too, which means a partner in your life.* 'You don't mention him much these days.'

Although her boss, DI Edwards, knew, Sara had not told anyone else at work that Chris had proposed to her the previous summer. She had turned him down, saying she wasn't ready for the commitment and wanted to carry on as before. To her considerable surprise, Chris had agreed to this.

'He's in yet another play,' said Sara, unable to keep the low-level annoyance out of her voice. 'Another Shakespeare thing. He's grown this little goatee for it.'

'Sounds ravishing,' said Aggie. 'Does it suit him?'

Sara nodded. Even if his beards came and went as the acting parts at the Maddermarket Theatre demanded it, Chris was a handsome man.

'I thought you liked seeing him in these shows.'

'I do. It just takes up so much of his time, and we don't get to see much of each other.'

'Whereas Mike and I see each other every day of the week.' Aggie shrugged. 'Sometimes you can get too much of a good thing.'

The office door swung open. Mike carried the coffee jug to the percolator, speaking over his shoulder to the other two members of the team following him in. 'No joy, then?'

'Waste of time,' said DI Edwards. 'These things usually are.' He dumped his coat in his office and came back to sit in the main room.

The percolator glugged as everyone selected and munched on their carrot cake.

'I hate these jobs,' Edwards said between mouthfuls. 'We can't prove anything if we can't get the evidence, which is inside these buggers' houses or businesses. We can't get a warrant to search because we don't have enough suspicious circumstances to merit one yet.'

The team was currently trying to find evidence against a car reselling racket. Stolen vehicles were being taken to one of a group of garages, where all identifying markings were removed or changed. They were then sold, often at the roadside, to make it look like a private deal. Edwards and DC Noble, the youngest team member, had been trying to interview a suspect.

Noble flopped into his chair and ran his fingers through his hair. Sara was tall by most standards, but Noble was taller than she was. He was thin, with long legs and arms that looked almost overstretched. 'He looked shifty, though. Kept biting his lip.'

'I know.' Edwards nodded at Noble. 'Your observation skills are coming along nicely. Notice anything else?'

Before Noble could answer, the phone in Edwards's office rang. Bowen doled out mugs of coffee as they listened through the open door.

'I see.' Edwards reached for a pen and began to scribble on a notepad. 'When was this?'

'Looks like something new,' suggested Sara. She popped some carrot cake into her mouth.

'Who's been alerted so far? Forensics? Pathologist?' Edwards scribbled the answers furiously. 'Tell them not to touch anything until the teams arrive. Especially the body. We're on our way.'

Sara forced hot coffee down her throat to clear the cake crumbs. It sounded as if something interesting might be happening at last.

CHAPTER 2

Of the few things in her life that Rose Crawford still managed to be grateful for, living in an out-of-the-way country cottage was one of them. It was larger inside than it appeared from the lane that ran past the two semi-detached homes. The pair stood down a twenty-metre bumpy dirt track, with small gardens guarding their privacy at the front and larger gardens at the back. A small copse shielded the rear, and high hedges prevented the neighbours or farmworkers in the field beyond from looking in. Rose hadn't been much of a gardener when she and her husband had bought the cottage soon after their marriage. She had been forced to learn when he had become too ill to deal with it himself.

It was one of those April mornings when the sun first breaks through with the promise of better weather, and it seems to most people that the dark of winter is finally being driven out. Not to Rose. She was angrily cutting back the spent daffodils that had grown through the lawn and across the borders. She threw the browning heads and floppy leaves into the plastic waste carrier next to where she was kneeling. 'Bugger those gardening experts,' she muttered. Pulling a clump of greenery tight into her fist, she snipped at the bases until they were all cut away. 'I don't care if I'm doing it wrong.'

Another fistful of rubbish hit the pile, and she sat back on her heels to survey the work still to be done. With a deep and resentful sigh, she struggled to stand up, stretching her back out to ease the ache settling just above her hips. Being tall and well built, she had begun to have trouble with her back during her menopause. Not to mention the searing hot flushes, uncontrollable temper outbursts and lack of sleep that had sent her to the doctor's for HRT within weeks of the symptoms setting in. Another mercy Rose was prepared to acknowledge was that the tablets had cured most of her symptoms in days, and five years later, she still took the things religiously every day.

Peeling off her gardening gloves, she dropped them and the secateurs on top of the waste. 'To hell with it.' She turned and headed to the kitchen. 'I need a break. Don't know why I started with this. There's so much to do.'

The kitchen was part of a modern addition at the rear of the eighteenth-century cottage. Despite being done in the 1970s, it was reasonably tasteful and well constructed. Large enough to house an old pine farmhouse table with ample room to walk around it and still cook a meal for ten, the kitchen took up one half of the new extension. On the far side, the other half housed a small utility room and her husband's study. In between was a conservatory with a seating area and a glass roof. The place was too big for her, now that she was on her own. Not that she had any intention of giving it up.

Following her ritual, Rose put a pot of fresh leaf tea on the table, carefully stacking a pile of work papers to one side, so she didn't spill anything on them. She had brought them home to cover up something she'd done wrong recently. If asked, she would blame it on menopause brain. God, it was awful being a 'woman of a certain age', even when you worked at a supposedly enlightened place like the University of East Anglia.

They'll never know, she thought, looking at the half-dozen buff-coloured files. *Most of them have no idea what I do all day anyway.*

With a sneer at the thought of the staff she worked for, Rose poured her tea using a strainer. She should have been at her desk this morning. Using her current circumstances as an excuse yet again, she had called in sick. Rose would have left the department a year ago when her daughter had died if she didn't need the generous salary. The job also served another useful purpose, though she hated the place, with its pretentious attitudes.

Her boss, Professor Chandler, had surprised her. When she'd tried to return to work after the funeral, he had guided her into his little glass cubicle of an office in the Sainsbury Centre and had sat her down on the sofa he used to hold informal tutorials.

'I can't imagine what you must be going through,' he had said, tucking his long legs out of the way, so he didn't crowd her. 'Your losses have been extraordinary, and you must take all the time you need to recover.'

He had given her an insipid cup of coffee, patted her hand and waited for her to cry. She hadn't. Chandler had fixed a look of empathetic concern on his fifty-something face, his straggly beard scrunched up. With his smart-casual clothes and fashionably frameless glasses, he looked the parody of a university lecturer. Rose despised him and all that he stood for. She had waited, careful to keep her face in neutral.

'Look, anytime you feel unable to come in, just leave me a message on the machine. Let's have a phrase or word you can use.'

He had pondered, gazing at the metal ceiling, chewing his lip. Rose had waited passively, although she'd been seething inside. He had turned the whole situation into a game. Intending to be kind, he had in fact been being self-indulgent, because he didn't know what to do or say to her. This was about making him feel better, not Rose. God, how she hated the man.

'Just leave a message saying, "black dog day",' he had suggested.

Rose had nearly snorted her coffee. 'Churchill or Led Zeppelin?'

Chandler had smiled at this. 'Yes, too obvious. Never was fond of Led Zeppelin myself. How about an "Eeyore day", then?'

She hadn't had the energy to continue with the conversation, so "Eeyore days" they had become. Truthfully, Rose had ached all over when her alarm had shocked her awake this morning. It had been a long and difficult night, with little sleep. She hadn't expected that. She had expected to feel better after getting that evidence away from work yesterday evening. But it hadn't brought the respite Rose had yearned for. So, today was an Eeyore day.

There were so many things to be done. After her break, a small garden fire would make her feel better. There were some old clothes that needed getting rid of. Rose could as easily burn them as take them to the recycling bins in the village. They were waiting in a plastic carrier bag near the back door.

Aiden, a local handyman-gardener who came in to help her two mornings a week, had left a pile of dead twigs and leaves in the compost area ready for the next bonfire. It would be simple enough to start.

She put the tray with the delicate bone china tea service for one on the work surface near the sink. Collecting the buff folders and the bag of old clothes, Rose headed to the bottom of the garden to get rid of the evidence.

CHAPTER 3

The village of Barnham Parva was hidden away in the lanes between the A47 and the A11. It was only five miles from the Norfolk Police's Wymondham HQ, so close that Edwards had no time to explain to Sara what they were attending for as he concentrated on the narrow road. They arrived in a matter of minutes.

Barnham Parva New Hall was anything but new. Sara was becoming used to the idiosyncrasies of rural existence and assumed this brick-built Elizabethan-looking building was simply newer than the one it had replaced centuries ago. It stood at the end of the long gravel drive, which ran downhill from the village road. A large expanse of manicured lawn was dotted with ancient trees and those expensive Lutyens benches she had seen in the garden centre. An elderly couple stood in the deep, stone-built entrance, watching the activity in front of them with obvious dismay.

Blue-and-white tape had been stretched between the line of trees at the entrance to the drive. A uniformed officer posted at the gate to log visitors in the crime scene book had directed Edwards and Sara to park immediately in front of the Hall. Bowen and Noble pulled in behind them. Forensic team vans and a shiny, dark-blue Jaguar were already there.

That belonged to the pathologist Dr Stephen Taylor, who had treated himself to the new car several months ago, much to the admiration of DI Edwards. White-suited forensic investigators huddled in conversation, pointing this way and that at the ground. The privacy tent stood in the middle of the lawn.

'That's bigger than the usual one,' said Sara. Edwards turned to see what she meant. This tent was twice the size and height of the ones normally used. The flaps at one end were fastened open.

'We'd better speak to the owners first,' Edwards replied. 'They look stunned.'

The man looked exactly like a country squire to Sara. His well-cut clothes bore all the hallmarks of an old-fashioned gentlemen's outfitters. Beige trousers, a check shirt, a mustard-coloured waistcoat — and was that a military tie? He looked like he had decided how he should dress in the 1950s and had never changed it since. His hair was fully white and slicked back on his skull, almost as if it was plastered down. Sara guessed he was in his seventies, but he looked fit for his age. His wife looked far more upset than he did. His arm was firmly wrapped around her shoulders as if he were supporting her.

Edwards introduced himself, proffering his warrant card as Sara did the same.

'James Gordon.' The man shook DI Edwards's hand and nodded at Sara. 'This is my wife, Paula.'

His wife turned worried eyes to Sara, bypassing Edwards completely. She began to shake. 'So horrible. It's all so horrible.'

James reached over and pressed her hand. 'Why don't you make the inspector and his sergeant a pot of coffee, my dear?'

'Yes, of course. Where are my manners? This way.' Paula turned her back on the garden and headed inside. Edwards nodded briefly at Sara to follow.

The door to Barnham Parva New Hall was made of ancient wood. The thickness of the timber made it look impregnable, although it moved with ease. Sara pushed it shut behind her.

'Victorian replica of the Jacobean original,' said Paula. The comment sounded well practised, something she was used to saying for visitors. It also sounded distant. When Sara turned, it seemed the woman had vanished.

Dark wooden dressers covered in pewter tankards and antique glasses lined the wide entrance hall. The flagstone floor was strewn with ancient-looking rugs. Though the walls were painted white, the space was still shadowy. A broad wooden staircase rose to one side, hinting at grand rooms upstairs.

Paula reappeared from the right of it. 'Sorry, I forget people don't know where the rooms are.' She waited until Sara joined her before turning along a wood-panelled corridor. 'Do you like coffee? Or would you prefer something else?'

'Coffee would be great. Thank you.'

The kitchen was as modern as the New Hall was ancient. Painted a cheerful yellow, with elegant fitted units and a large contemporary table surrounded by chairs, it was the sort of room Sara assumed only existed in trendy magazines.

'You look surprised,' said Paula.

As her host filled the kettle, Sara saw that she looked painfully thin. Her delicate hands looked almost see-through. Her clothes were simple and chic. No doubt they were also expensive.

'I am,' agreed Sara.

'Modern kitchen in a sixteenth-century house? Can't bear to be without a decent kitchen. It was my only condition when we bought the place.'

Paula sounded more confident as she bustled around, finding the cafetière and the grinder. Having something to do was obviously good for her. She smiled at Sara and pointed to the table. 'Do sit down, my dear.' She placed mugs and the freshly made coffee on the table before sitting opposite.

'Can you fill me in on what happened this morning?' Sara asked.

'Certainly. Although I haven't actually seen . . .' Paula paused. 'It was Stuart, you see.'

'Stuart?'

'This is such a big place.' Paula's hand gestured to the house around them. 'We can't manage it on our own. We have a live-in couple who help us. Sort of household staff, if you will. Although they are more like friends than staff.'

'Stuart is one of them?'

'Yes.' Paula rolled her eyes heavenwards. 'He had hysterics when he saw it. Not that I blame him. What a terrible thing to find. But he is prone to hysterics. Rich took him off to their quarters.'

'Rich?'

'Stuart's husband. They have a flat at the top of the house.'

Sara nodded. 'We will need to speak to them urgently.'

'They know, or at least I think they do. Anyway, Stuart came blundering in here sobbing. We couldn't make head nor tail of it, to begin with. Just kept saying that the lid was lying on the grass, and it shouldn't be. He was perfectly right about that.'

'Lid?'

'You haven't been told anything, have you?' asked Paula. She smiled and plunged the handle on the cafetière. 'It's the Alec Clifton funerary urn.'

Sara frowned. What on earth was that? A memorial of some sort? Or some old grave marker?

'Such a talented young artist,' said Paula. 'We first saw his work when we were still in London, at an ICA ceramics exhibition. After we moved here, it seemed such an obvious choice for the lawn, being weatherproof and so on. Such a wonderful statement piece.'

Sara felt as if the world had shifted slightly off its axis. Paula smiled at her, as though she took it for granted that Sara knew what the hell she was talking about. Pulling out her pad, she began to scribble notes.

'Naturally, it isn't intended to be anything other than a work of art,' said Paula. 'Nor should it be allowed to fill with water, hence the lid. In fact, you can't open the lid if you don't know how. There's a locking mechanism. It's very clever.'

'You said the lid had been removed?'

Paula lost her smile, and worry filled her face again. 'It was lying on the grass next to the urn. Someone had opened the piece and used it in the manner its name suggests, but for which it was never actually intended.'

'For a funeral? What did Stuart find inside?'

'The body of a young man. And it wasn't there when we went to bed, I can assure you of that.'

CHAPTER 4

Dom Wilkins's office was on the top floor of the Lower Common Room building, at the end of the Street on the University of East Anglia campus. Built during the 1960s, the campus was a Brutalist architect's wet dream. In practice, this meant that the concrete-and-glass construction looked interesting in good weather and drearily depressing when it rained.

Unfortunately, it was raining this morning. Dom checked his online diary and email inbox. There were a couple of new assistance application forms to go through before he headed off to meet with a professor in the "teaching wall" who was worried about a student's mental health. A fairly normal day for April. The students had just returned for the summer term after the Easter break. As a student disability advisor, most of his clients were settled in now, and only the potential pressure of exams might bring a spike in workload. It would ramp up again come the autumn with the new student intake. Dom intended to make the most of the few weeks of slack time.

For some reason, the flesh above his prosthetic leg was itching today. He scratched at it, the fingers of his good hand failing to make much difference through the fabric of his expensive jeans. It was no good. He would have to get at it by dropping his trousers. He selected a tube of cream from his desk drawer, checked he had his wallet in his back pocket and picked up his reusable coffee cup.

The toilets on this floor were suitable for disabled use, as you would expect in this department. Locking the door, Dom relieved himself and then his itch with the cream. Making himself respectable, he glanced in the mirror to make sure he hadn't missed anything. He washed his hands and dragged his wet fingers through his mop of blond hair to make it look a little spikey. He'd been up late this morning and hadn't had time to gel his hair as he usually did. He looked at his reflection with a smile.

The amputation of his left leg below the knee five years ago had been an appalling blow at the time. Now Dom knew it had opened doors for him that might otherwise have never been available. For one thing, he hadn't known what to do with his economics degree apart from being an accountant. Far too boring. He had taken a dull job in the UEA's administration team to finance his sporting ambitions.

The car accident had seemed to put a stop to everything. As well as his left leg, his left arm had been damaged, leaving him with issues from the wrist downwards. The hand and fingers, which looked unharmed, would never move properly again. There was only modest sensation or feeling in them. He'd learned to live with the fear of accidentally hurting himself without realising.

Who would have thought such an awful situation would be the making of him? Now he had exactly the right job, helping other disabled people navigate their adult education and the support that was available to them. Dom could guide them from personal experience. Within a year of the worst day of his life, he was back to his sport, making the most of being a parathlete. Over the last three seasons, he had made so much progress that he was a national champion in his category and in line to go to the next Paralympics.

He liked to think of his prosthetic leg as his best-kept secret. Unless he wore shorts, as he did when racing, it was hard to tell it was there. He wore identical shoes and there was no limp in his walk, except when he had overdone the training, like today. Dom was sure it was staying too long at the track last night that had made his amputation scar itchy.

With a cocky wink at his handsome face, Dom headed to the café on the Street. He was queuing for his coffee and sugar fix when his mobile rang. He paid for his doughnut and fished the mobile out of his pocket. *Taryn Deacon.* Dom hadn't spoken to her in days.

'Good morning,' he said. It was a good day, and Taryn wasn't going to be allowed to spoil it, no matter how excessively worried she was over some triviality or other.

'Dom, are you at work today?'

'Of course.'

'Can you come down to my office? I've just heard this rumour, and you ought to know.'

Dom grimaced. She was in panic mode again. 'I've got a meeting at eleven at the School of History. Can I pop down after that?'

'Can't you come now, before your appointment?'

'Is it that urgent?'

'I'm not sure.' Her voice wobbled a little. 'That's why I wanted to talk to you.'

'All right.' He took the reusable coffee mug and levered the rubbery top securely on. 'I'll be there in a few minutes.'

He bought another doughnut, then tucked the bag into his jacket pocket. Dom went down the lesser-used staircase that led to the service road behind the Street. It was the quickest route to the Sainsbury Centre, where Taryn was one of the exhibition curators.

She was hovering by the glass doors at the entrance waiting for him. Her face was even paler than usual, the fringe of her dyed-black hair emphasising her lack of colour. The lacy hem of her gothic corset dress fluttered around her legs in the breeze of the door opening. Doc Marten boots in black patent leather completed the outfit.

'Thank you,' she said quietly.

He followed her into the office she shared with another curator. The man was absent, so Dom flopped down into his vacant chair. Taryn pulled the door carefully closed, then began to pace up and down the small space. She had to step around stacks of art reference books and piles of files to do it.

They had been friends since university, when they'd met as part of the Rock Music Society, sharing a taste for live gigs and alcohol, even if they differed in which bands they followed. For a while, Dom and Taryn had been an item. It hadn't lasted, but when he'd been in hospital, she had been the one to visit regularly and listen to his woes.

Dom pulled the doughnuts out of his pocket and plonked them on the desk. 'Here. Eat one. You look like you need it.'

Taryn shook her head, then looked longingly at the sugary lump.

'Oh, go on,' Dom urged. 'One won't hurt you. What is it?'

She took one of the squashed doughnuts and sat at her desk. 'It's Joe,' she said. 'He's disappeared.'

'Not the famous Joe Summerhill?' Dom sounded amused. 'Winner of the largest research grant this year?'

'Yes. Our Joe. He hasn't been seen since Sunday. I tried calling him loads of times. There's been no reply. Now I can't get through at all.'

'And this rumour?'

'Someone's found a body out at Barnham Parva New Hall. What if it's him?'

CHAPTER 5

The coffee had gone cold by the time Paula Gordon had explained their art collection to Sara. Far from being a country squire, James Gordon had been a city financier with a taste for contemporary art. He was a knowledgeable and avid collector, with purchases going back over thirty years.

'We wanted to retire to the country,' said Paula. 'James has family up here, so when this house came on the market, we thought it was perfect.'

She had led Sara on a grand tour of the downstairs rooms, pointing out various paintings and sculptures as she went. Some were by people so famous even Sara had heard of them, and she had no interest in the subject at all.

'We buy from galleries, exhibitions and auctions. Depends what takes our fancy. Always British artists, though. James insists on that.'

Sara wondered what kind of income and investments the couple must have had to create a collection of this prestige. The one thing she knew about art was that it was highly expensive. 'Your insurance bill must be huge,' she commented, as Paula showed her a small Lucien Freud portrait.

'It is. Our security systems are pretty good too. The insurers insist on that.'

'CCTV?'

'Of course.' Paula took her into a room at the rear of the house. It was small and packed with computers, screens for camera feeds that seemed to cover every conceivable angle, and panels of winking lights for fire or security breaches.

'This covers the grounds too?'

'You would have to ask my husband or Rich,' said Paula. 'It's part of Rich's job to monitor it and do the backups.'

Sara looked at the six screens that stood neatly on a long shelf along one wall. At least two of them appeared to show garden views, including a clear picture of the investigation circus unfolding on the front lawn. The views changed on a regular rotation, providing good coverage of the outside of the house.

'Do you have much artwork in the garden?'

'Several pieces of note. Most of them from up-and-coming artists, apart from the Barbara Hepworth. That's in the white room.'

'Is that an outbuilding?'

'At the side and back of the house, the garden is laid out in several "rooms", as they call them.' Paula pointed as one of the screens flickered and changed viewpoint. 'The white room has only white-flowering plants, and the Hepworth is in the centre. Naturally, it has its own security markers.'

'I'd like to see that,' said Sara — if only to work out why it was so special, given that it looked like a large lump of metal with a hole in the middle. She jotted the artist's name into her notebook. The camera overlooking the front garden switched viewpoints, and she saw Dr Taylor waving DI Edwards over. 'I'd better go and see what they've found.'

'I'll sort out some more refreshments.' Paula vanished down the panelled corridor and Sara let herself out of the front door. James Gordon had disappeared. Perhaps it was all too much for him.

Pulling protective clothing from a pile on the driveway, Sara went to join the others. Forensics had laid stepping plates out on the lawn, which Sara was careful to use. No point in antagonising them. She was the last to get inside the tent, which was busy despite being larger than normal.

The sculpture stood in the middle of the tent on a two-tier stone plinth. Made of layers of terracotta, it rose in several bands of material to form the shape of a giant vase. There was an inward-turning lip at the top with a small section cut away. The urn itself was at least five feet high, and with the addition of the platform, Sara thought it must be getting on for six feet to the lip. Presumably, this was where the lid should have been fitted. It lay on the grass next to the urn and had the only decoration, some form of hieroglyphs in a dense spiral. A crack ran across the surface. The urn seemed to be glazed, although there was a patina of weathering on the outside surface. God knows how much the thing weighed.

Dr Taylor was standing on a short pair of steps so that his waist was level with the top of the urn. DI Edwards stood next to him, looking over the rim to where Taylor was pointing. The two DCs stood opposite. Bowen, being shorter than Noble, was straining on tiptoe to see inside. Noble was turning pale.

Don't throw up in the bloody urn, Sara thought, watching him try to step back. Forensic officers were impeding him. One was packing up the specialist camera kit, while another was logging evidence bags. A short woman in a white suit was working at a temporary table, putting items into a plastic crate for removal to the lab.

Taylor looked up as Sara entered and nodded in greeting. He pulled up his mask to speak. 'IC1 male,' he began. 'Early to mid-thirties. Dumped in here while still alive, though I doubt if he was conscious.'

Sara stood next to Edwards and peered into the urn. The contorted body of a well-built young man with brown hair lay inside.

He must have been pushed in bottom first. His hips had jammed in the tapering shape, causing his legs to point upwards against one side of the urn. His back was supported by the inside wall on the other. His arms were pulled in front of him while his head lolled sideways, eyes wide open. There was a long gash on the front of his neck. Blood had poured from it down his chest, soaking the front of his shirt so much that it would have been impossible to tell the colour of it except for the cuffs. A ragged smear of blood on the inside of the urn looked to have come from a wound on the back of his head. From the smell, it seemed that he had evacuated his bowels.

Sara stepped back, for once in sympathy with Noble. The combination of the old blood, bowel contents and rainwater had created a revolting stink.

Dr Taylor glanced at her without acknowledging her reaction. 'We'll get him out when we can,' he said. 'I'd like to take the urn as well.'

'You'll need to be careful with it, Doctor Taylor.' Sara tapped the side of the artwork, which thudded dully. 'It's worth rather a lot of money.'

'How do you know?'

'Mrs Gordon has been telling me all about their art collection. This one has a current valuation of thirty-five to forty thousand pounds. You'll need specialist help to move it, she says.'

'In any event, it will need a full examination and cleaning out in the future.'

'It's going to smell for ages.' Bowen wrinkled his nose. 'Good job it's outside.'

Dr Taylor glared at Bowen before he continued. 'Our victim is still in full rigor mortis, so it will be a while before we can lift him safely. However, that does indicate that he has been in here eight or more hours.'

'You say the poor sod was alive when he went in there?' DI Edwards asked.

'That seems most likely.' Dr Taylor pointed to the position of the body. 'He would have been very heavy and messy to lift if he was already dead. Cause of death is obvious. Sharp blade to the throat, followed by exsanguination.'

Sara heard Noble rapidly brushing past the tent flap and striding off, taking raspy deep breaths as he went. Bowen watched him go, then caught Sara's eye and shrugged. 'You think he was awake long enough to crap himself?' He was never one for subtle words.

Dr Taylor shook his head. 'Not necessarily. It's not uncommon for a body to evacuate from all orifices immediately after death, even when someone dies peacefully in their bed. Given the stress of the position, that might have happened here.'

Steeling herself to look again, Sara peered into the urn. She couldn't see any personal effects at all with the body. 'No mobile, no wallet, no keys. Nothing?'

Taylor shook his head.

'That's going to make identifying him interesting.'

'That's not quite true,' said Dr Taylor. He climbed off his little steps and walked round to the table where the investigator was packing items for the lab. He reached into one of the crates and held a bag aloft. 'There's this.'

It seemed to be a toy animal. There were four long legs and a long neck, with a pointed tail, long muzzle and a pair of erect ears. Sara couldn't see it clearly enough to decide what it was made of, but it looked beige.

'What the hell is that?' asked Edwards.

'At this moment, my best estimate is that it's a toy llama.'

CHAPTER 6

James Gordon had reappeared and initially taken the team into the kitchen. DC Noble still looked green as the man offered them drinks, which they all declined, wanting to get on with what they could. The couple looked shaken, although they seemed willing enough to help.

'You say Rich looks after the CCTV?' asked the DI. 'Could you show DC Bowen and DC Noble what you have and give us copies?'

'No problem,' said James. 'I'll take you to our surveillance room, and my wife will find Rich.'

'We also need to talk to Stuart.'

'You might find he's more comfortable in his own quarters,' said Paula. 'This way.'

James led Edwards and Sara up the wide ornamental staircase. Paula strode ahead while the two DCs waited downstairs. Walking the length of the house on the first-floor corridor, they went past at least ten doors. Sara counted them off as she brought up the rear, assuming they must all be bedrooms. They reached a less obvious door, painted and wallpapered to match the end wall. James knocked and almost immediately a handsome, trim man in his forties answered the door. Behind him, another set of stairs, smaller and more functional, turned out of sight.

'Ah, Rich,' said James. 'Let me introduce you.'

Formalities over, Edwards stepped forward. 'We'd like to speak to your husband about what he saw this morning.'

Rich hesitated, glancing back up the stairs. 'Stu is still in a bit of a state. Perhaps I ought to be with him.'

'We really need your expertise on the CCTV, along with Mr Gordon's input.'

'I could sit with Stu,' suggested Paula. She guided Rich by the shoulder. 'You go and sort out the computer with James. You're the only one that understands the thing properly.'

With a shake of the head at his wife's comment, James went back downstairs with the reluctant Rich. Paula led Sara and Edwards up to the next floor. Sara had never been in bona fide servants' quarters before. The contrast to the main house was significant. A narrow central corridor had little natural light, a low ceiling and several plain doors.

They followed Paula into a decent-sized sitting room with an open-plan kitchen at the far end. It was beautifully decorated with dark wallpaper covered in tiny flowers and birds on a trellis. Light streamed in through windows that started at floor level, growing in angular stages into the curve of the roof. Three soft sofas stood around a huge coffee table covered in glossy magazines and recipe books. A thin man lay on one of the sofas, propped up on a mountain of embroidered cushions. His arm was draped across his face in what Sara thought was a consciously theatrical pose. Hearing them, the man raised his hand a few inches and glanced at them through his long, slender fingers.

'Oh, Paula,' he said in a wavering voice. 'Who is this? I can't cope with visitors.'

'Well, you're going to have to cope with these.' Paula tapped Stuart's leg gently and indicated another of the sofas, encouraging Sara and Edwards to sit down. 'Come on, Stuart. You're a witness, and these are the detectives.'

Stuart groaned again. 'I couldn't possibly.'

Sara felt Edwards bristle at Stuart's obvious grandstanding. She got in before, as he would put it, he started 'getting northern' with the man. 'We're so sorry to disturb you, Mr, er—'

'Stuart Read.'

'Thank you, Mr Read. I believe you were the person who found the unfortunate young man this morning?'

With a heavy sigh, Stuart sat up on the sofa. He was shorter than Sara expected from seeing him lying down. He would have had trouble looking inside the urn.

'Can you tell us what happened?'

When Stuart shuddered, Sara shot a warning look at Edwards. These days, he usually left the more vulnerable interviewees to her.

'I can understand that it must have been a traumatising thing to have witnessed,' she continued. 'The truth is, if we are to have any chance of catching this killer, these first few hours are vital.'

Stuart chewed his lip. 'I'm a key witness?'

'Of course.' So, he wanted to be the centre of attention, did he? Not as vulnerable as he was making out, but easy enough to encourage. 'Essential,' she added.

Stuart sat up straighter. 'Rich usually helps with the gardens and the security stuff. I do the food, help with the admin and around the house.'

'Stuart is wonderful,' said Paula. Obviously, she also found the best way to deal with Stuart was to butter him up. 'He's a godsend. Don't know how I'd manage without him.'

'Not really,' said Stuart, his smile betraying his false modesty.

'You were out in the garden this morning?'

'I went downstairs to check on breakfast. I'd made fresh croissants. Are there any left, Paula?' He waved his long fingers in Sara's direction. 'This lady might like to try one.'

'I'm sure I would later on,' she replied. 'What made you go out into the garden?'

'It had been raining overnight. There were damp coats everywhere, so I went to tidy them up.' Sara thought about the rack of coats and wellingtons near the front door, the boots lined up with military precision. 'I just happened to glance into the garden and saw that the lid was off the Alec Clifton.'

'The artwork on the lawn?'

'Yes. I thought everyone would be cross because it would have got wet inside, which isn't supposed to happen. I went to check it out.'

'To put the lid back on?'

'I'd struggle to lift it on my own. I just wanted to see if it was full of water.'

'What did you see?'

'I could see something poking out of the top of the urn. Like a toy, or something. Which was all wrong. So, I looked inside.'

This time, Stuart's reaction wasn't stage-managed. His face turned grey, and he looked close to vomiting. He drew a deep breath.

'And what did you find?'

'That poor man.' Stuart gulped. 'He was all scrunched up. He'd been shoved in there like an old rag doll. No respect for him at all. This animal thing was on his head, like it was deliberately peering over the lip to keep watch or something. And the smell. That terrible smell.'

Paula approached with a mug of herbal tea, which she placed in front of Stuart. 'Here, this will settle your stomach.'

'What did you do?'

'Came inside. Everyone else was in the kitchen, and I went there. Told everyone what I'd seen.'

'And then?'

'My husband rang the emergency number.' Paula patted Stuart on the back of his hand as if to tell him he had done well. 'It was only a matter of minutes before two officers turned up. Once my husband had shown them, they immediately rang for help.'

'The lid was on the grass. I didn't touch it,' insisted Stuart. 'Whoever moved it must have pushed it off from above and onto the steps below. I'm surprised we didn't hear it fall. There must have been quite a crash. It's broken in two.'

CHAPTER 7

Dom's meeting with the tutor in the School of History took longer than expected, but he felt that her concerns were justified. The two of them left a message for the student in question to get in touch, their unstated intention to persuade the young woman to go for counselling. In its parkland campus, four miles outside the city centre, the university didn't suit everyone, and this student from a much larger city seemed to still be struggling to adapt socially.

'It's the only thing I didn't experience myself,' said Dom. 'Because I was a local boy, I never stayed on campus. I lived at home for the first year and with friends in a shared house after that.'

'Did you feel doing that cut you off?' The tutor frowned. 'How did you manage your social life? Were you sporty?'

'Still am.' Dom smiled. His reputation as a triathlete obviously hadn't reached the history department. 'I joined several societies. The one that stuck with me the longest was the Rock Music one. I made friends there, and we spent rather a lot of time in the LCR or at the Waterfront.'

'Perhaps we should see if my student has a personal interest she's not using in a social context?'

Typical tutor, thought Dom. *Why not just say, "Let's find out if she has a hobby"?* 'It's a start, but a couple of counselling sessions might avert a crisis. We took on an extra staff member to do just that, so it's not difficult to arrange a slot.'

It was past lunchtime when Dom headed up to his office. He was unsurprised to find Taryn hovering in the foyer of the building.

'No luck?' he asked.

She shook her head. 'I've tried several more times, but his phone is just cutting out. It doesn't even go to voicemail.'

They sat around his desk while Dom tried for himself. Taryn was right. His call was shut down immediately. He typed a jokey text and hit the send button. The wheel at the top of the message circled for a while before telling him that it could not be sent. It couldn't be the signal, as it was good all over campus. Taryn tried on her phone with the same result.

'I'm not up on mobile technology,' she confessed. 'Does this mean his message box is full?'

'Maybe his phone's just run out of juice, or he's out of range. I don't know. What about his housemate? Is he still in the same place?'

'Yes, sharing with Rhys. Don't know why he hasn't got a place of his own.'

'Like you have?'

'It's not much, but it's mine,' she replied defensively. 'I don't have to let anyone in unless I want to.'

Dom didn't question how Taryn had managed to be the first of their circle to afford her own terraced house off the Unthank Road. Her mother would have been part of it. She'd married money the second time around and had more than enough to help her daughter. Perhaps she'd even bought it for her as a gift. In his opinion, all this goth rebellion stuff was spoilt-little-rich-girl syndrome. Quite frankly, he could have managed a mortgage himself these days. He just didn't want to. Living at home with his parents was the easier option.

Joe shared a house with a fellow researcher from the Climatic Research Unit, UEA's world-leading climate change institution. Both were dedicated to their work to the exclusion of much else. The recent grant Joe had received was to fund a project for a long-term study on the effects of rising sea levels on Britain's coastal communities and had been a major coup for the entire department. But even if Joe was away doing some research, Dom would have expected him to respond to Taryn's numerous messages. He might be single-minded about his work, but he wasn't cruel.

'When I rang Rhys yesterday, he was visiting his family in Wales,' Taryn said.

'Let's try again. He may have heard from Joe by now.'

Although Rhys wasn't part of their inner circle of friends, Dom had his number and dialled it. He answered after a couple of rings.

'Rhys, I'm sorry to bother you,' said Dom, 'but we're worried about Joe. We haven't been able to reach him at all. Have you heard from him?'

'Not a peep.' They could hear Rhys's footsteps. 'As luck would have it, I've just got back. Hang on a minute.'

Rhys was opening a door. The sound of his voice dampened as he went inside and yelled, 'Joe? Joe? You home?'

There was clearly no reply.

'Why are you so worried?' Rhys asked.

'It's just not like him to vanish. He usually says if he's off to work on something.'

'Have you spoken to Taryn?'

'She's here with me n—'

'He didn't leave a note or anything?' Taryn interrupted anxiously.

'Why would he do that? Joe's his own man. He doesn't need to tell me where he's going.' They heard him drop a bag of some sort on the floor. 'It's odd that he won't answer his phone, though, isn't it?'

'You've been trying too?'

'A couple of times. No luck.'

'Does it look like he might have gone off somewhere?' Dom wasn't going to assume the worst just yet. 'Something to do with this new project?'

'That's possible, I suppose,' said Rhys. 'Let me check.'

He walked some more and they heard the fridge door open. 'Looks like Joe didn't take any food with him if he did. I can check with Professor Huxley. He's supervising the new project, so he should know.'

'I didn't think they'd got that far.' Taryn's voice wobbled with emotion. She dropped her gaze to her mobile. 'We had dinner last week to celebrate the award, and Joe said there was lots of planning to do before he could go out in the field.'

Dom felt a rush of jealousy. Since when had Joe and Taryn been dinner companions? Why hadn't he been invited as well? 'What about his room?' he asked.

'I don't go in there,' said Rhys. 'And he doesn't go in mine.'

'Is it locked?'

'No. Why would it be? We trust each other not to invade personal spaces.'

'Then I think you ought to have a quick look,' said Dom.

Taryn squeaked in protest.

'Why not?'

'Well, it's personal,' she stuttered.

'What if he's lying up there ill?'

With a dramatic gasp, Taryn said, 'What if he's lying up there dead?'

'Oh, for God's sake, Taryn.' Dom's patience with her was wearing thin, as usual. 'It's been days. Rhys would be able to smell something if he'd been lying up there dead for that long. The stink would be horrible. I just meant that we might be able to tell if he's packed a bag.'

'I never thought of that. I'll go and check his room.'

They listened as he climbed some stairs, then knocked at a door. There was no reply.

'Oh my God!'

'What's the matter?'

'Joe's not here. He's not the tidiest person in the world, but he'd never leave his room in this state. Your dress is still hung up, Taryn. Maybe they don't share your taste.'

'Your dress?' Dom demanded. Taryn squeaked again, and he grunted in displeasure. Why the hell were any of Taryn's clothes in Joe's bedroom? An angry flush rose up his neck. 'When did you last see him?'

'Friday night. I told you, we went for dinner.'

'And you stayed the night?'

'Hey,' interrupted Rhys from the mobile's speaker. 'That's none of your business.'

'Never mind all that. What do you mean? About the room?' Dom rushed on.

'It looks like it's been burgled or turned over. There's stuff everywhere, even the duvet is on the floor, and he always makes his bed.'

'Don't touch anything,' said Dom. 'We need to report this to the police.'

CHAPTER 8

It didn't take Rose long to burn the clothes and files. She added some garden clippings and dead leaves for good measure, which created a slow-moving plume of white smoke that drifted above the trees in the copse and across the farmer's field. Luckily her neighbours were away for some months. 'The cruise of a lifetime,' they had boasted to her. A retirement present to each other that stopped at various Caribbean islands then circumnavigated South America. She had agreed to keep an eye on their house while they were away, which hadn't seemed much of a chore in principle. Until the man had turned up back in February.

Rose knew that homelessness was a problem, even in rural areas. The previous summer, a man had camped out in the copse behind the house for a couple of weeks in a torn tent. He had moved on when the neighbours had threatened to call the police, though he had been no trouble. He'd asked for permission to draw water from her garden tap, and she'd readily agreed, for once feeling virtuous for helping another human being. She'd occasionally left him cartons of milk or tins of food by the tap, which had always vanished by the next morning. No, the poor chap was no problem, but next door had become wary of him being there, so had moved him on.

She didn't think the February man was the same person. For a start, he didn't have as much stuff. He looked taller and more powerful. The night he arrived was bitter, and he had broken into the old wartime hut that stood at the bottom of her garden. It was one of those corrugated metal prefab buildings that had survived all over the county. Her husband had liked it, and fixed it up as a workshop and man-shed for when he retired. Not that he'd ever been able to use it in the end. Rose rarely went in it these days; only Aiden went in there regularly to bring out the lawnmower or garden tools. It was Aiden who had disturbed the man, who he'd found sleeping in the second room at the back of the workshop area.

'I didn't even know that was here,' she had said when Aiden had shown her the back room.

'I told him to bugger off,' the gardener had assured her. 'Not to come back. Or tell his mates.'

Rose had bought a solid lock and chain to close the back room off. But someone else had used it again at the weekend, mercifully only for a couple of nights. Being here on her own so much, the idea upset Rose. Not only were her neighbours away, but Aiden was also absent for three weeks, off seeing his daughter in Canada, where she had emigrated a couple of years ago.

I'll get Aiden to do a better job when he gets back, she promised herself. *I suppose I'd better clean it up first.*

The peculiar little room had no windows. Perhaps, during wartime, it had been for storing something they wanted to keep secret, like cans of petrol. When her husband had done up the shed, he had run electricity down to it, and the space was lit by a single light bulb. Opening the door to it now, Rose was offended by the stink the visitor had left behind. The bastard had used the floor as a toilet.

Fetching her household cleaning gloves, Rose inspected the old mattress and pile of blankets in the corner. There was unfinished food on paper plates, which she carted straight round to the dustbin. A quilted outdoor coat and fleecy mud-stained jumper lay next to the bed. Thrown in a different corner was a newish-looking mobile phone. The clothes went on the bonfire with the rest of the rubbish. Rose piled more bits of dead wood around them to make sure they caught well enough. She dragged the mattress and blankets round to the back of the workshop.

Rose decided to deal with the phone next. The man may be gone, but this was damning evidence of his visit. Though the battery was long dead, the police could trace it, no doubt. She put the phone on a workbench and selected a large hammer from the tool rack on the wall.

With a grunt of effort, she brought it down on the mobile. The screen fractured. She lifted the hammer higher the second time, imagining the phone was the face of her boss and other people who had offended her. It took several hard blows to smash the thing to pieces. It was almost cathartic, hammering the plastic and glass into fragments. She swept the bits up in a dustpan and threw them in the bin too. The SIM card went on the bonfire.

Now there was the room to clean. She dragged the garden hose to the door and sprayed all the walls with the jet setting. There were stains everywhere. The man had been disgusting. Soon, the earth floor was swimming in dirty water, but that would quickly drain away. Determined to do a thorough job, Rose brought a bucket of warm water liberally dosed with Jeyes Fluid. Car-cleaning brush in hand, she scrubbed the walls as high as she could reach before throwing neat cleaner down in the corner, which the man must have used as a latrine. The bucket, the bottle of cleaning fluid and the brush all went in the bin, which was due to be emptied tomorrow.

Giving the area a final spray of clean water, Rose put the hose back where it belonged and refitted the lock and chain on the outside of the door. It was nearly teatime, and the light was failing. *No one else is getting in there*, she vowed.

A good day's work, Rose congratulated herself as she showered to get rid of the reminder of her disgusting visitor. When she was done, there would be plenty of screen time left. She was behind with her online self-help bereavement course.

38

Professor Chandler had suggested it to her and, for once, he had been right. It was actually full of good ideas to help her deal with her years of mourning, the grief her boss 'couldn't imagine that she had to live through every day'.

Rose was determined to complete every one of the suggestions on the course in her own way. Then, perhaps, she might finally be free of all this anger.

CHAPTER 9

Rich had given Bowen and Noble a memory stick with all the recordings from the previous night. Once they had organised formal statements, there was little else the team could do until Dr Taylor brought the body back to the mortuary for the full post-mortem.

'It will take a while, I'm afraid,' the doctor had explained to James and Paula. Privately, he had said more to Sara and Edwards. 'It's a difficult decision. I don't know if I should lift him as he is or wait for the rigor to wear off. I don't want to lose any evidence if I wait, but being folded in on himself like that is very unhelpful, forensically speaking.'

They left him to decide and headed back to the SCU office. Aggie had prepared the whiteboard with photos already sent through from Forensics. It wasn't an easy sight.

'I've checked for missing persons locally,' she said. 'No one in this age group, or even matching descriptions in a different age group.'

'Let's find out what we can about this couple and this piece of so-called art,' said Edwards. 'Mike, Ian, you get cracking on that CCTV stuff.'

Sara nodded and fired up her computer. Like her boss, she didn't understand why this art was so sought-after or expensive. Aggie volunteered to research the couple and the house.

It didn't take either of them very long. The artist had a prominent website, which showed pieces for sale and listed his exhibitions. The home page had a short essay from some art critic that explained why Alec Clifton was such an important contemporary sculptor. It was written in a pretentious double-speak that Sara found both frustrating and vacuous. The prices of the available works were jaw-dropping, given that they looked like giant flowerpots with screw-on lids. Paula Gordon had been right in her estimate. A new piece of similar size and construction to the one on the lawn of Barnham Parva New Hall was listed with a guide price of £40,000. Sara doubted if this one would be worth that much now. Having had a dead body shoved into it might affect its valuation, downwards probably. Although you could never tell with some people. What about that shredded Banksy she'd seen on the news? It was worth more now it was in bits than it had been before.

Drilling down further on the website produced a list of current owners of Alec Clifton artworks. Sara printed off a copy. He had been selling the funerary urns for the best part of ten years and other artworks for several years longer than that. She pulled up a photo of the artist, who looked at least in his late thirties, although there was no guarantee it was a recent picture. The list revealed one thing. The Gordons were not the only people to own an urn in this area.

She knocked on the door frame outside Edwards's office. 'Boss,' she said through the open door. 'Seems there's another of these things at the SCVA. Worth a look or a chat with people there?'

Edwards nodded. 'Could be. Any others round here?'

'Not locally. There are about forty on the list. It would seem that each one differs from the others, mostly on the lids. Scattered all over the place, though. There are even a couple that went to America.'

Aggie joined them. 'The Sainsbury Centre? That would make sense. They do like to keep up with contemporary artists.'

'You go there often?' Edwards asked, sounding amused.

'I like the exhibitions, and there's a nice café. Two actually.'

Sara glanced out of the office glass panel to Bowen, who was hunched over a computer screen with Noble. She wouldn't have had him down as a natural art gallery aficionado. Clearly, Aggie was broadening his horizons. They had recently confessed to going to the theatre together as well.

'The Gordons have lived at Barnham Parva New Hall for about nine years.' Aggie waved a couple of printouts. 'The interesting thing is that their collection is quite well known. They have open days to raise money for various charities several times a year.'

She handed the paper to Sara, who checked the dates. 'At least one in each season.'

'Shows off those gardens too,' suggested Aggie. 'You have to book online in advance. You can't just turn up. Then it looks like you get shown round in small groups, including the main rooms of the house.'

'I wonder if they have lists of attendees,' mused Edwards. 'That could be useful. Whoever put that man there, it wasn't a random act, was it? They didn't just drive past and decide it looked like a good site to dump a body.'

'You can't see the lawn from the road,' Sara reminded him. 'I doubt you can see the Hall through those trees, especially at night.'

'You might see headlights down there, though. Aggie, can you ask the Gordons about open-day lists and then see if there are any traffic cameras on that road?'

Sara doubted such a minor lane would be covered. There weren't any street lights for miles around. It was one of the benefits of living in the Norfolk countryside. The night skies were amazing in the right conditions.

'How are you getting on with the CCTV?' Edwards moved back into the main office.

'Slowly,' said Bowen. 'The cameras switch cover every thirty seconds.'

'Why?'

'They're trying to make six cameras do the work of a dozen,' said Noble, sounding frustrated. 'I don't get it. Why penny-pinch on a thing like that when you have all that expensive stuff to protect.'

'And no doubt loads in the bank,' added Bowen.

'So far, I've found them going out at about seven o'clock.' Noble checked a pad of paper he was scribbling notes on. 'Both couples. Two cars corresponding with the ones in the drive this morning. Then it gets really dark, and the rain sets in.'

'I wonder where they were going?' said Sara. 'I'll check that out, sir. It might help.'

The office door opened, and the top half of genial desk sergeant Trevor Jones hesitantly peered round.

'Hello, Trevor,' said Aggie. 'There's some cake left if you want it.'

'That would be a nice bonus,' he said with a smile. He edged into the room, holding up a piece of paper. 'It's not why I came. DI Edwards, are you still looking for a John Doe?'

'We are. You got something?'

'I look after the misper log sometimes when there's not much else to do. This one came in about half an hour ago. Some chap from the university went into the City Central desk and said his housemate was missing.'

'Another student? Probably just off on a bender or found a girlfriend to stay with.' Edwards didn't sound very interested.

Jones looked at the report and shook his head. 'Not a student. A researcher from the climate unit. In his thirties. His flatmate is also his colleague. The chap hasn't been at work this week. His boss said they were expecting him to be.'

'He wasn't missed at the house either?'

'Housemate says he just got back from a few days away in Wales, visiting his family. He also claims that the man's bedroom looks as if it's been burgled.'

'What's this man's name then?'

'Summerhill. Joe Summerhill.'

CHAPTER 10

Sara and Edwards drove to the housing estate that surrounded the UEA. Although half the homes belonged to local families, the rest were multiple-occupancy student accommodation. It was a lucrative market.

They easily found the semi-detached house where Joe Summerhill lived. The front garden was covered in old grey flagstones. Weeds pushed between the joints, the rubbish bins stood by the front door and dirty net curtains obscured the downstairs windows. It looked uncared for. Sara knocked on the front door, which was swiftly answered by a young man with dark, tightly curled hair. Stubble turned his chin even darker. Skinny brown arms hung from an overlarge T-shirt.

'I'm Rhys Davies,' he said. There was a pleasant Welsh lilt to his voice that belied the anxiety of his tone. His worried eyes glanced at their warrant cards without real comprehension. 'I didn't think you lot would take me seriously. Come in.'

The hallway had a bike parked in it. Sara and Edwards climbed round it to reach the kitchen. Rhys opened the fridge door.

'No food, do you see? He hasn't taken any food, and this lot is going off.'

Sara looked inside and could see clumps of rancid fat bobbing in the plastic milk carton. A packet of cheddar had mould growing on it. Her nose wrinkled at the smell drifting off the shelf.

'How long is it since you last saw your housemate?' Edwards asked.

'I went home to see my family in Cardiff on Thursday,' said Rhys, closing the fridge. 'That's the last I saw of him. I'll have to clean that lot out soon. It stinks.'

'Has anyone else seen him since?'

'He and Taryn went out for dinner on Friday. Her dress is upstairs, so I assume she stayed the night. Although that's new . . .' Rhys's voice trailed off, and he frowned.

'Is Taryn his girlfriend?'

'Well, she wasn't, I don't think. It's complicated.'

'What do you mean by that?' asked Sara. 'Who is Taryn?'

'Taryn Deacon,' said Rhys. Sara scribbled it in her notebook. 'She's one of the group, you see. They've been mates for ever. Well, since they all came here to uni.'

'Perhaps you'd better start from the beginning,' suggested Sara. 'How do you all know one another?'

Rhys sighed and sat on a kitchen chair, running his hands down his face as if trying to clear his thoughts. 'Joe and Taryn are part of a group of four friends.'

'And you're not?' interrupted Edwards.

'Not as such.'

Sara wished Edwards would let the young man talk. She tried to steer the conversation again. 'These four friends?'

'Joe, Taryn, Dom and Junina. They met when they came here as students — it must be twelve or thirteen years ago. Used to go to gigs together and somehow managed to stay in touch after they graduated. In fact, Dom never left the uni. He's local, anyway. The others went off to do courses elsewhere and gradually drifted back over the last few years.'

'They all work at the university?'

'Apart from Junina. She lives and works in London.'

'I'll need all their contact details.'

'Yeah, sure.' Rhys reached for his mobile and began to scroll before rattling off mobile numbers for the friends. 'I don't have Junina's details, sorry.'

'Taryn and Joe are an item?' asked Edwards.

'They weren't really, unless something changed that I don't know about. It looks like she stayed over, so it might have.'

'You say they went out for a meal on Friday?'

'To celebrate. Joe had been awarded this huge grant to do some long-term research. The department are thrilled. It's big stuff. Really important.'

'If there are four friends, why did only Joe and Taryn go?'

'I don't know about Dom. Junina has young kids. You'll have to ask Taryn.' It sounded as if Rhys was getting a bit cross with Edwards.

Sara intervened. 'How do you know Joe?'

'I did my base degree at Exeter,' said Rhys. 'In our field of speciality, everyone dreams of working here. They were the first to open up the field and are world-leading experts. I was beside myself when they accepted me to do my doctorate. Student advisory put me in touch with Joe. He was looking for someone to share with. It's great because we're both in the department, if not exactly the same field.'

'How long have you been sharing with him?'

'This is my final year. My third year. I've still got to finish my thesis, which is another year, and I may stay in Norwich for that. I like it here.'

Sara knew that lots of students who came here never went home again. Norwich was a vibrant and welcoming place. She'd have stayed in the city herself if she hadn't inherited the cottage near the coast.

Edwards was moving round the room, poking at stuff on the work surfaces. He must be getting bored. Sara tried to hurry the story along. 'What made you report Joe as missing?'

'It was Taryn who was worried about Joe. She said she'd been trying to call him for days and no reply. They asked me to check his bedroom, so I did.'

'And?'

'It's been trashed. Stuff thrown all over the place, papers ripped up, drawers open and all that. Joe is basically a tidy chap. He would never leave his room like that.'

'We'd better go and have a look.'

They followed Rhys upstairs, and he opened a bedroom door wide. Sara could see that the young man's assessment was right. The room had been turned over.

'Have you been inside?' Edwards asked, surveying the mess from the landing.

Rhys nodded. 'Just to look.'

'Did you touch or move anything?'

'No, I was too shocked. I didn't understand why it was just Joe's room. My room, the living room, the kitchen, bathroom — none of it has been touched.'

'You don't think that you've been burgled as such?'

'No, I don't.'

Sara peered into the room. She could see an expensive laptop still perched on the desk. 'They weren't very efficient if they were stealing, sir. His computer's still on the desk.'

Edwards perked up at this. 'Personal, then?'

'I don't get that either,' added Rhys. 'I can just about understand if Joe was personally targeted, but not why they left the computer behind.'

'Why would you think Joe was being targeted?'

'Social media shit. We all get it sometimes. You know, climate change deniers, conspiracy theorists, alt-right garbage. You just have to ignore it.'

'Did Joe ignore it?'

'Usually. Recently it started getting really nasty, and I know Joe was worried by it. That's why the grant thing meant even more to him. He felt validated by that award after what those buggers said to him.'

'Such as?'

'Death threats. Persistent and detailed. He told me they knew things about him that weren't public. They threatened Taryn and the others too.'

CHAPTER 11

Fortunately, Dom had chosen to drive that morning. With the soreness on his leg, he had decided to go for a swim after work rather than cycle in. His car was in the main car park, which was the closest to his office, and he guided Taryn out there as she sobbed uncontrollably. He dropped her handbag in the footwell and almost had to force her into the passenger seat, leaning over to clip in the seat belt.

'Come on,' he said. 'I'll get you home.'

Taryn continued to cry all the way. 'It's him. It must be.'

'There are lots of reasons why he could be missing,' he replied. 'Out of range on the north coast, you know what reception's like up there. He might be camping. He might have broken his phone. We don't know.'

'Except that none of that is like him.' Taryn turned on him. 'He would have let me know if he was going off. Or told Rhys, or you.'

'I'm not so sure. It sounds like the pair of you have been keeping secrets from me.' Dom tried to parallel park on the street near Taryn's house, anger making him misjudge the manoeuvre, which made him angrier still. 'How long have you two been sleeping together?'

'A few weeks.' She looked down at her hands, a sheet of black hair obscuring her face from him.

He drummed on the steering wheel, jealousy running icy fingers across his forehead. 'Are you ashamed to talk to me, then? And when were you going to tell me?'

'When we felt like the time was right,' snapped Taryn. 'It's none of your business, anyway. You and me haven't been an item for years.'

'An item?' His tone was sneering. 'God! You're so upper middle-class, Taryn.'

'Not exactly a working-class hero yourself, are you?'

'At least I work for a living, despite all this.' He gestured to his amputated leg and injured hand. 'You never had to go through anything like this. And you can hardly call what you do work. At least I help people, instead of pretending to be the bloody undead and flouncing around the place in widow's weeds.'

Taryn's eyes sparkled, not with tears but with anger. Somehow, she managed to keep her voice even. 'Well, that's a nice little tantrum, isn't it? That is exactly why we didn't say anything to you. We knew that you would be jealous.'

'Jealous?' He roared the word all the louder because he knew Taryn was right.

'Yes. A green-eyed, angry little monster.' She opened the car door and climbed out. 'I think you need more anger management sessions. Thank you for the lift.'

She let herself in without a backward glance in his direction. He snorted with derision as he tried to get out of the parking space. 'Bloody woman! She's never changed.'

He needed some exercise. That would make him feel better. It was only a few minutes back to the university and its sports park. Grabbing his holdall from the back seat, Dom slammed the door with more force than was necessary before heading into the changing rooms.

The lifeguard nodded in recognition to Dom. He swam here two or three times a week as part of his training. One of the few sensations his injured hand did register was the rush of water through his fingers. It told him that his extremities were still alive, a much-desired comfort right now. Diving into the fast lane, he began to plough up and down at speed, working off his rage. It took fifty lengths for him to calm down enough to pull himself back onto the side of the pool and catch his breath.

He *was* jealous, to be honest. Which was definitely unfair. He'd had other girlfriends in the past, although none since his accident. The idea of being naked in front of some woman when part of him was missing was more than his pride could cope with. As a young man, he still had plenty of sexual urges to go around. There were ways of dealing with that, and Taryn often had a leading role in those moments, though only in his head. Dom made sure to keep those images locked firmly up in his imagination, not to allow them to affect the friendship he maintained with her — or at least, he thought that was the case. Did he still have a sense of ownership, then? Had Taryn suspected him of wanting something more? Why did she think he would be jealous if he hadn't given her some cause?

Dom shook his head in frustration, unable to sort out his thoughts. Taryn was just a friend. Especially now, if she was going out with Joe. Anger began to creep over him again at the thought of them in bed together. He grabbed his towel and wrapped it around his waist. He just hoped it hid the erection that had accompanied the mental picture of Taryn and Joe having sex. Little green-eyed monster of jealousy indeed.

Dom's mobile was blinking with a voicemail when he pulled his holdall from the locker. With water-wrinkled fingers, he opened the message and listened.

I hope this is the correct number for Dominic Wilkins. I'm Detective Sergeant Sara Hirst of Norfolk Police, and I would be grateful if you could call me back when you receive this. The matter is quite urgent. Thank you very much.

The woman left a contact number, which showed on his missed calls register. With a twinge of fear, Dom knew this was about Joe. He dragged on his clothes and dealt with his prosthetic as quickly as he could.

Escaping the swimming pool building, he dialled a number and waited. He had made sure that Taryn was safely home. Now there was someone else he had to check up on, someone else who needed to know what was happening. After a couple of rings, he heard the voice he wanted.

'Junina, are you still at work? We need to talk.'

CHAPTER 12

Rhys had no pictures of Joe, and neither Sara nor Edwards wanted to go into the room to search for one.

'I'll get a forensic investigation team round,' Sara told Rhys. 'Don't touch anything in here until they've been, will you?'

'No problem. Can I clean out the fridge?'

'Better leave it until they've had a look, just in case.' Sara assured him as Rhys grumbled about the smell. 'We'll book it immediately, but it might be tomorrow morning before they can come.'

They still weren't sure if Joe Summerhill was their victim, and the FI team would only prioritise it if he was. The online death threats were worrying, though. They would need to go through his computer carefully. If that was the reason someone had turned over his room, why had they left it behind?

Sara rang Taryn Deacon, got her address and arranged to visit immediately. As Sara drove, Edwards tried to encourage the forensic team leader to go out, even though it was late in the day and they were still working out at Barnham Parva New Hall. He wasn't winning.

The streets bordered by the Unthank Road and the Earlham Road were known locally as the Golden Triangle.

Terraced houses lined the cramped streets, ranging from upmarket Georgian to working-class Edwardian, with different sizes of garden according to their status. Rows of old shops had been converted to boutiques, hipster coffee bars and gastropubs. It was the natural home of the academics and the socially ambitious middle class of the city. You could pay significantly more for a house here than one of the same size on the other side of the Dereham Road, just a few hundred yards away. Taryn Deacon's house was on Calais Street, in the heart of the area.

She must have been waiting for them, Sara realised, as Taryn wrenched open the door before she'd finished knocking. Despite her thick black eyeliner, the young woman looked as if she had been crying. Her eyes were bloodshot, her nose bright pink where the pale make-up had been wiped off. She led them into a sitting room dominated by dark-blue walls covered in gold stars before plonking herself down onto a black leather sofa to blow her nose again. A pile of wet tissues lay on the wine-red carpet at her feet. A second, smaller black sofa stood at right angles, and in the corner by the window was a highly decorative red-and-gold chair that looked as if it had come off the set of one of those 1950s technicolour horror movies.

'May we?' Sara pointed to the second sofa, and Taryn nodded.

'Sorry. Yes, sit down. I'm just . . .' The words petered out.

'You're a close friend of Joe Summerhill, I understand?' Sara asked as she settled on the leather seat, making it squeak embarrassingly. Edwards perched on the sofa arm, seeming reluctant to make a similar noise when the matter was potentially so serious.

'Y-yes,' Taryn stuttered. 'We've been friends for years. Have you found him? I'm so worried about him.'

'More than just friends?'

'What?'

'We've been to see his room and spoken to his housemate, Rhys Davies.'

'Oh, my dress. Well, yes.'

'Yes?'

'Do we have to go into that? Dom will get even angrier if he finds out any more, and Rhys has already dropped me in it.'

'Dropped you in it?' When she got no reply, Sara tried her best empathetic look.

Taryn sighed and blew her nose again. 'Joe and I have sort of become an item recently, but we hadn't told Dom. Dom and I used to go out years ago. We weren't sure how he would take it. Rhys mentioned it when we spoke on the phone today, and Dom was listening.'

'You went for a meal with Joe on Friday, didn't you?' Edwards asked. Taryn turned her attention to him. 'Just the two of you.'

'Yes, to celebrate his research grant.'

'And you stayed with him?'

'Joe usually stays with me when we've been out. As Rhys was away, we didn't think anyone would see us.'

'And then?'

'My dress got torn.' Taryn gazed down at her fingers as they twisted the snotty tissue. 'When I came home on Saturday, Joe lent me a tracksuit and said he'd get the dress mended because it was his fault.'

Their relationship was clearly a passionate one, Sara mused, unlike her own these days. 'Was that the last time you saw him?'

'We were supposed to be having coffee on Monday morning.'

'Where were you due to meet?'

'At work,' said Taryn. 'I mean, where I work, not at his department.'

'You work at the university?'

'Attached. I'm one of the exhibition curators at the Sainsbury Centre. I wanted to show Joe what I was working on. My office is in the Art History department in the centre of the building. Some of the paintings I had arranged to borrow had arrived. I was so excited, and I wanted to show them to him.'

'He didn't turn up?'

'When he wasn't there by lunchtime, I kept ringing and leaving messages. Nothing. There wasn't much I could do. I went to their house to check after work. There was no one there at all.'

'Did you report Joe missing?' asked Edwards.

'I tried to, but the man I spoke to said Joe wouldn't be considered missing for several days as he was an adult.' Neither of them was surprised at Taryn's reply. It was standard procedure. 'I kept trying and trying. I've been so worried.'

'What changed today?'

Taryn looked at Edwards and then back to Sara. 'I heard something this morning. A rumour. That a body had been found at Barnham Parva New Hall. Is it true?'

'Why would you think it was him?'

'I don't want it to be.' Tears were running channels in the woman's pale foundation. Her body was shaking with distress. 'It just seemed like too much of a coincidence.'

'Why?' Sara moved across to the other sofa and sat next to the distraught woman.

'We all went there, back in the spring.'

'To an open day?'

'Yes. I think the others thought it would be a treat for me, which in a way, it was. I'm not so up to date on contemporary art as they think. It's not my specialist area.'

'What is your specialism?' Sara was genuinely curious.

'Futurism. You know, Boccioni, Marinetti, Severini, even Goncharova and all that. Italian and Russian early-twentieth-century dynamic art. It's what I did my doctorate on.'

'You're a doctor?' Edwards sounded surprised.

Taryn lifted her chin momentarily in a defiant gesture. 'Just because I'm a goth, doesn't mean I'm stupid. Yes, strictly speaking, I'm Doctor Taryn Deacon. Just don't ask me about a broken wrist or your kid's rash.' She dropped her head again. 'When I heard the rumour, I realised we had been there recently, and I panicked. I got Dom to speak to Rhys and check Joe's room.'

'Which made Rhys report him missing?'

'That and his phone is dead. None of us can get through. We've all been trying.'

Sara looked round the sepulchral decorations in the living room. The bookshelves were jammed with large, expensive art tomes mixed with gothic novels and horror film DVDs. The mantlepiece was cluttered with faux skulls, picture frames with joke ghosts draped around them and candlesticks with used candles in them. A black, Victorian-looking top hat decorated with steampunk paraphernalia and dark feathers sat on an old phrenology bust.

'Do you have a recent picture of Joe?' Sara asked.

'Sure.' Taryn reached for her phone. 'This was us on Friday night. At the Holly.'

Sara examined the picture. The couple were clinking champagne glasses and smiling. Sara recognised Taryn in the steampunk top hat, while the man opposite her looked fit and happy. He also looked a lot like the body in the Alec Clifton funerary urn.

CHAPTER 13

Rose had stopped cooking for herself when her daughter, Lily, had died. Before that, she had struggled to make food interesting for her husband coping with MS, and later as he battled with cancer and lost. There were four years between the two deaths. Endlessly long years, when Rose had tried her best to keep a home going while she worked full-time and looked after her disabled daughter. Now this was her time to use as she wanted.

After her shower, she headed for the kitchen, the rumbles in her stomach warning that without something to eat, the evening would be wasted through faintness and lack of energy. Her fridge and cupboards were full of convenience foods. The stuff was flavourless and bad for you. Not that Rose cared about that. There was little to live for apart from her self-help plan. Looking after yourself was, understandably, part of the bereavement course. Rose simply parked that bit for later, should later ever arrive. She selected a pre-made tuna salad in a foil dish and chose a fork. Without even bothering to decant the stuff into a bowl, Rose slumped into an easy chair in the glass-roofed atrium. She flicked on the television, although it was just noise and colour. It meant nothing.

The light outside faded and the heating glugged into action. The radiator in Lily's room knocked as the first of the water circulated. It was on the ground floor, overlooking the garden, and had been adapted to accommodate her daughter's needs.

One of the things the self-help course recommended was to enlist the help of a friend to clear away items that caused too many memories or pain. Things that were good memories should be retained, such as photos of the loved one smiling or achieving something. These could be given pride of place. Things that were not useful or acted as triggers could be donated to charity shops (such as clothes, shoes, books, DVDs) or even sold to raise much-needed money (cars, furniture, music systems, et cetera).

Rose had done this when her husband had died. Then Lily had returned to live with her after respite care elsewhere. Lily's pain had rapidly increased, and her mobility had kept reducing. Her creative mind, which had produced such wonderful visions, was gone. She became little more than a vegetable, in Rose's opinion. If Rose hadn't got her up and dressed or fed her, Lily would simply have shrivelled up in her bed and died. There had been no quality to her life at all. Sometimes, Rose wondered how or why the shell of a body that had been her daughter had kept drawing breath. Every small movement had brought pain, which she communicated in moans and groans when touched. Sometimes, when Rose had offered food, mushed up like the rubbish you spooned into babies, Lily would open her mouth. Other times, her head would turn partially away in refusal. Finally, she had needed adult nappies, the ultimate indignity in Rose's mind.

Paying a daytime carer had allowed Rose to escape to work. Only in the evenings when Lily was propped up in her bed, and Rose talked to her about her day, did any semblance of the old Lily show in her eyes. That was why Rose had stayed at the Art History department and attended talks about the Sainsbury Centre collection. It had given her something special to talk to Lily about.

The tuna salad had gone, though Rose had little recollection of eating it. She threw the foil tray in the bin, then made herself a cup of tea.

Three rituals kept Rose going. One of them was making a proper cuppa, using loose leaf tea and beautiful antique china teacups and saucers. Nor had she let the situation turn her into a dirty person. All the rooms she used regularly were kept tidy and clean. Her clothes were washed, her hair trimmed, her shoes wiped. No, Rose hadn't let her standards slide since Lily's death.

Her second ritual was to spend some time in her daughter's room each day, which she kept exactly the same as it had been when Lily was alive. Rose would sit in the armchair by Lily's bed and talk to her daughter about her day or the latest art exhibition, just as she had in the past. Turning on the bedside light, Rose settled to look at the pristine, unruffled bed.

'It's been a difficult few days,' she said with a nod. 'I think you know that. I'm so glad of your company when there are such horrible decisions to be made.'

The duvet didn't answer. Rose watched as tiny motes of dust spiralled up in the heat from the radiator and gently fell through the warm light to the floor.

'I'll clean again on Saturday,' she promised. 'You know I'd do anything for you.' She sipped from the cup. 'You'd like this one. It's called "Queen Mary Blend". Fortnum, of course.'

When had they started ordering packs of tea from the famous Fortnum and Mason's London store? Rose mused. Sometime during her husband's illness. When he was still working, he had occasionally taken them there for afternoon tea. Both she and Lily had developed a fondness for the ritual and the tastes. That had been before multiple sclerosis had left him wheelchair-bound and jobless.

'I'm so grateful that the professor suggested that course. It's helped me make a lot of changes. Perhaps I should do a little more tonight.'

Rose carefully put the cup back in its saucer. She plumped up the pillows and settled the large toy panda against them as though it were sleeping. Drawing the curtains to keep out the dark, she put on the night light. Its red bulb glowed out of the tiny doors and windows of the porcelain fairy-tale house. Inside, a family of miniature pottery rabbits sat at a table eating their tea, fully dressed, just like a picture in a child's storybook. No matter how long she'd lived, Lily had still needed the red glow to help her sleep, to keep the monsters at bay.

Rose closed the door and left her cup and saucer in the kitchen. She selected a key from the rack and crossed the living area to her husband's old study. This was her third ritual. The one that had kept her going the most.

She kept the small room locked whenever she was out of the house. It was just as she had left it last night. Papers were filed in brown buff folders and placed in a special order on the desk. Notebooks bulged with cuttings and photos. Pots of pens stood ready to use. The desk and computer were turned to one wall. The printer winked, its feeder full of paper. The second wall had once had a wide window to let in the light. Someone had boarded it up and painted the wood with white gloss. The other walls were also white. Each had been divided into sections so that there were several giant columns. Maps, photos, printouts, academic and newspaper articles were pinned up. Items from one area were cross-referenced to others with pink legal tape.

Rose turned on the computer and the table lamp. The icon for the self-help bereavement course popped up. She minimised it. First, her regular trawl — checking the list of newspapers, academic journals and other websites. This would be followed by a visit to her social media sites, where she posed as an art history academic or a climate change activist to befriend younger people in the same field. There was no point in sending any emails today.

'Let's see what they've been up to today,' Rose muttered to herself. 'Let's see if there's anything to add to my gallery.'

CHAPTER 14

Thursday morning was as bright and clear as Wednesday had been grey and wet. The team gathered for morning orders and information-sharing at eight o'clock. After the interview with Taryn Deacon the previous evening, DI Edwards had made Joe Summerhill's raided bedroom and his shared home a priority for the forensic team. Rhys had gone to stay with Taryn at Sara's suggestion.

'DNA tests have been arranged from items in the room,' she said. 'Tech have the laptop and are looking into the threatening social media angle this morning. See what they can trace.'

Aggie was pinning a picture of Joe onto the board. 'His poor mother. As soon as the university personnel office is open, I'll get his family details.'

'Please do,' said Edwards. 'But hold off contact until we have DNA confirmation. I want to be certain.' The team looked at the picture of the crumpled body and the smiling young man in Taryn's photo. 'It looks like a fit, but there isn't much to connect him with Barnham Parva or any reason why the place should have been used to dispose of the body.'

'Doctor Taylor says he's got the body back to the mortuary.' Sara was speed-reading another email. 'He'll do the PM this morning. We can go later today.'

'Assuming this is Joe Summerhill,' said Edwards, 'where the hell has he been all weekend? We know his housemate was away from Thursday until yesterday.'

'And that Taryn last saw him on Saturday morning,' added Sara. 'There was no one to miss him until Monday, when he was supposed to be meeting her at work.'

'So, missing from Saturday lunchtime until Tuesday night, when he ends up at Barnham Parva New Hall. Let's start with his mobile and see if it shows us where he got to. Mike, get onto the phone company. Sara has the number.'

Bowen nodded.

'CCTV from the Hall?' Edwards continued.

'Lots of nothing, and it's very dark,' said Noble. 'The rain doesn't help. Outside lighting gets triggered now and then by passing wildlife. I'm up to half past ten.'

'So, neither couple are back by then?'

'Doesn't look like it.'

'Aggie, give them a call and check what time they think they got back,' instructed Edwards. 'Chase those open-day lists as well. Did you hear from that other friend, Sara?'

'Dominic Wilkins?' Sara shook her head. 'No, he didn't call me back last night. Taryn said he also works at the UEA as a student disability advisor. We could go to his office and catch him that way.'

Edwards checked the time. 'He should be in by nine, I suppose. We'll go there after coffee. Aggie, can you check where his office is?'

'If we're going to the UEA, shall I arrange a visit to the Sainsbury Centre?' asked Sara. Edwards frowned. 'In case you want to view the other Alec Clifton in the area?' she added.

'See if we can speak to someone about it,' he agreed. 'They might know about the one at the Hall. Did you look into that toy animal?'

'On it now, boss,' she said. According to the website, the head of collections at the SCVA was Emilia Thornton. Sara assumed she was Taryn Deacon's boss.

The department's PA set them an urgent appointment. With time to spare, Sara began to trawl the internet for information on the toy.

Dr Taylor seemed to have been right in his suggestion that it looked like a llama. There were dozens to choose from. Furry and stuffed, knitted or crocheted, plastic or "calma llamas" to cuddle in bed. Take your pick. Nothing seemed to match the one in the urn, the picture of which Sara had taken from the board and put on her desk for comparison. Too small to be a pinata, it did seem to be made from strong paper or possibly straw. No doubt the forensic team was already looking at that.

'I wonder if that's tourist tat.' Aggie pointed at the photo as she gave Sara a map of the campus with a building marked on it. 'The student advisory offices are here. Top floor of the Lower Common Room, at the end of the main street.'

'Main street?' It was impressive that the place was big enough to need a map to get around.

'You'll see when you get there.'

A further search brought up a possible answer to the llama mystery. It seemed that just about every Central and South American country could provide an eager tourist with a range of llama figures, from keyrings to hand-carved artisan models. The ones that looked closest to theirs seemed to be either from Mexico or Peru.

'Might be useful,' said the DI when Sara showed him the screen. 'Our perpetrator might have been there on holiday.'

'Possible,' agreed Sara. 'They're not hard to buy online, though. I'd say that this tends towards folk art or crafts rather than children's toys.'

Edwards rolled his eyes. 'When did my team come over so artistic? Either way, the main question is, why is it there? Why did someone go to all this trouble to dispose of the body in such a difficult place and then leave a bloody llama with it?'

Sara couldn't answer that any more than Edwards could.

Aggie had managed to raise Mrs Gordon at the Hall, and they could hear her apologising about the early call. Grabbing a notepad, she scribbled a question of her own and pushed it into Aggie's sightline. She looked up at Sara and nodded while jotting down an email address.

'Could I just ask you to hold for a moment, Mrs Gordon?' Aggie put a hand over the receiver. 'Would you like to ask yourself?'

'Sure.' Sara waited until Aggie transferred the call to her own line.

'It may not be important, Mrs Gordon, but I just wanted to check about your absence from the Hall on Tuesday night,' she said.

'Good morning.' Paula sounded half-awake. 'Yes, I see . . . We got back just after midnight. That's late enough for me these days.'

'Where had you been?'

'The Sainsbury Centre. They were opening a new exhibition, and we were all invited.'

'All four of you?'

'Yes. It's a courtesy thing. We offer private tours of our collection to their art history students should they wish them. In return, we get invited to attend the launch parties for the visiting shows. Stuart does the organising for the visits, so they get invited too.'

'You went in two cars?'

'The boys were going on somewhere else afterwards,' said Paula. 'I can't remember where. To see friends, I think. I must have been asleep when they got back.'

'And you are sure the lid to the artwork was in place when you returned?'

'I think so.' Paula paused to consider before carrying on. 'It was a filthy night, wasn't it? Raining really hard. The outside light wasn't working properly, so the lawn was partly in the dark. I can't be certain.'

'We'll need to find out where your employees went and who saw them,' said Sara. 'Can you remember anything else about your journey or getting home?'

'There wasn't anything remarkable that I can think of. Hold on.' A man spoke in the background, and Paula repeated the question before the phone was passed over.

'Good morning, DS Hirst,' said James Gordon. 'There was one thing that happened. In some ways it was not unusual, given the state of some people's driving on quiet roads at night.'

Wanting to forestall a rant about bad driving, Sara said, 'I suspect there isn't much traffic on the roads near you.'

'Hardly anything. That's why I was rather shocked. It was at the crossroads, just outside Barnham Parva village. Fortunately, I was slowing down to turn left. A van turned out suddenly in front of us.'

'You didn't see it coming at all?'

'Not with all that rain. And they hadn't put their headlights on until they saw us.'

CHAPTER 15

Dom had rung Taryn last night to ensure she was still coping. He'd been surprised when Rhys answered. The news that he was there taking care of her because the police had forensic investigators doing a detailed analysis of Joe's room was a sop to Dom's emotions. He felt that Taryn should have asked for him, even if they had parted with difficult words. It wouldn't have been the first time.

He hadn't answered the message from the detective, so he was unsurprised to find the same woman and her boss waiting for him when he reached his office first thing on Thursday.

'Sorry I didn't ring.' He unlocked his office and arranged a couple of chairs for the detectives to use. 'It was late when I finished training, and I didn't think you would still be working. It was the first thing on my to-do list this morning.'

'Training?' DS Hirst looked him up and down as if assessing his fitness. 'For anything in particular?'

'I'm a triathlete. In fact, I may make the Olympic squad if I keep up the standard of my performances.'

DI Edwards now assessed him as well. 'Impressive. I thought athletes at that level were full-time professionals these days.'

'Paralympics,' said Dom. 'We don't always get the same support.'

'Really?' The DI didn't seem convinced.

Dom pulled up the leg of his jeans to display his prosthetic leg. 'You can't see when I've got my trousers on.'

'I watched that at the last Olympics,' said Sara. 'The times are pretty amazing. You must have to train hard.'

Dom sat behind his desk and pushed the trouser leg back down. 'I do, although having the three disciplines means that I get plenty of variety.'

'Have you always had this?' Edwards waved at his own legs. 'I mean, was it from birth, or did something happen later on?'

'It was an accident,' replied Dom. He was starting to feel cross at these personal questions. 'You might know, actually. I was the victim of a hit-and-run five years ago. Your lot never managed to solve the crime. Now, how can I help you?'

'We're sorry to sound nosy about your private life,' the DS apologised. 'We're here about your friend Joe Summerhill.'

'Have you found him?' snapped Dom. 'Or is that going to be another thing you can't solve?'

He smiled a little as he watched the DI purse his lips and shuffle in his chair. Dom had managed to rile the old bugger. Serve him right for asking about his leg. Advantage Wilkins. Sara seemed less put out. Dom shifted his attention to her. She was rather good-looking when he viewed her properly. Not that she would be interested in him, no one ever was these days. Who wanted a half-man?

'Can you tell us when you last saw or spoke to Mr Summerhill?' she asked.

'About a week ago.' Dom leaned forward on his desk. 'He'd just been told that he'd won this big research grant. We met for a drink at lunchtime to celebrate. Wednesday or Thursday, I can't be exact.'

'No contact since then?'

'We don't see each other that often.'

'Even though you both work here at the university?'

'I'm usually training in the evenings,' said Dom. 'It's a big responsibility, representing my country like this. I wasn't aware that he was missing until Taryn contacted me yesterday.'

'That's when you called his housemate?' DI Edwards prompted. Dom flicked him a look, then returned his attention to Sara.

'Yes. Taryn was very worried, especially when Rhys said it looked like his room had been burgled. I assume he reported him missing?'

'He did.'

'I've heard the rumour about the body at Barnham Parva New Hall. Is that why you're searching his room? Do you think it's him?'

'I can't say, sir,' said Sara.

'Out of interest, sir,' said the DI. 'Where were you at the weekend?'

Dom felt his hackles rising in anger. He gripped the edge of his desk with his good hand as he stared at Edwards. 'As a matter of fact, I was competing in an early season event. In Leicestershire.'

'All weekend?'

'On Sunday. I drove over on Saturday and stayed in a hotel, because the race started early.'

'Did you come home after the event?'

'Yes I did.' Dom was furious now, barely able to stop himself from swearing at the man. 'So there are witnesses to my being there and you can ask my mother what time I got home.'

The DS tried a conciliatory smile. 'We have to ask everyone, Mr Wilkins. I'm sure you understand. Can I ask, did Mr Summerhill mention anything about online threats he had been receiving?'

They had been doing their homework. Dom admired them for that. If only the other coppers had been as diligent about his accident. 'It had been going on for ages. Once you stick your head above the parapet on climate change issues, all sorts of nutters come out of the woodwork. Fake science and keyboard warriors.' He almost snarled these last words.

'Was it more than that?' Sara persisted. 'We believe you and Doctor Deacon might have been included in some of this.'

'Yes, we all were, sometimes. Actually, that only started about six months ago. One of the regular haters started to go a bit loopy.'

'How did they know about you?'

'None of us could work that out. At first, we wondered if it was someone we knew doing it, thinking it was a joke.'

'They didn't say anything that might help you identify them?'

Dom thought about this. 'Nothing specific. They keep ranting on about our achievements. How we didn't deserve them. How we were useless and deserved to die.'

Sara frowned. 'Were the messages only sent to Mr Summerhill?'

'I think so. I never got anything directly. Nor did the girls, as far as I'm aware.'

'Girls?'

'Surely someone has explained about the Famous Four?'

'Not as such,' said Sara. 'Enlighten us.'

This was going to sound arrogant, but what the hell. Dom grinned at the DI. 'It's the nickname we gave ourselves. Years ago, when we were still at university together. It was meant to be a joke.'

'You weren't famous?'

'Infamous or notorious, more like. We all joined the Rock Music Society in Freshers' Week. For three years, we went together to every gig we could afford. It didn't matter if we knew who the bands were. Let's just say that alcohol was consumed and high jinks may have been had.'

Hirst raised her eyebrows a little. 'Did you manage any study?'

'Enough,' said Dom, still smiling. 'We all managed to get through our various courses. Some with better results than others. The other three went off to do master's degrees of one sort or another. I stayed here.'

'Why was that?'

'I was more interested in sport than what work I did.'

'What happened to the others?'

'Taryn went to the Courtauld until she got her doctorate. She came back here to curate exhibitions, as you must already know. Junina went to the Inns of Court to study for the bar. Joe did his masters at York, came back to do his PhD and stayed to do research.'

'You've all returned to work here in some way?' asked Sara.

'Junina is still in Temple. She's a big-shot defence barrister. That's the irony of it, the name sort of fits these days. I suppose each of us, in our own ways, have become famous.'

'Did anything happen or change six months ago?'

Dom shook his head. 'Nothing, apart from a reunion dinner. Just after I came back from Mexico. Would that count?'

CHAPTER 16

When Sara probed for more information, Dom Wilkins explained that he had been in Mexico competing at an international paratriathlon, representing England. Before flying home, he had purchased four toy llamas from a craft shop near their training base. One for each of the Famous Four, each had a different colour of blanket on their backs. When Sara showed the photo of the llama from the urn, he looked shocked.

'I gave Joe one with a red blanket,' he said quietly. 'I had the blue one. Taryn's was purple, and Junina's was green.'

Sara couldn't help but wonder why he could remember so specifically who'd had which colour. She didn't think she would have retained a detail like that. The one in the picture had no blanket or saddlecloth at all. 'As a precaution, can we arrange to take a DNA sample? In case it's one you have touched?'

Wilkins reluctantly agreed. He looked shaken as he showed Edwards and Sara out of his office and down to the Street. Edwards steered them past the shops to a square set inside an amphitheatre of steps, which students were using as a meeting place. Groups sat on the steps or stood near the café, chattering and being boisterous. Sara phoned Aggie to arrange for the DNA swab to be done, striding behind

Edwards, who clearly couldn't wait to get away from the crowds of youngsters.

'Place is a nightmare,' he grumbled. He shoved the map at Sara, and it crumpled as she caught it. 'Can't make head nor tail of that.'

Smoothing the thing out, Sara orientated herself. 'We go left along this walkway.'

Sounding more confident than she felt, they climbed a set of concrete steps, then descended another and passed along the main building until they reached the end of the pavement. A small spiral staircase led to the ground, while a metal walkway headed towards a door halfway up the wall of a long hangar-like metal-clad building. Edwards trotted energetically down the spiral, and Sara was forced to follow him as he marched towards the long metal wall. There were three sets of glass doors set at intervals along it.

'I assume this is it,' she said.

'Amazing, isn't it?' asked Edwards. Sarcasm dripped from every vowel. 'Bloody place has won awards and everything. Looks like it belongs on an RAF base, if you ask me.'

The first set of doors swished open. Inside was a distinct contrast to the outside. The metal framework of the building was clearly visible reaching up to the roof. There was a gentle hum of some sort, perhaps air conditioning, while the grey walls and carpet gave a sense of mellow calm. Voices could be heard, though none were raised or angry. There was cheerful chatter and the tinkle of crockery from somewhere.

Edwards had already reached the reception desk and was demanding in a raised tone to see Emilia Thornton. Sara caught him up before he could annoy someone and explained about the appointment. The young man on the desk returned her smile before checking a staff list and picking up the phone.

'Ms Thornton will be along in a moment,' he confirmed. 'She suggested you pop into the café to wait.'

Behind the desk was a small shop, beyond that tables and chairs for the café. Sara left Edwards staring round in bemusement while she sorted out some drinks. As she waited for their order, she looked at the gallery spaces clearly visible on either side of the café. Windows stretched above the entrances, and the end wall of the building was made entirely of tinted glass, allowing natural light to diffuse around the space. There were cases with ethnic artefacts in them. Moveable screens of varying heights created wall-hanging spaces for paintings. There were sculptures and display cases of pottery, next to tiny drawings and wartime sketches. Each item was clearly prized and cared for equally. Although it surprised her, Sara realised she could like the place. It felt calm and welcoming. Perhaps Aggie was right about visiting here.

Edwards was sitting with his back to the larger gallery. Sara nodded behind him. 'Unless I'm very much mistaken, that looks like the Alec Clifton.'

The DI swivelled round to look, then grunted. 'I'm not sure how this is going to help.'

'Just seems the easiest way to find out more about where the victim was left. It might give us some insight as to why.'

They had finished their drinks when a short, blonde woman approached them. Her fashionable floral dress was topped with a pale-lemon cardigan. It looked smart without being intimidating. Even so, she had authority in her manner and walk. You couldn't doubt that she was in charge of something.

'Emilia Thornton.' She shook their hands firmly. 'How can I help you?'

After a brief explanation from Sara, Emilia led them along a short barrier and into the gallery. The soft grey carpet muffled the sound of visitors walking around the displays. A guide was talking to a small group of adults standing in front of a brightly coloured painting. They passed them to reach the tall raw pottery urn on a large square dais.

'These two galleries are free to access,' explained Emilia. She pointed to a glass wall with offices partway down the building. 'Beyond that wall is the Art History department offices. Some of my curators also have workspaces there. My office is on the mezzanine floor above that. At the far end is the main restaurant. Here we are, Alec Clifton.'

Edwards pursed his lips. He looked disdainfully at the large urn. On its stand, it was almost as tall as the two detectives. 'This one has no lid.'

'No, the artist doesn't always make them with lids,' agreed Emilia.

'Would it be waterproof?' Edwards asked.

'I doubt it. I don't think he began to make them suitable for outdoor display until later on.'

'So, the one the Gordons have is a later model?'

Emilia winced. Edwards had made the artwork sound like a cheap car. 'Yes indeed. By several years. Why are you interested?'

Edwards looked to Sara. 'You may have heard the rumours?'

'That a body has been found at Barnham Parva New Hall? Hardly a rumour anymore. It's been on the local radio this morning.'

Edwards sighed and muttered, 'For God's sake. How did that get out?'

Emilia raised a neatly sculpted eyebrow. 'I'm sorry this has happened. Mr and Mrs Gordon are great supporters of us here. They are good friends to us. But why this?'

Sara pointed to the display dais. 'May I?'

'Only if you absolutely have to, and try not to touch it.' Emilia didn't take her eyes off Sara as she stepped gently up and peered inside the urn.

'Not as big inside,' she said to Edwards. 'Wouldn't work with this one.'

She carefully stepped down again.

The head of collections eyed her beadily. 'Has this something to do with the body?'

'Yes, I'm afraid so,' said Sara. The woman was obviously going to be bright to hold down a job like this — there was no point in denying it.

'They put the young man's body inside an Alec Clifton?'

Sara wasn't sure if the outrage was because the man was dead or at the sacrilege of leaving a corpse inside a valuable

74

artwork. 'I'm afraid so, but that information is strictly not for public dissemination at this time.'

'Of course.' Emilia nodded and stood back to look at the urn. 'Poor soul. That would have been quite a problem, wouldn't it? Lifting a dead body that high without pushing the urn over. I mean, these artworks are heavy, but they wouldn't be completely stable if you tried to heave a heavy object into the top.'

'It's certainly a problem we have to solve.' Sara reached into her pocket to retrieve the photo of the toy llama. 'This is another.'

Emilia Thornton took the picture and studied it. 'Why?'

'It was left on the body, and we don't yet know why. Any suggestions?'

Edwards mumbled about needing to leave. Sara deliberately ignored him. The DI turned his back to look at a nearby painting, which from the set of his shoulders, Sara assumed he didn't much like either.

'I might,' said Emilia after a long couple of minutes. 'Come with me.'

Edwards strode after them as the small woman headed off past the display cases and paintings to the far end of the gallery.

'The collection has a wide-ranging ethnographic content,' she said. 'This is one of our most popular pieces with the visitors.'

In a protective case that raised it to eye level, and lit from below, glittered a silver model llama. It was larger than the toy they had found, but the shape and form were nearly identical.

'It was made by the Incas,' explained Emilia. 'They left them in formal burials as offerings for the dead. Beautiful, isn't it?'

Sara nodded in agreement.

'This one is most unusual,' Emilia continued.

'Why?'

'Normally, they were much smaller than this. About a quarter of this size, in fact. And this one wasn't found in a normal burial. It was found with a ritual sacrifice.'

CHAPTER 17

Rose was in later than usual on Thursday, grabbing the last space in the staff car park for the Sainsbury Centre. The department was already working, office lights were on, and a tutorial was taking place in the central work area. The main gallery was also open, and a few visitors could be heard beyond the wall of offices.

The building had its own particular ambience. The low-level background hum from the air conditioning was pleasant enough. Sounds echoed up into the metal girders of the roof, where they usually became dispersed and muted. Even the noise of people in the cafés or galleries was suppressed by the ceiling height. Rose opened her tiny glass-fronted office and turned on her computer.

A loud guttural sound, part howl, part anger, suddenly came from Chandler's office.

'Bastards! They shouldn't be doing that,' he said so loudly that the partition between their offices might as well have not been there.

Dropping her things, she walked swiftly next door, her eyes wide in astonishment. She had never heard her boss speak like this, didn't think he had it in him.

'Can't we stop them?' Chandler demanded. He waved at Rose to enter his office and shut the door behind her. 'He hasn't been officially identified, has he?'

The voice at the other of the phone warbled more news. Chandler murmured and muttered until finally killing the call.

'Whatever is the matter?' Rose knew she sounded rather shocked.

'I'm sorry, Rose,' said Chandler. 'I didn't mean to startle you. How are you today?'

Rose shrugged. 'I'm here. Whatever is going on?'

'You may not have heard,' said Chandler. 'They've found a young man's body at Barnham Parva New Hall. Rumours were flying all over the place here yesterday.'

'You mean dead?' Rose's voice became a squeak. 'That's terrible.'

Chandler nodded. 'Now it seems that the local press have got hold of it. Broadcast it on the radio first, now on the local news. That means the Gordons will be hounded by television crews, no doubt.'

'The poor things,' said Rose. She sank into the visitors' sofa.

Chandler suddenly moved to sit next to her. 'How stupid of me,' he said. He patted Rose's hand awkwardly. 'After your Eeyore day.'

'Why would it be a rumour here?'

'They say it's one of the staff. A researcher from CRU. Taryn has been worried about a missing friend for a couple of days. Her boyfriend, in fact.'

Rose let her eyes widen as if she had just put the two suggestions together. 'It might be her boyfriend? Is that what they're saying?'

'He's still missing, and she's come into work this morning.' Chandler glanced over his shoulder and through the glass wall. 'I was amazed. Would you feel up to chatting with her? On Emilia's and my behalf?'

For a moment, Rose bridled at the idea that he was using her to have a conversation he wanted to avoid. Then curiosity got the better of her. 'I'll pop in to see how she's getting on.'

'Thank you.' Chandler sounded relieved. 'Of course, it might not be her boyfriend at all. Tell her she can go home if she would prefer. I would understand. Look after her for me, will you?'

He probably wouldn't understand, Rose thought as she returned to her office. *He's never had a bereavement. At least he tries to be a good boss, I suppose.*

She made sure everything was up and running, glanced through her emails for anything urgent, then went further along the row of offices to find Taryn. Rose found the whole goth thing unconvincing in this doctor of art history, although she conceded that it suited Taryn as a look. Rose just thought it pretentious.

There was no need for white make-up this morning. Or black eyeliner. Taryn looked as if she had been drained by one of those vampires she so loved to emulate. Her skin was pale and waxy. There were deep, dark bags under her eyes. For once, she was wearing a pair of jeans and a simple roll-neck jumper, although they were, of course, black.

Although she was sitting at her computer, Taryn's fingers lay on the keyboard, trembling and unmoving. When Rose tapped on the open glass door, the young woman visibly jumped, her body jolting away from the desk and back into her chair. Momentarily, her eyes closed.

'Oh, my dear,' said Rose. She went into the office, climbed over the piles of books on the floor and held out her arms. 'Do you need a hug from a mum?'

Taryn nodded, tears seeping down her cheeks. Rose pulled her into a gentle embrace and, after a small hesitation, Taryn wrapped her arms around Rose's waist with a sigh.

'It has to be Joe, doesn't it?'

'I don't know,' said Rose. 'How can we find out?'

'His parents.' Taryn straightened up to wipe her eyes with a tissue from a box in her desk drawer. Even the carton had comic Halloween pictures on it. 'They said they'd let me know if they heard anything.'

'Haven't the police been in touch with them?'

'Only to ask if they think he's missing. I spoke to them last night when Rhys was with me.'

'And did his parents think he was?'

'They thought he had been working.'

'Typical of the police,' said Rose.

Taryn looked up at her. 'What do you mean?'

'To call and say something guaranteed to make you worry, then say they can't confirm anything. I don't think they realise how crass that is when you're a parent.'

Taryn nodded. She knew a little about Rose's losses. 'Was it like this when your daughter had her accident?'

'Yes.' The words grated out between Rose's teeth. 'Called to ask if we knew where Lily was. As if they didn't know she was in A & E. Didn't come round for a couple of hours after that to find us. It was too late by then. We had already rung the hospital and gone to be with her.'

'That's awful.' Taryn's eyes were hollow with shock. She began to weep again, reaching out to pick up the small toy llama sitting next to her computer screen. Turning it over and over, Taryn allowed it to settle in her palm and began to pick at the tiny purple saddlecloth draped over its back. 'Dom gave us all one of these when he came back from Mexico.'

'I remember you telling me,' said Rose. 'A lovely present.'

'The only one he ever gave me.' Taryn squeezed the toy hard. 'He said it was to be a symbol of our lasting friendship as a group. Joe had one with a red saddle.'

'If I might say so, I don't think this is the best place for you to be while you wait for news.'

'If I go home, I'll only be on my own. What good is that? I can't face going on the bus looking like this.'

'That's not a problem. I can run you back in my car and stay for a while, if you'd like me to. Perhaps you should take the llama home with you, as it means so much.'

'A lift would be wonderful.'

'I'll just get my keys.' Rose headed back to her own office to fetch her handbag.

CHAPTER 18

Edwards drove Sara to the hospital mortuary, which was no more than a few minutes around the university park. Dr Taylor was waiting for them, the victim's body carefully stretched back into a normal shape and covered with a sheet. The head was propped on a stand to prevent it from pulling backwards. They gathered around the examination table.

'We'll have formal DNA confirmation later today, I hope,' Dr Taylor said. 'The hairbrush samples show a match to the victim's hair colour. Now we can see his face properly, he looks like the man in the photo you sent through to me. To be honest, I'd be surprised if this isn't Joe Summerhill.'

'What have you got that we can work with?' asked Edwards.

'There are scratches down the back and rear of the legs. I'd say they were from where our victim fell or was pushed into the urn.'

'Fell?'

'I'm convinced that he was alive when he went into the thing.' Taylor chewed his lip reflectively. 'Not necessarily conscious, though. Could have been really woozy or completely out of it.'

'So how did he get up there without knocking the thing over?'

'You should speak to the forensic team about that,' said Taylor. 'There were some bizarre wheel tracks cut into the lawn that went up to the side of the urn. That might help.'

'Do you think he'd been drinking?' asked Sara.

'No, the tox screen shows no evidence of alcohol. I think our victim may have been drugged. Again, there's nothing specific showing on the tox screen, but that doesn't mean it wasn't there.'

'What do you mean?'

'There are certain date-rape drugs that are easily put in drinks, which become untraceable in the gut very quickly. They give certain side effects that the perp might have found useful, like sleepiness and disorientation. I've sent away some other samples to test for those.'

'Joe Summerhill has been missing since Saturday afternoon,' said Sara. 'Could he have been imprisoned somewhere, kept drugged and quiet, perhaps?'

'That's a lot of effort.' Edwards sounded sceptical.

'It's a lot of organisation,' agreed Sara. 'He would have needed to have been hidden somewhere no one other than his jailer could access.'

'Somewhere he couldn't be heard shouting?' asked Dr Taylor.

'Or where no one would see them coming and going,' added Sara.

'It's a big county,' said Edwards. 'Lots of empty places you could use.'

'So, this dumpsite is carefully and specifically chosen,' said Sara with a grimace. 'And whoever our perp is, they've kept the victim locked up for up to three days. That takes a lot of planning. And you think he was definitely alive when he went in?'

'Yes.'

'So how did he die exactly?' asked Edwards.

'This is just a working theory, you understand,' began Taylor.

They both nodded.

'I think he was drugged and taken to the site. Somehow, he was persuaded to sit on the lip of the urn or stand beside it. Then he was placed or pushed inside.'

'Still conscious?'

'Possibly.' Taylor pointed to the long gash across Summerhill's throat. 'Then whoever was with him lifted his head and slashed his throat, possibly with a cut-throat razor. He bled to death.'

Sara was aware that her mouth was open. She quietly closed it. There was a long silence in the examination room. None of the three moved as the detectives tried to navigate the information. If Taylor was right, this was a bizarre killing.

Sara let out a noisy breath. 'They would have been covered in blood.'

'Indeed. A deep cut here would have created a wide spray of blood from the main artery. Of course, the rain would have washed away some of it at the site. Much of it was inside the urn. I don't envy the crime scene cleaners dealing with that.'

'Would the perp have to be strong to do all this?'

'Depends how they got him up there,' said Taylor. 'Not much strength would be required to lift the head, and the cut would be easy if the razor was sharp enough.'

'I've never heard anything like it!' Edwards paced to the end of the mortuary and sat heavily on one of the high stools by the workbench. 'What the hell is going on?'

Taylor followed him. 'It's extreme,' he agreed. 'Did you get anywhere with that toy animal?'

Sara pulled the sheet over Joe Summerhill's face and joined them. She explained the link to tourist items from South America.

'That makes even more sense.' Taylor clicked on the computer and opened a newspaper website. 'Look at this article.'

Sara read aloud. '"Mummified body of an Incan maiden." I think I've heard of this. They found it at the top of a mountain, didn't they?' She read on. '"Ritual sacrifice . . . drugged and plied with drink . . . left to freeze to death."'

'That doesn't add up.' Edwards moved to look at the screen. 'Our victim wasn't left to freeze to death.'

'It was cold and wet,' countered Taylor. 'This artwork is also modelled on ancient Inca funeral urns. Did you know that?'

'We spoke to the head of collections at the Sainsbury Centre,' broke in Sara. 'She showed us an Incan silver llama that was left at a ritual sacrifice. Could this one have been left for the same reason?'

'It's elaborate,' said Taylor. 'It's obscure. It's also deliberate and well planned. Whoever did this was clearly sending a message.'

'Either way, it looks like a ritual killing,' Edwards said. 'Dear God. It looks like we have a nutter on our hands. An educated and organised one.'

CHAPTER 19

Edwards and Sara relayed the PM results to a stunned team. Aggie looked as if she might pass out. Noble sat rigidly upright in his chair, his eyes unfocused. Only Bowen seemed to be thinking rather than being emotional.

'Whoever and whatever this is about,' he said, 'it's taken a lot of planning and research. It's hardly a spur-of-the-moment thing, is it?'

'It doesn't seem a random choice of victim to me, either,' said Sara. 'Joe isn't the target of generalised insanity. He wasn't just someone in the wrong place at the wrong time. He was specifically chosen.'

'Indeed,' said Edwards. 'So was the dumpsite. Does that narrow it down to someone who knows or knew Joe in the past?'

'Or a close friend?' Sara smiled. 'Who had reason to be jealous?'

Edwards grinned at her. 'Dom Wilkins? Perhaps.'

'Did he know about Taryn and Joe sooner than he's claiming?'

'It could be someone who researched him specifically,' suggested Aggie. Her voice wavered with suppressed emotion. 'As a representative of the climate change community.'

Sara narrowed her eyes as she worked through an idea. 'It's certainly someone who knows about the Gordons' art collection. Not just the contents but its significance. Is that the best place to start?'

'Open-day visitors,' said Edwards. 'Did you get those lists?' Aggie nodded. 'Can you get back in touch and ask about these visits by the art students too? See how many of those there have been in the last twelve months.'

Aggie distributed copies of the visitor lists. 'This is shocking,' she murmured. 'Even by our standards.'

No one contradicted her.

'Same with the llama toy,' Sara continued. 'That's significant too. Unfortunately, anyone who visits the free gallery at the centre could have read up about that.'

'Worth bearing in mind,' agreed Edwards. 'Mobile records?'

'The company are sending them through this afternoon,' said Bowen.

'How's the CCTV coming on?'

Noble was jolted out of his visualisation. 'Very well, sir. We were going to show you when you first came in.'

He brought up a grainy CCTV video on his screen, and they all gathered round to look. It was timestamped at 23.25. The rain was bucketing down, and the lens of the camera that overlooked the front of the Hall was blotted with rain droplets.

Noble ran the sequence. 'This van comes in. Might be white, might be light grey. Couldn't see any signs or trade advertising on the side. It's a box type, but I don't recognise the model, and you can't see the number plates. Then it does this.'

The van had its headlights up full. The driver parked it at a precise distance and angle so that the lights blinded their view.

'Damn,' breathed Edwards. 'Planned and deliberate.'

'Then this happens. There's no sound, by the way,' said Noble. 'The camera isn't as high as you might think. It's over that entrance porch and easily accessible from a ladder.'

After a minute or so, a hand in a dark glove appeared from below the lens. It briefly held a piece of fabric that was swiftly wrapped around the camera.

'That stays there for the better part of fifteen minutes.' Noble ran the image forward until he reached another change. The timer now said 23.39, and the piece of cloth was suddenly removed. 'I can't see a hand this time. So, I guess it was pulled down somehow.'

The van still faced the camera, its lights on full and swung around. The headlights flicked off and it carried on up the driveway, too far away and too dark for the rain-soaked camera to pick up the number plate. The outside light for the Hall came on too late to help.

'I'm sorry, it's not much use.'

'It's extremely useful,' replied Edwards. 'For a start, we have an exact time frame now. We know the victim was brought in a van and that it took a significant amount of time to deposit him. We also know that the driver knew where the house CCTV cameras were.'

Noble brightened up.

'Get me as clear a sample of the van picture as you can,' said Edwards. 'Graham in Forensics keeps a useful list of likely vehicles. I bet he can identify the make and model.'

'It tells us something else too,' said Sara. 'Whoever was driving had a good idea that the occupants of the Hall were going to be out. They couldn't risk turning up and anyone hearing them.'

Edwards turned to Bowen. 'Mike, I want you to speak to Stuart or Rich. Find out where they went after this reception. Sara, I think we need to chat with whoever organised that evening event at the Sainsbury Centre, don't you? Find out who that is.'

'What about these email threats? Shall I head down to Technical afterwards?'

'Good idea. I'd better go up and report to ACC Miller before he has to ask for an update.'

Edwards vanished upstairs while Sara rang the university.

'Guest lists are agreed by Ms Thornton,' said the PA. 'There are a number of standard invites, including Mr and Mrs Gordon. Then others who would be specifically invited to the given exhibition.'

'Do you send these out?'

'The practical stuff is usually done by Rose Crawford. Sends out the invites, keeps the reply list up to date, organises the buffet and all that kind of thing.'

'Rose Crawford?'

'She's Professor Chandler's assistant. She'd be the best one to speak to. Unfortunately, she's out at the moment. I think she'll be back later this afternoon.'

'Can you ask her to call me?' asked Sara. The secretary agreed and took the number.

Sara headed downstairs to the Technical Forensics team with an impatient sigh. Their office was at the end of an open-plan area that reached from the canteen wall to the edge of the HQ plot. The windows were shrouded outside by dense greenery, which formed an impenetrable hedge. It also gave the area a weird dark-green glow behind the strip lights and desk lamps. She was directed to a middle-aged man called Rob.

The man was hunched forward, his shirt pulled out of his trousers at the back and carelessly hanging down. A food paunch strained at the buttons on the front. Wire-rimmed glasses were rammed up to the bridge of his nose. It looked to Sara as if a haircut wouldn't go amiss. Joe Summerhill's laptop was open on his workbench, the screen scrolling through endless streams of data analysis, watched intently by Rob.

Sara introduced herself. 'Found anything yet?'

'Some good stuff.' Rob hit a pause icon, then opened one of the multiple tabs at the top of the screen. 'The emails were easy enough to get to. I've separated the threatening stuff.'

He showed Sara a few samples. 'Most of it is the usual keyboard warrior fare. "You're all liars, climate change doesn't exist, you don't deserve to be alive", et cetera, et cetera.'

'Whoa.' Sara flinched from the email she'd just noticed. '"You should kill yourself for your lies. If you don't, I'll come round and do it for you."'

'Standard,' shrugged Rob. He opened a different file. 'These are the ones you'll be wanting.'

Sara had to agree that this selection was different. As she scanned through the messages, they began to sound familiar in tone. 'Sounds like one person wrote these, doesn't it? Where has this all come from?'

'I've run a few diagnostics,' said Rob. 'The warrior stuff comes from the usual sources. Hard to trace as they've been bounced off servers in Russia or the Far East. Some of it's even generated by computer robots. If you need me to be more accurate, I can be?'

'I don't expect so,' said Sara. 'What about these ones?'

'They're hidden behind a series of redirects. I'm still working on them, but it should be possible to drill it down.'

Rob flicked on the tabs to reach the screen with the analytics and unpaused it. The lines of programming screed began to roll again. 'That's what I'm trying here. This author is a very experienced hacker or fake news generator. That makes it more of a challenge, just as I like it. I'll find them.'

CHAPTER 20

The interview with the officers hadn't worried Dom too much, although they had asked for a lot of details about his trip. For some reason, they were interested in the gifts he had brought back as well, though they wouldn't say why. He shrugged it off and worked through the rest of his day as usual. It was going to be a fine, clear evening, perfect for a long training ride. Until a text arrived on his mobile.

Police have confirmed body is Joe. Taryn is melting down. Can you go round now? Rhys

It was almost time to finish, and Dom knew no one would notice if he left immediately. As he headed for the car park, he called Rhys.

'I thought you were with Taryn,' he said.

'Had to come into work,' Rhys replied. 'Taryn did the same.'

'She came into work today?' Dom was shocked. 'Surely they would have let her have a day off under the circumstances?'

'Taryn insisted.' Rhys sounded defensive. 'I gave her a lift in.'

Dom skidded to a halt. 'She's at the SCVA?'

'Nah. Couldn't cope. Some secretary ran her home. Been sitting with her all afternoon as well, while they waited for news about Joe.'

'Who?'

'Someone called Rose?'

'Oh, I know,' said Dom. He was relieved. 'Professor Chandler's PA. Nice lady. So how do you know?'

'This Rose person called me. Apparently, Taryn had a message from Joe's parents. The police confirmed it to them. They're already on their way up, and I've got to try and find them a hotel.'

'Okay, you deal with that. I'll get to Taryn,' said Dom. Realising that this sounded high-handed, he added, 'Thank you for what you're doing.'

'No problem.' Rhys was tapping at a keyboard in the background. 'I'm on it now. I'll go back to Taryn's place when I've done this.'

'See you there.'

Dom pulled out into the rush hour traffic. Angered by the queue of cars inching along Bluebell Road, he turned towards the city centre down an estate road. It was a rat run for those in the know, although it probably didn't save him any time. As he sat behind some cars at a set of traffic lights, he counted the number in front of him. Six. Four got across on each change. He let go a roar of frustration. His hands began to shake. Sweat broke out on his forehead and trickled down his cheeks.

'Damn it to hell!' he swore.

It wasn't sweat. It was tears. Taryn wasn't the only one who had lost a friend. So had he. He momentarily forgave the news about the growing relationship between Joe and Taryn. Dom longed to sweep his friend up in his arms and hold her until they both felt better.

Parking on Taryn's street was always difficult. Dom swung into the car park at the pub on the corner, vowing to square it with the landlord later on. They drank there often enough.

It was the professor's PA who answered the door. She seemed to recognise Dom, although he might not have returned the favour, meeting her out of context like this. She had a practical air about her, although she looked worried.

'Taryn's in the living room.' She pulled her cardigan around her chest and folded her arms. 'Poor thing's very upset.'

'Rose, isn't it?' Dom squeezed past the woman into the hallway. He could hear Taryn's sobs through the dark-painted door.

'That's right.'

Taryn was hunched on the sofa, bent almost in half. Her arms were laced around her knees, her head bowed, forehead tucked under. A sideways glance brought her head up when she recognised Dom. Then he was on the sofa beside her. They wrapped their arms around each other, hugging so tightly that Dom could hardly breathe.

'I'll put the kettle on,' said Rose from the doorway. She pattered down the hall to the kitchen at the back of the house.

'H-he's dead,' stuttered Taryn. 'His father told me. It's definitely Joe.'

'Shhh, there, there,' he murmured, perhaps for himself. Their tears were mingling. He'd never held a baby, but Dom found himself instinctively rocking for comfort. As his breathing began to slow, he unlocked one hand to wipe his face. Feeling the gesture, Taryn looked up.

'Tissues.' She pointed to the coffee table.

Piles of used ones littered the carpet, overflowing from the wastebasket at the side of the sofa. Dom blew his nose and tried his best to regain composure. He cleared his throat, took deep breaths and patted Taryn gently on the back.

More baby gestures, where did they come from? Dom wondered. A deep memory surfaced of himself lying in a hospital bed, newly awake after the operation to amputate his leg. Connected to drips and machines, Taryn and his mother had held one hand each. When he had tried to sit up, it was Taryn who had pulled him into a hug, rocked him, patted his back.

'I'm so sorry,' he said.

Taryn slumped into the sofa. 'He was your friend too.'

'Yes,' said Dom. 'But he was your boyfriend.'

Taryn nodded gently. 'Thank you.'

Rose returned with mugs of tea on a tray. There was sugar in a black bowl and milk in a jug shaped like a raven. He smiled. 'Nevermore.'

Rose looked confused. Dom pointed to the jug.

'*Thus quoth the raven, "Nevermore."*'

'*Quoth*,' said Taryn. Her eyes were closed.

'What?' Dom glanced at her.

'Everyone thinks it goes, *Thus quoth*. It doesn't. It's just, *Quoth the raven, "Nevermore."*'

'If you say so.'

Rose sat down opposite them. The chair creaked, and Taryn's eyes flew open.

'What are you doing?' she demanded.

Rose shot up from the gilded seat with its blood-red cover. 'I'm sorry. I was only trying to help.'

'No one sits in that chair. No one.' Taryn's voice was broken but full of force. 'It's a genuine prop. I have the provenance from the auction and everything.'

Wide-eyed, Rose turned to look at the chair with its gothic embellishments. The high back had a triangle form with carved tracery and a spike on either side at the top. The gold paint that covered it was rubbing away here and there. The velvet seat cushion was worn in patches. Splinters of wood were shaved out of the armrests.

'Prop? I'm sorry, I didn't realise,' said Rose. She looked unsure what to do, then shrugged her shoulders. 'I'll get my coat.' She went out into the hall.

Dom handed Taryn a mug. 'Steady on,' he said. 'Rose has been looking after you all day.'

Taryn nodded. Her eyes closed again. When Rose returned to collect her handbag, Taryn tried to force a smile.

Dom escorted Rose to the door. 'I'm so sorry about that,' he said. 'It's very precious to her. It came from the Hammer horror film studio props sale. We watched their films to see if it had been used. Which it had, rather a lot, including in the first *Dracula* with Christopher Lee. Taryn's a big fan of his.'

Rose nodded, although she still looked confused. 'I can see that it meant a lot to her. I'm sorry if I made things worse.'

'I'm just so grateful that you have been here all day. It's so kind of you.'

'No problem. Can I suggest that you contact Taryn's doctor? She may need some help sleeping tonight.'

'Good idea.' Dom agreed.

'I'll be off, then.'

As Dom opened the door for her, the front garden gate rattled. At the bottom of the footpath stood the female detective who had interviewed him that morning, although there was no sign of her boss. She opened the gate for Rose to leave, then stepped up to the front door. 'I've come to see Taryn. Is she available?'

'I don't know if she'll speak to you. But if you've come to tell her that Joe Summerhill is dead, you're too late. We already know.'

CHAPTER 21

'Could I speak to her anyway?' asked Sara.

Wilkins directed her to the living room and shut the front door with a bang. Taryn was slumped on the sofa, her eyes closed and her face ravaged by weeping. As she asked if she could sit down, Taryn's eyes flew open. 'Not on there,' she snapped, indicating the gothic prop chair.

Sara perched on the second black leather sofa. 'You seem to have heard that we have confirmation of the identity of our victim,' she began, hearing herself sound impersonal and pompous.

Wilkins sat next to Taryn, pulling her against him. 'Joe's parents rang,' he said. His jaw was locked.

'I'm sorry you heard that way.' Sara dropped her voice, hoping that she sounded less officious that way. She was trying too hard. She needed to be more natural. 'I wanted to tell you myself so that you could have time to process this before things got more difficult.'

'How do you mean?' Taryn shifted away from Wilkins and sat up. 'It wasn't an accident, was it? It can't have been.'

'I'm afraid not.' Sara shook her head. 'It is definitely murder. What we need to do now is find the culprit, and I'm afraid that we will need your help. Both of you.'

'We'll do anything, whatever it takes,' swore Taryn. 'Won't we?' She turned to look at Wilkins, who nodded slightly.

'Of course,' he said.

Sara thought he sounded reluctant. 'If you would like, I can organise a family liaison officer for you. Joe's parents will certainly need one, and it could be the same person.'

'His mum and dad can stay with me.' Taryn's eyes glittered. 'It's the least I can do.'

'Rhys is organising a hotel for them,' said Wilkins. 'I think it's best.'

'We'll see about that.' She shrugged Wilkins's hand away, which had been calmly stroking her back.

'Do you know where?' Sara asked.

Wilkins shook his head. 'I'll give him a call and let you know.'

'Thank you.' Sara stood up. 'Are you going to be all right for now?'

'I'll stay,' said Wilkins. 'Rhys said he would be here later on.'

'Then I'll leave you in peace,' said Sara. 'We will need to speak to you both in detail tomorrow to take formal statements. Oh, one thing — can I ask if you still have the gift Mr Wilkins brought you back from Mexico?'

Taryn frowned as Wilkins asked, 'What is it with the bloody toy llamas?'

'It's there.' She pointed to the mantlepiece over the Victorian fireplace, with its fashionable log burner. The fire surround and the burner were both black, in keeping with the décor of the rest of the room. The pale-coloured llama stood out against the dark-red walls behind the collection of knick-knacks, candles and photo frames.

Sara picked it up. 'This one?'

'Yes.'

The toy was less than half the size of the one they had found with Joe's body. Sara turned to Wilkins. 'Were they all the same size?'

'Of course. Why?'

Sara placed the llama back on the mantlepiece. 'Thank you.'

Wilkins took her to the door with formal politeness, making Sara feel as if she were being escorted off the premises.

'One last thing for now,' she said before stepping out. 'Who was the lady who left as I arrived?'

'Rose Crawford,' said Wilkins.

'Professor Chandler's PA?' Sara was surprised.

'Taryn works in the same area. Rose kindly brought Taryn home and stayed with her until I could get here.'

At least I know what she looks like, Sara thought as she thanked Wilkins and headed back to her car. *Think I might make Mrs Crawford a priority tomorrow.*

Back in her car seat, she fired up her mobile and rang Chris. He answered quickly. In the background, she could hear street noise.

'You finished for the night?'

'Just locked up,' he replied. 'Heading home.'

'Despite a new investigation, it looks like I have the night free. How about you?'

There was a pause. Sara heard him unlock the door, the change of noise level indicating he had gone inside the block of flats where he lived. Then he began to climb the stairs. 'I have a rehearsal.'

'I thought you were taking a bit of a break.' Sara sighed. Chris loved to act, and these days he seemed to go from show to show at the Maddermarket Theatre, Norwich's premier amateur dramatic society.

'I am.' A door slammed in the background. Chris seemed to have reached his flat on the first floor. 'It's just that I promised Mel that I would help with her lines for the next show. She's rather worried.'

'Can't it wait until tomorrow?' Her frustration came through her words. 'I may not get much time off for the next few weeks.'

'No, it can't,' snapped Chris. 'I made a promise, and I intend to keep it.'

'What about your promise to me?' Sara demanded.

'Or yours to me? Oh, wait! You haven't made one. You turned my offer down.'

'I thought we'd been through all that. Agreed to leave things as they were for now.'

'If you didn't live all the way out on the coast, life would be so much simpler.' Chris sounded as frustrated as Sara felt.

'I'm not sure this is a conversation we should be having over the phone,' she said, trying to sound calmer. 'Let me take you out for dinner.'

'Shouldn't that be me asking you that? Leave me some pride.'

Sara gasped. Chris hurtled on before she could say anything. 'No, I don't want dinner. No, I'm not free tonight. I've made other arrangements, which I intend to honour.'

Sara's reply of 'I'll call you soon' was cut off as Chris ended the call.

CHAPTER 22

It had been a near miss. Rose sped down the street outside Taryn's house and climbed with inelegant haste into her car. Thankfully, the traffic was moving, if slowly. It only took a few minutes to reach the ring road. At the traffic lights, Rose checked behind her but couldn't see any car that might have been an unmarked police car following her. She was even more certain by the time she got through Long Stratton, after which she turned down the network of lanes that led to her home.

'Don't be stupid,' she scolded herself. 'I was just helping a colleague in a time of crisis.'

Dropping her handbag on the kitchen table, she reached to fill the kettle and carry out her calming tea ritual. She was home earlier than usual, which gave her time to think and cook, for once. She scrubbed a potato for the microwave.

'Got to keep my strength up,' she said. 'At least for now. Afterwards, it won't matter a damn.'

She carried the tray to her seating area and turned on the television. Some quiz show or other mumbled away in front of her as Rose strained the tea into the pretty cup. A pure silver teaspoon tinkled against the fine bone china as she stirred. It was the last vestige of civilisation to her.

Half an hour later, Rose finished her meal of cheese-filled baked potato. It was filling and sustaining. She washed the pots by hand. There were too few these days to bother with the dishwasher. Before long, she was settled in the chair in her daughter's room.

'I'm going to have to bring the next event forward,' she said to the empty bed. 'That idiot girl might say something incriminating.'

Thinking of Taryn's grief, Rose felt only contempt. What did the stupid child know of real suffering?

'Besides, I don't want to run out of time. What do you think?'

Rose paused as if listening to the answer.

'It was so easy the first time round. It all went precisely to plan,' she continued. 'Now the police are sniffing around. Of course they are. Good job I was prepared for emergencies. It will be all right. You'll see.'

She stood and picked up the large stuffed panda. Cuddling it, Rose wandered about the room, touching objects and looking at pictures. A large painting stood on an easel. Blues, blacks, greens and browns raced and swept around the canvas. Sometimes the colours fell off the edge, while other areas looked like vortexes, with the colours sinking down into the centre until they became a dark morass.

'So talented.' Rose breathed softly. 'You were so talented. They stole your life and your mind. Destroyed everything you lived for. They deserve to be punished.'

With tears in her eyes, she tucked the panda into the bed, turned on the night light and left the room. There were still several hours before she could put her revised plan into action. There was also one hurdle to get over if tonight was to be useful. Plenty of time to do her nightly online trawl.

Clearly, the Norfolk police had given a statement about Joe Summerhill to the press. The internet was alight with the story, from the local newspapers to the darker parts of the web, which was already rife with speculation and conspiracy theories, so bizarre was the placing of the murdered boy.

Even the national news channels were getting in on the act. With luck, their trucks would go and camp out at Barnham Parva New Hall. It was bad enough with the police getting under her feet, without the television crews being all over the place. With a shudder, Rose recalled the fuss the news people had created in Ipswich when those girls had been murdered a few years ago.

Rose carefully printed each report and entry, filing it into her system. She also printed a nice picture of the Hall, with a talking head of a reporter imposed on it. Waiting for it to dry, she felt cross with herself. This information-gathering campaign had consumed her for so long. The planning itself had taken months of research — learning to hide her online activities, sourcing illegal items from the dark web and local drug dealers. When her neighbours had announced their lengthy cruise, she knew the time had come for action. Now she realised that having become locked into her own private world, she had failed to consider some very practical obstacles.

As she stuck the picture up in one of the columns on the wall, Rose felt a rush of anger. 'Grief!' she shouted. Her hands clenched, the knuckles almost bursting through the skin. 'I'll give them grief like they've never known. Even that won't match mine.'

Rose raised her arms and struck down at the column of information. Pins, staples and paper edges scratched her palms as she swept through the accumulated press releases, photos and social media entries she'd printed. The temptation to pound her fists on the wall until they bled overwhelmed her. Her voice stuck in the back of her throat, only issuing a scratchy wail as her hands stilled.

Enough! Rose told herself. *Discipline! That's what will get you through.*

She picked up the debris, put it on the office chair and went through to the kitchen to clean up the cuts. Her heart stopped racing and her breathing settled. She sat in her armchair and waited.

At precisely nine o'clock, Rose rang Taryn's home number. Dom Wilkins answered it.

'I just wanted to ask how Taryn was doing,' she said in her gentlest tone. 'I am so worried for her.'

'That's kind of you. Rhys spoke to the doctor like you suggested.'

'Oh, my dear, is she so distressed?'

'Yes, she is rather,' said Dom. 'He prescribed her some sleeping pills, which Rhys bought from the pharmacy.'

'And has she taken them? Will she get some rest?'

'Knocked her out. I've just been to check on her, and she's sound asleep.'

'You won't leave her alone, will you?' Rose held her breath.

'I've got to go home tonight,' replied Dom. 'Rhys has volunteered to sleep in the spare bedroom in case she wakes up.'

'I couldn't help but notice there was a bottle of wine in the kitchen if you two needed a drink for the shock.'

'We've already found it. Shock is as good an excuse as any.'

'Thank you for talking to me,' said Rose. 'I'm so glad that Taryn has such wonderful friends.'

Difficult, but not impossible. Rose made her decision. Tonight would do. At midnight, she pulled on an old pair of gardening jeans and a dark-grey sweatshirt. Her work clothes went in the washing basket. She collected a sports bag from the study and checked the contents. Everything she needed was there.

She used a torch to get down the garden path to the workshop. Behind it was a patch of dense brambles and dead bushes. Aiden kept promising to clear it, but neither of them knew quite where to start. As it backed onto the copse beyond, it was waste ground in any case. Anything here was completely out of sight.

Pulling at a dirty old piece of tarpaulin, Rose uncovered a tall white van. Its number plates were deliberately obscured with mud. The wheels and sides were also spattered. Dropping the bag into the passenger footwell, she climbed into the driver's seat and started the engine.

CHAPTER 23

Sara had spent last evening watching television and feeling miserable. Chris hadn't spoken to her like that for ages, despite her having turned down his marriage proposal in the summer. He'd helped her in the cottage, taking her dad's old furniture to the tip or slimming down the bookshelves for the charity shop. The place still needed decorating, but between them, they had made it feel like Sara's home rather than her late father's house.

She had always been somewhat resentful of the amount of time Chris spent at the Maddermarket Theatre. Lately, she couldn't fail to have noticed that he was spending ever more time there. Keeping a relationship alive with someone who wasn't in the police force was tricky for many officers. Theirs wasn't the best combination. She just didn't know what she wanted to do about it.

Sara had arranged to meet DC Bowen and Dom Wilkins at Taryn Deacon's house at eight this morning to take statements. She was the first to arrive. The curtains to all the windows at the front, downstairs and upstairs, were still drawn. It looked as if no one was awake yet. Wilkins was the next to arrive, climbing out of his car looking tired and worried.

'I thought the tablets would have worn off by now,' he said as they stood looking up at the drawn curtains of the front bedroom. He explained about the doctor prescribing sleeping tablets for Taryn. 'Even if she's still asleep, I would have thought Rhys would have been up. Shall we go in, or should we wait for your colleague?'

'I guess knocking wouldn't hurt,' she said.

Wilkins brandished a bunch of keys. 'Spare set. I borrowed them last night.'

Sara's detective instinct jangled. Why would Wilkins have taken a set of house keys? He hadn't spent the night here, and he had expected Taryn to be awake by eight.

Wilkins knocked first, then, receiving no answer, unlocked the front door. 'Taryn! Rhys!'

There was no reply. In fact, the whole place felt oddly empty. There was also a smell that Sara hoped she didn't recognise. She placed a restraining hand on Wilkins's arm. 'Can you wait a minute.' It wasn't really a question. Wilkins nodded.

Sara climbed the stairs. 'It's the police, Taryn. DS Hirst. We made an appointment. Remember? Rhys, are you awake?'

'He was going to sleep in the spare bedroom,' called Wilkins from below.

Sara opened the first bedroom door. The room presumably looked over the back garden, as was common in these Victorian terraces. The room was gloomy, the curtains drawn. Someone was in the bed, wrapped in a duvet. It looked like Rhys to her, although she could only see the back of his head.

'Rhys? Mr Davies?'

Stepping closer, Sara could see that he was breathing deeply. He appeared to be sound asleep. If this was acting, he was good at it. She went to the window and drew back the curtains. The morning light filled the room without disturbing the sleeping man. Sara left him to it while she went into the front bedroom. It was much bigger, and given the décor, she assumed it was Taryn's room. The bed seemed to have been slept in, as the duvet was dragged to one side, and clothes were scattered across the floor. Sara returned to the other room. Rhys had turned over and was blinking sleepily in the daylight.

'Mr Davies?' Sara asked from the open doorway. 'Rhys, where is Taryn?'

Rhys frowned. 'In bed. Dom and I helped her to bed last night after she took the sleeping pills.'

'In that room?' Sara pointed along the corridor.

'Yes.' Rhys still seemed half-asleep and was struggling to sit up. 'She fell asleep pretty quickly. Isn't she there?'

'Then what did you do?' Sara felt a growing sense of unease.

'We had a bottle of wine,' said Rhys. 'Dom and me. Found it in the kitchen. Then Dom went home.'

Downstairs, Sara heard Wilkins impatiently set off down the hall. She shot out of the bedroom. 'Don't move!'

She was too late. Wilkins was standing in the living room doorway. He let out a moan of horror.

'Don't touch anything,' Sara shouted. She ran down the stairs.

Before she could reach Wilkins, he shot through the hall to the kitchen. Sara could hear him fumbling with the back door as he retched. He wrenched it open and rushed into the garden, where he was violently sick. Sara didn't follow him.

Given his reaction and fearing the worst, she pulled on a pair of nitrile gloves. Pushing the living room door gently open, the metallic stench of blood hit her, rapidly followed by the more basic smell of urine.

She dialled for backup as she stepped into the room. The sight stopped her, phone in hand.

From the speaker, a female voice called with increasing panic, 'Hello? Hello? Can you hear me? Do you need assistance? Officer? Do you need assistance?'

Sara did need assistance. But she was too rigid with shock to say so.

Taryn was sitting in the golden gothic chair, the one she prized so much. One leg was crossed over the other, her hands folded in her lap. She had been tied to the back of the chair by a long, purple scarf wrapped around her chest and upper arms, which prevented the body from falling forwards.

Her throat was gaping open. Blood had run down her front, soaking the scarf and her pyjamas, spilling onto the chair and the floor. In her lap, nestled in her hands, lay a beige-coloured toy llama.

Sara's eyes flickered to the mantelpiece. The toy that Wilkins had brought from Mexico was missing. The one on Taryn's lap looked larger and had no saddlecloth, just like the one left with Joe Summerhill's body. It also looked free from blood.

The operator on the line was still calling out. 'Caller, I've identified you as Detective Sergeant Sara Hirst. Can you hear me? Give me an indication of your whereabouts. I will summon assistance.'

'Yes. Send backup. Tell DI Edwards in SCU.' Sara reeled off Taryn's address. Behind her, she heard Rhys walking heavily down the stairs as if he were still not really awake.

'What's going on?' he asked.

'Don't come in here,' said Sara. 'Go out into the garden and help Mr Wilkins.'

'If you say so.' Rhys shuffled past towards the kitchen as the letterbox in the front door pushed open.

'Good morning,' called a voice. 'Police here. Is everything okay?'

For once, Sara couldn't have heard a better person than stable and steady DC Mike Bowen. She strode to the door and let him in. 'In here. Put on gloves.'

Bowen did as she said before walking up behind her. He stiffened in disgust at the sight.

'Fucking hell! It's like something out of a horror film.'

CHAPTER 24

Dom vomited until his gut was empty of the breakfast he'd eaten before leaving home. Then he retched some more, bringing up bitter bile while his brain flared up the vision of Taryn's body tied to the chair in full technicolour. Rhys tried to comfort him by patting his shoulder in a supposedly manly way before bringing him a glass of water.

'What's going on?' asked Rhys.

Dom shook his head, unable to begin to put it into words.

'I'll put the kettle on.'

'How English of you,' snarled Dom through gritted teeth. He sipped the water then spat it out on the floor. 'Can't even get that right.'

Rhys stepped back uncertainly. 'What? It's just water.'

Dom threw the glass, shattering it against the wall of the house. 'It was you, wasn't it? You fucking did this to her!'

'What are you talking about?' Rhys held up his hands as Dom advanced. 'Did what? To Taryn, do you mean?'

'Of course I mean Taryn!' Dom had backed Rhys up against the fence. His voice grew louder. 'You did it, didn't you? I should never have left you alone with her.'

'I didn't do anything.' Rhys tried to move sideways, but Dom caught his arms and pinned him against the wood.

'Dom, mate. I didn't sleep with her. You know I wouldn't do that.'

'You think this is about sex? You're not fit so much as to kiss her on the cheek. You killed her, you bastard!'

Dom pulled his head back, intending to headbutt Rhys on the nose. Rhys turned his head away and Dom felt an arm suddenly around his neck, pulling him backwards.

'Come on now, son,' said an older man's gruff voice. 'None of that.'

With one arm around Dom's neck and the other hand holding one of Dom's arms firmly up his back, the man frog-marched him down the narrow garden path. He gave a gentle push, and Dom staggered a few steps forward. Turning angrily, he could see the man holding something up. How dare the man drag him about like this? Didn't he know who he was?

'DC Bowen.' The man waved a warrant card. 'Stay where you are.'

Dom recovered his balance with some of his temper. He held up his hands. 'Okay, okay. I'm not the killer here. He is.' He jabbed a finger in the direction of Rhys, who was leaning on the outside ledge of the kitchen window.

'You look a bit unsteady there, sir,' said Bowen. 'Did he hit you?'

Dom huffed in exasperation.

'No, no.' Rhys rubbed at his forehead. 'I just feel a bit strange.'

'He stayed here all night, or so he claims,' said Dom. 'If anyone knows who did this, it's him.'

'You were here when DS Hirst found the victim?' DC Bowen turned back to Dom.

'Yes.'

'Then we'll need to take statements from you both immediately. I'll make the arrangements.'

He looked at Rhys again. 'Those your only clothes?'

'No. I have some other bits upstairs.'

'Let's get you dressed, then. I'll have to come with you. I'll need those things to be checked, you understand?' Rhys nodded. The DC reached into his pocket and sorted out a plastic evidence bag. He looked at Dom. 'Same goes for you.'

'Why me? I haven't done anything.'

'You were inside the crime scene perimeter,' replied DC Bowen with exaggerated patience. 'Got a change of clothes?'

'No.'

'We'll sort it out at the station. Wait there.'

Dom sat down on a garden bench. The DC escorted the unsteady Rhys inside. From the street at the front, he could hear vehicles arriving and an argument developing about the road being shut off by a neighbour trying to get his car out to go to work. The number of voices inside the house grew. Dom could hear equipment being unpacked. He was shivering with shock. Sirens wailed up the main road, bringing more officers.

Luckily it wasn't raining. After several minutes of growing impatience, Dom heard voices in the kitchen. DS Hirst stepped out, looking pale under her natural colour. She took a couple of deep breaths. Her boss followed her out. They spoke quietly together before approaching him.

'Mr Wilkins,' the DI said. 'DS Hirst tells me that you entered the crime scene before she could stop you.'

'I just went in to draw the curtains,' mumbled Dom.

'Despite being asked to remain in the entrance hall?'

Dom nodded. 'I was going to tidy up the glasses if Rhys hadn't remembered.'

Edwards looked him up and down. 'Two reasons? Why did you want to remove something from the crime scene?'

'I didn't know it was a crime scene, did I?'

DI Edwards remained impassive. 'Did you actually touch anything?'

'No. Absolutely not.'

'Can you account for the blood on your shoes?' Edwards pointed to the toes of Dom's trainers. One had a dark-red splodge on it, which had to be blood.

'I don't know.' Dom was confused. He looked at his trouser leg. That also seemed to have a dark wet patch on it. 'I was ill. I threw up.'

'So ill that you attacked your friend, Mr Davies?'

'He killed Taryn!' shouted Dom. 'You can't pin this on me. Haven't I suffered enough? He was here all night. He must have done it.'

'And gone back to bed afterwards, perhaps?' DS Hirst asked sarcastically. Dom winced as the DI glanced at her. She raised a hand to make a gesture like she was injecting herself. 'Or without getting covered in blood?'

'Let's get him tested,' said Edwards.

'It was hard to rouse him, sir,' said Sara. 'Claims he hadn't heard a thing.'

'Well, he would say that. What if he had an accomplice? Anything could be going on.' Dom was becoming hysterical. 'What if he let someone in? What if—'

'All things we will be looking at, sir,' said the DI. 'Along with your own eagerness to contaminate or clear items from the scene.'

'I didn't do it on purpose!'

'Are you willing to accompany us to the local station?'

Before Dom could answer, there was a crash from upstairs. With a glance at her boss, DS Hirst strode back into the house. After a few seconds, they saw her stand near the window in the back bedroom on her mobile.

Dom sighed. 'Now what?'

They waited in silence until Sara returned to the garden.

'I've sent for an ambulance,' she said. 'Mike was just getting the clothes for analysis when Mr Davies collapsed.'

CHAPTER 25

Dom Wilkins was reluctant to accompany Sara for an interview until DI Edwards pointed out that the alternative was for him to be arrested and interviewed under caution. He sat on the garden bench to wait, a uniformed officer keeping him company. The house was full of people. The forensic team was already there in force, as was Dr Taylor and his photographer assistant.

'Not much doubt as to the cause of death,' he said to Edwards and Sara in the hallway. 'She will have bled to death in seconds with a cut like that. I'd say that the killer got the jugular. The spray patterns and the autopsy will confirm that, of course.'

'How apt,' said Sara. The two men looked at her in surprise. 'She had a thing about vampires and stuff like that. The chair was something to do with Hammer horror films, apparently.'

Edwards looked thoughtful. 'We should check that out. Perhaps her position in the chair is meant to echo something in one of the films.'

'I'm surprised she didn't resist,' said Taylor. 'That scarf is only there to hold the body up. It could easily have been removed. Her hands were free.'

'I understand that she'd taken sleeping pills,' said Sara.

'I'll get a tox screen done. That may have meant that she was asleep with any luck. Horrible death, either way.'

'Time of death?' asked Edwards.

'Guestimate at this point,' said Taylor. 'Sometime between midnight and four in the morning.'

'Good enough to get going with, thank you.' Edwards and Sara headed upstairs.

In the spare bedroom, Rhys Davies was sitting on the bed. His head was hanging loosely on his chest, his arms limp by his sides. Mike Bowen was standing next to him.

'I've found his mobile,' he said. He held out the phone to Sara. 'Who should we call for you? Rhys?'

Rhys raised his head wearily and tried to focus on Bowen. 'My mum. She's in Cardiff.'

'Anyone closer?'

It was a question too far, and Rhys keeled backwards onto the bed, eyelids fluttering. Sara bagged up his phone, then went out onto the landing to call Aggie. Two paramedics strode up the stairs as she requested another long-distance contact visit.

Edwards joined her. 'Mike, you'd better go with him,' said the DI. 'Save on confusion when he comes round. Request blood samples, because it looks like this fella has been drugged to me.'

'I agree, sir,' Sara nodded. 'And not many people would have had the opportunity apart from Dom Wilkins.'

'Let's get this parathlete down to Bethel Street and find out what's really going on between this lot.'

Bethel Street was the most local station. It occupied one wing of City Hall, which overlooked Norwich's market. The interview rooms were unlikely to be much in use first thing in the morning. To Wilkins's clear disgust, they were soon occupying one. He sat in a white paper boiler suit, having been relieved of his own clothes for testing.

'Thank you for helping us,' said Edwards. Sara could hear that he was using his formal tone. Sometimes she had her doubts about her boss. He could be abrasive without being aware of it, or get angry if he thought he was being taken for a fool. But no one could run an interview quite like him.

'No choice, have I?' Wilkins sounded like a truculent teenager.

'You are under no obligation at the moment,' Edwards replied. 'You are also welcome to have a representative with you if you wish.'

Wilkins sighed. 'I have nothing to hide. I've lost two friends in a matter of days, and you people need to find out what the hell is going on. Let's just do this, shall we?'

'I agree.' Edwards flicked on the recorder after explaining its use. 'Let's start with yesterday. When did you find out about Joe Summerhill's death?'

'Rhys sent me a text. Asked me to come and look after Taryn while he helped Joe's family find a hotel.'

'You went straight from work? No detours?'

'I drove straight there.'

'What did you find?'

'Rose Crawford was there. She'd been there all afternoon, keeping Taryn company.'

'She left as I arrived, sir,' confirmed Sara.

'Taryn was upset. We're all upset.' Wilkins glared at Edwards, who returned the look placidly. 'I thanked Rose and said she could go home.'

'How long did you stay?' asked the DI.

'Until about half past nine. Rhys arrived about six, then we called the doctor.'

'Doctor?'

'Taryn was hysterical. We thought she might need some sleeping pills. Luckily he prescribed her something. Rhys picked the tablets up at the late-night chemists.'

'And Doctor Deacon took these pills?'

'She did. Then we helped her go to bed, hoping she would sleep. What are you implying?'

'Nothing at all.' Edwards glanced at Sara, who nodded to confirm she would look into Wilkins's story. 'What happened then?'

'There was a bottle of red wine open in the kitchen. *Rhys*—' Wilkins emphasised the name — 'suggested that we should have a drink. So we did.'

'And then you drove home?'

'I only had half a glass,' Wilkins said.

'What time did you arrive there?'

'Just before ten. You can check with my mother. And then I went straight to bed, before you ask.'

Edwards paused and turned to Sara. 'DS Hirst?'

'I'd like to ask about your friends at university,' she said.

'The Famous Four? Do you think that's what this is about? Why one earth would it be that?'

'We need to consider all possibilities. What about your relationships within the group?'

'We were young.' Wilkins frowned. 'We went out, drank too much, as students often do. Taryn and I were together for a while.'

'It didn't last?'

'A few months. She was getting into that whole goth-punk thing, and I didn't get it. Eventually, she found a bloke who wandered around dressed like a vampire, which seemed to make her happier.'

'Her finding another boyfriend didn't break up the group?'

'Actually, that was after she'd moved to London.'

'What about the rest of you? Did you have relationships outside the four?'

'Not so much,' replied Wilkins. 'Joe was always off birdwatching or stuff like that. I was getting into my sport. Junina was a swot.' He smiled. 'She always studied more than the rest of us.'

'We don't know much about Junina,' said Edwards.

'Junina Kaur Nagra. Married to another hotshot barrister, destined to become a QC before long. Flat in Kensington.'

'You've all kept in touch, though? You gave her a llama too?'

Wilkins frowned. 'Bloody llamas. Wish I'd never bought them. There was one on Taryn's lap, wasn't there?'

'You need to keep what you saw in that room to yourself,' said Edwards.

'Of course. What do you take me for?'

'Can I ask about Taryn and Joe's relationship?' interrupted Sara. 'Had it been going on for long?'

'I don't know. I only just found out about it.'

'How did that make you feel?'

'Mind your own business!' Wilkins's neck began to turn bright red, the flush rising rapidly up to his cheeks. 'What are you on about?'

'Three of the Famous Four are back at UEA,' said Edwards. 'Only things are different this time, aren't they? Two of them are going out, and you've had a life-changing accident.'

'We were the best of friends,' snapped Wilkins. 'That hadn't changed.'

'Rhys Davies didn't become the fourth member?' Sara suddenly asked. 'To replace Junina?'

'No one could replace Junina. Rhys was just Joe's housemate. I thought he was all right. How wrong could I have been?'

'Yet you had a drink with him last night after you helped Taryn to bed?'

'I told you, Rhys found a bottle of red wine in the kitchen.'

'Rhys drank a whole bottle on his own?' *That might also explain his unsteadiness this morning*, Sara thought. 'Is he used to drinking that much all at once?'

'It wasn't a full bottle. Taryn must have had a couple of glasses out of it the night before. Can't say I'd blame her if she had. What has this to do with her death?'

'We just want to get to the truth,' Sara assured him.

'You lot aren't interested in the truth. If you were, then you'd be talking to Rhys bloody Davies. Isn't it enough that you never found the bastard who deliberately ran me down without trying to pin two murders on me?' Wilkins looked between the two detectives. 'I don't think I can help you any more. I don't like where this is going.'

'Why did you attack Mr Davies this morning?' Edwards's voice was growing hard.

'Because he has to have done it.' Wilkins's hands balled into fists. 'He was there all night. I trusted him to look after her.'

CHAPTER 26

Sara arranged for Dom Wilkins's mother to bring him some shoes and clothes, then take him home. At first, she was surprised that he still lived at home, given his age. Then she assumed it was because of his accident and subsequent treatments.

'What do you think about Dom Wilkins, sir?' she asked as they reached their office back in Wymondham.

'I think we need to check out his alibis for both murders, frankly,' said Edwards. 'Just because he left the house, it doesn't mean he couldn't have come back later.'

'He does seem very keen to place the blame on Rhys Davies,' she added. 'Why did he take the spare door keys? Why would he have needed them?'

'And why did he say he wanted to move the wine glasses? It's all adding up for him to be my favourite suspect so far.'

'I'd also like to pull up the details of his accident,' she said. 'He goes on about it so much. Might be of interest.'

'In any case, these two murders have to be connected,' said Edwards. 'Right, let's get an update.'

DC Bowen was at the hospital with Rhys Davies. Sara rang him while the rest of the team gathered at the table to replenish their caffeine levels.

'Bowen says that Davies has come round,' she told them. 'Davies agrees he had some wine with Wilkins last night, then the latter left the house saying he was going home. Davies went to bed feeling really tired and only woke up when we arrived. They're doing blood tests, including a tox screen. Bowen's asked them to send a copy to Doctor Taylor.'

'Doesn't mean Wilkins actually went home,' said Edwards. 'Or that he didn't come back later. Aggie, can you find out about CCTV in the area and request them for a window from 9 p.m. when he says he left and 8 a.m. this morning.'

'Of course.' Aggie scribbled on her notepad.

'Being disabled doesn't mean he isn't capable of murder. In fact, he's the fittest of the lot, and the strongest.'

'Would he have been able to lift Joe's body into the urn?' asked Sara.

Aggie perked up. 'Forensics' best guess is that there was some kind of lifting equipment, or perhaps mobile ladders.'

'Like a forklift truck?' asked Noble.

'No, more this sort of thing.' Aggie pinned a couple of pictures to the incident board. One was a heavy lift mechanism, the other a set of steps with wheels.

'That one would need power.' Sara pointed to the lifting machine. 'It can't be that. Where does it say these other ladder things get used?'

'Warehouses, libraries, archives and museums.' Aggie read the list from her notes. 'They fold down so that you can move them from one place to another more easily.'

'I think you've uncovered something important.' Edwards smiled at Aggie. 'Just as you always do.'

'Even with those,' said Sara, 'it would take a strong person to carry an unconscious thirty-five-year-old male up the steps and push them into the top of the urn.'

'Ruling out female suspects?' asked Noble.

Sara bristled at the implied sexism.

'Not necessarily.' Edwards shook his head with a smile. 'I don't want to rule out anyone at this stage. However, I think we have to be looking for someone fit, healthy and strong.'

'Women can be strong.' Sara glared at Noble, who ducked his head down. 'I could have manoeuvred him, even if he was out of it.'

'Would these ladders fold down small enough to go in the back of the van we saw?' Edwards swiftly changed the subject.

Aggie rattled off some dimensions. DC Noble proffered a photo of a van. 'Graham in Forensics reckons it's a Ford Transit, nineteen or twenty model,' he said. 'Unfortunately, there's thousands of them on the road.'

'Many of them stolen recently?' asked Edwards. 'Check that out, Ian. How are you getting on with Summerhill's mobile?'

'The company sent through a list of pings,' said Noble. 'Unfortunately, the phone seems to have either been turned off or run out of juice on Sunday morning. After that, there are no traces.'

'Where was the last one?' asked Sara.

Noble consulted the list. 'Norwich city centre, at 10.32.'

'So we have no idea where he got to after Sunday morning?'

'Not on mobile traces,' confirmed Noble. 'I checked if he had a car, but he doesn't. So ANPR is no help either.'

'Eco-warrior,' murmured Sara. 'He probably cycles everywhere.'

'Mr Summerhill vanishes on Sunday morning,' said Edwards, 'only to reappear at about half past eleven at Barnham Parva New Hall on Tuesday night. That's two and a half days, for God's sake. Where was he all that time?' The DI turned back to Aggie. 'How are you getting on with those lists?'

'I put round copies of the names of ticket purchasers for the last four open days,' she said. 'I'll start to follow them up if you can let me know what you're looking for in particular.'

'I'm not sure,' admitted Edwards.

'I also asked about the student visits,' Aggie added. 'There have been three in the last twelve months with half a dozen students each, which seems to be average. The visits began four years ago as an initiative between the Gordons and Professor Chandler of the Art History department.'

'Can we get hold of lists for those too?'

Aggie checked her notes. 'It's organised by his secretary, Rose Crawford. I imagine she might have the names.'

This grabbed Sara's attention. 'Same woman who organises the gallery opening guest lists? Bit of a coincidence.'

'Definitely time to speak to Rose Crawford,' said the DI. 'Any joy from Technical about those death threats to Joe Summerhill? This could still be about those emails, after all.'

'I'll check with them,' said Sara.

Edwards turned to the board and picked up a pen. 'So where are we? Who would we put our money on?'

'Dom Wilkins,' said Sara. 'Despite his restrictions, he's fit and strong enough to have lifted Summerhill's body with the aid of steps. If Summerhill was missing all that time, we know Wilkins was back in the county from later Sunday. We need his alibi for Monday and Tuesday, don't we?'

'If he has one. And Taryn?'

'Jealousy. If they used to be a couple, perhaps Wilkins thought they might become one again.'

'Okay.' The DI circled Dom's picture on the board. 'What else?'

'Whoever sent those death threats by email might be local,' said Noble. 'Probably nutty enough to do something weird like this if they've lost control of themselves.'

'They included Joe directly and Taryn by association,' agreed Edwards. He wrote *Death threat emails?* on the board and put a box around it. 'They also included the other two of the Famous Four. That could have been done to create a cover story. We need to interview Summerhill's colleagues at CRU.' He wrote *CRU interviews* next to the box. 'Anything else?'

'What about the university connection?' asked Aggie. 'They both worked there.'

'Agreed.' Edwards wrote *UEA/SCVA* and drew a circle round it.

'Have you seen the crime scene pictures yet?' asked Sara. 'There was something odd about the way Taryn was left. Deliberately posed and with one of those blasted llamas on her lap.'

Aggie turned pale. 'They came through a few minutes before you got back. I didn't have the heart to print it out.'

'Can we get a picture of our victim in happier times?' suggested Edwards. Sara glanced at him. This was rather a concession from him. He never usually minded graphic stuff on the walls if it helped.

'I imagine so,' said Aggie. 'I'll look for one.'

'Even so, I think we should look into that pose. Noble, can you trawl stills from Hammer horror films and other stuff from the same era? Our goth doctor was deeply into that kind of thing. There may be some connection or other. Someone like this vampire character that Wilkins mentioned as a previous boyfriend. See what you can find.'

'On top of the stolen vehicle search?' Noble sounded a bit overwhelmed.

Edwards pursed his lips. 'You're right,' he said after a moment. 'This is going to be a big investigation. We'll need to interview all of Taryn's work colleagues as well. I'd better go and speak to ACC Miller and request some help. He'll be waiting for an update anyway.'

He wrote *Toy llama/ horror/ goth* on the board and put a box round that as well. 'Right, let's get to it.'

After he had left, Sara pulled up the crime scene photos, which were attached to an email. They were definitely graphic, but then so was their victim's death. They were used to seeing all manner of things, all police officers were. Aggie, however, never went to crime scenes or road traffic accidents. Edwards was trying to spare her having to look at this mess all day.

Sara ran a search for Dom Wilkins's accident. It was marked as unsolved and still open. It had also been shelved as unsolvable — something the force had neither the time nor the resources to look into, as a resolution was highly unlikely.

Sara sighed. It happened all too often with years of cuts to police funding.

Running through the file, she read through the various reports. Whoever hit Wilkins had driven off, leaving him unconscious on the floor, leg smashed to pieces and arm damaged. Fortunately, another driver had found him before anyone else could accidentally run over him and had rung for an ambulance. The only time frame was the emergency call record. They didn't know how long Wilkins had lain there. It was a stormy night, and he had been soaked through, which suggested he had been there a while. With no traffic cameras and a network of unlit minor roads connecting the lane to the main roads, it had been impossible for the investigating officers, hence the shelving of the case.

In his statement, Wilkins claimed that he had been deliberately run down, though he had no idea why someone would have targeted him in this way. His subsequent injuries, along with a lengthy stay in the hospital, must have coloured his memories. But if this claim were true, it was an act of real violence, and Sara could see why he was so frustrated about the lack of resolution.

She closed the file with a sigh. Reading it hadn't offered any help. Trouble was, Sara wasn't sure that she believed anything that Dom Wilkins claimed.

CHAPTER 27

Rose arrived at work at exactly nine o'clock on Friday morning. There were dark bags under her eyes, and she yawned as she walked across the grass to the SCVA. The gallery and cafés were opening, although it didn't seem very busy yet. The Art History department central office space was empty.

Heading for her own desk, she realised that everyone was gathered in Professor Chandler's office. She dumped her things and slipped in at the back of the gathering to listen.

'Are we all here?' Chandler scanned round the staff. 'Ah, Rose. Could you close the door? I know it's a bit of a squash.'

Moving a couple of people forward, she managed to get the door shut. The atmosphere in the room was decidedly tense.

'I'm afraid I have some very bad news,' said Chandler. He was standing behind his chair, hands gripping the dark leatherette of the headrest. 'There is no easy way to say this, so I'm going to get on with it.'

A worried murmur ran between the lecturers and office staff.

'Redundancies,' one of them whispered to Rose. 'Has to be.'

Rose doubted that and shrugged in reply.

'The police called me this morning,' Chandler went on. 'I could not actually believe what they told me, so it has taken me a few minutes to process this enough to pass it on to all of you. Our esteemed colleague Doctor Taryn Deacon has passed away.'

The group broke out into shocked chatter. Rose rubbed her face with both hands. Her tiredness was making her head pound, and it felt weird hearing this news from her boss. Chandler held up a hand to quieten the noise.

'The police tell me that her death is being treated as suspicious and they will be undertaking investigations accordingly. As we all work with — sorry, worked with — Taryn . . .' He paused to draw in a shaky breath and regroup. Rose doubted he had ever had to deliver such an announcement before.

'As colleagues, we will, naturally, want to help as much as we can,' he continued. 'The police will be joining us soon to gather initial statements from each of us. I've placed the meeting room at their disposal, so please don't try to use it for the next few days. Or however long this all takes. Any questions?'

'What happened to her?' demanded a voice from the middle of the group.

'I don't know,' replied Chandler. 'And if I did, it's hardly appropriate for me to say. Let's just all do our best to help. Anything else?'

There wasn't. Rose managed to reopen the heavy glass door, and people filed out, muttering and gossiping. One or two seemed genuinely in shock, especially the other curator with whom Taryn had shared an office. His face was pale as he wandered past with uneven steps.

'Rose,' called Professor Chandler. She stepped back inside his office. 'Close the door, please. Have a seat.'

When they were both perched on his teaching sofa, he went so far as to gather one of Rose's hands in his.

'Thank you for looking after Taryn yesterday,' he said. 'How did it go?'

'She was really worried, obviously.' Rose glanced down as Chandler patted the back of her hand in an unconscious gesture. 'I stayed until we heard from her boyfriend's dad. It was bad news.'

'Joe Summerhill?'

'Yes.' Rose gently removed her hand and gripped the other to stop it from shaking. 'I rang Taryn's friend. A chap called Rhys, who'd been looking after her the previous evening. He'd had to go into work.'

Chandler nodded. 'Good move.'

'He'd also spoken to Joe's parents and was trying to help them. So he got another friend to come round to relieve me. Dom Wilkins.'

Chandler frowned.

'He's a student disability advisor.'

'Ah, of course,' Chandler replied. 'Knew I recognised the name.'

'When he arrived, I left them to be together. It didn't feel right with me getting in the way.'

'And how was Taryn when you left?'

'Deeply upset, obviously. Glad that Dom was there but, quite frankly, not very grateful to me for spending the day there with her.'

Chandler frowned. 'How so?'

Rose told him about the Dracula chair. 'I left after that.'

'We often focus on the littlest thing when we're grieving,' said Chandler.

Rose had to stop herself from physically slapping him, so great was her indignation. What the hell did he know about real grief?

'Can I ask, did Taryn seem at all suicidal to you? Or likely to self-harm?'

'What makes you ask that?' she said.

'I'm sorry, that was too bald a question.' Her boss shuffled uncomfortably. 'It was just something that the detective who rang me said.'

Rose sat more upright, sensing a chance to rehearse a moment for her police interview. 'She didn't say anything directly. I just got the feeling that it might be possible. When Joe's father called, she began to hit herself on the chest with her mobile phone. Like she was punishing herself. I had to grab her hands to stop her from doing it. Even when she calmed down a bit, she seemed completely in despair.'

That might do it.

Chandler sniffed and wiped a tear from his cheek. 'I promised Emilia I would keep an eye on her people down here. I should have noticed she was so upset.'

'Surely not.' It was her turn to pat the back of his hand. His head hung down, apparently in the agony of anguish. Gritting her teeth, she forced herself to say, 'You're a good boss, you know. I've really appreciated all you've done for me. And you made sure she wasn't alone. What else could you have done?'

'Thank you,' he said. 'I try my best, even if I'm clumsy at times.'

'I know you do. Shall I get you a coffee?'

'Yes, thank you.'

Rose left him slumped on his sofa and headed for the café. Two takeaway proper coffees were in order, she felt. One for the professor having a maudlin moment of self-pity and guilt, and the other for herself so that she would be ready when the police arrived.

CHAPTER 28

DI Edwards angrily dumped his car in a disabled persons' bay outside the Sainsbury Centre. Sara winced as DC Bowen followed suit. Noble unfolded his lanky legs from the passenger seat, and the entire team headed for the Art History department. Edwards strode ahead, looking furious, making Sara wonder what ACC Miller had said.

The door swished open.

'Got the agreed list of questions?' asked Edwards.

Bowen waved his notepad. Noble was carrying a tablet computer, something Bowen teased him about.

'Make a note of anything that might seem odd or out of place. I want to know what our victim was like at work, who she was friends with, what they thought of her appearance. We'll get the formal statements done after tomorrow when the ACC has organised more help. Understood?'

Bowen looked at Edwards with a hurt expression. 'I've been at this game longer than you, boss.'

'Yes, sorry.' Edwards sounded irritated, not apologetic. 'This investigation is rapidly getting out of hand, apparently. We need to get it moving.'

They were clearly expected. Professor Chandler emerged from his office as soon as they approached the long row of filing cabinets that formed part of the barrier between the workspaces and the gallery and restaurant to keep the public from entering.

'My staff will make themselves available as you require,' he said. He took them to a meeting room that had been set aside for interviews. 'I've told them you wish to see them all.'

'We'll need two rooms,' said Edwards. 'And I want to start with Rose Crawford.'

'No problem.' Chandler pointed to another office. 'You can use my office. I'll sit in the meeting area in case you need me. Rose has made up a list of all the departmental staff you might want to speak to. Meanwhile, I'll organise some refreshments.'

No one discouraged him, and he strode off to an office opposite.

'Damn it,' said Edwards. 'Why did the stupid bugger tell them we were coming? Now they've had time to get their excuses in order.'

'Keen, isn't he?' remarked Bowen. 'I wonder why.'

'Trying to be cooperative?' suggested Noble.

'Trying to look like a good boss,' said Sara dryly. 'Or watches too many TV dramas.'

Bowen snorted a laugh. A few minutes later, a woman appeared that Sara recognised. She had a sheaf of papers in her hand. It took a moment or two to hand round the staff lists and decamp Bowen and Noble to the professor's office.

'Sit down, Mrs Crawford,' said Edwards.

'How can I help?' The woman settled in a chair on the opposite side of the table to them. She looked the picture of calm efficiency.

'This is just a preliminary inquiry,' explained Sara. 'We will take a formal statement tomorrow.'

'I'm sure I'd like to help as much as possible,' said Rose.

'Didn't I see you at Taryn Deacon's house yesterday evening?'

Sara wasn't sure if Rose winced slightly before she answered. 'I was looking after her during the day. When her friend turned up, I thought it best to leave them alone. We passed in the doorway, I believe.'

'Why would you be there at all?' asked Edwards. Sara inwardly sighed as Rose cast a wary look at the DI.

'Doctor Deacon had been upset for several days,' she said. 'Her friend was missing, and when you began to search his house, she became extremely worried. The professor and I were surprised when she came to work yesterday morning. It was clear she wasn't really capable, so Professor Chandler requested that I take her home and look after her.'

'Did you want to?' Edwards asked.

'Why not? I was in a position to help. She's a nice enough person, and it was distressing to see her like that.'

As Edwards started to snap out another question, Sara hurried in. 'Did you like Taryn?'

'As a colleague, she was fine. Although strictly speaking, we didn't work together.'

'What do you mean?' rapped Edwards.

'There are two departments here.' Rose waved at the space behind her. 'The Art History department, which is a teaching school. Professor Chandler is in charge of that. He teaches MA students mostly. I work for him.'

'And the other?'

'That's Collections and Curations. Emilia Thornton is the head of that department. They have other offices on the mezzanine floor and workshops in the bunker, with overspill staff in here. We have more space, you see.'

'Bunker?' Edwards sounded surprised.

Rose smiled to herself. 'It's not so well known, but we have a bombproof bunker under the building where we store items from the collections that are not on display. We also do some conservation there too.'

'For paintings? A bombproof bunker for pictures?' Edwards sounded outraged.

'It's also temperature and atmospherically controlled,' said Rose. She seemed to enjoy exposing the DI's assumptions.

'It has top-level security and is completely firewalled. The collection is rather valuable, after all.'

This made Edwards stop, giving Sara a chance to speak again. 'Mrs Crawford—'

'Rose. Please call me Rose.'

'Thank you. Can I ask you about your work? You say you primarily work for Professor Chandler, but don't you also organise things for the exhibitions?'

'Yes. Technically my job was only part-time. Being on my own, I really needed full-time, so it was arranged that I should do some of the organising for the exhibition opening events.'

'You organise the visits to Barnham Parva New Hall as well?'

'The student visits, yes.'

'Do you go with them on the visits?'

'Usually. It seems only polite. I help with the refreshments.'

'Are you involved with their open days?'

'No.' Rose sounded firm about that.

'Can you provide me with lists of students who attended these outings?'

'So long as Professor Chandler agrees, then I can run those off for you.'

'This is a murder investigation,' snapped Edwards. Sara mentally rolled her eyes. 'What we require supersedes any data protection issues.'

'A murder investigation?' Rose looked shocked by this. 'I didn't know. I thought, perhaps, she might have . . .' Both detectives let the silence hang until Rose continued. 'Professor Chandler was asking me if I thought she might have hurt herself. I never imagined someone else had hurt her.'

'Can you think of anyone who might have wanted to hurt her?' asked Sara gently.

'No, I can't. Unless . . .' Rose frowned. 'She had recently started going out with Joe Summerhill. She was quite excited about it but worried as well.'

'Why?'

'Oh dear, it was a confidence. Taryn asked me not to say anything.'

'If there's anything that might help, please tell us.'

'Do you know that she used to go out with Dom Wilkins?'

Sara nodded. 'Years ago, wasn't it?'

'Initially. Taryn came back here to join the curating team about five years ago, about the same time Wilkins was knocked off his bike and injured. She told me that she spent time visiting him in the hospital. Later on, they saw a lot of each other. Taryn supported him through physio and getting back into his sport. They became close.'

'How close?'

'That's the thing she was worried about. Taryn felt Dom might be angling for a relationship with her, but she didn't feel like that about him.'

'Because she was going out with Joe Summerhill?'

'Exactly.' Rose looked directly at Sara. 'They had kept their relationship secret from Dom. She said that Dom has had anger management issues ever since his accident, and they were afraid of him finding out.'

CHAPTER 29

After his mother brought him home, Dom showered. No matter how hard he scrubbed or how hot the water was, he couldn't wash away the image of Taryn tied to the Dracula chair with that blasted llama in her lap. Nor could he control his emotions — his revulsion at the blood running down her front from under her chin like a nauseating scarf, his anger at the perpetrator, the aching of his heart. He combed his damp hair, took care of his stump before strapping on his everyday leg and then pulled on a tracksuit. His hand was aching worse than ever, and he massaged some ibuprofen cream into the back of it. That would have to do for now. He couldn't face going into work today.

'I rang your boss,' said his mum. 'I didn't think you'd be up to being in your office for a few days.'

'Thanks.' There was a pot of coffee on the kitchen table, and they sat down together to share it. Freshly baked scones sat on a plate between them. Dom couldn't face them either.

'What's going on?' she asked when they were nursing their mugs. 'I know it's about Taryn. But why did the police arrest you?'

'They didn't arrest me,' Dom said. 'I was there when she was found. I'm her best friend. They were bound to have questions.'

'I suppose.' Dom's mum looked angrily away. 'Pity they didn't do more after your accident.'

'I know. I told them so myself.' Dom sighed. 'It's all so long ago. The police shelved the investigation years back.'

Unable to settle, Dom wandered around their large back garden, idly looking at the spring flowers. His mum kept the place immaculate. She was a keen gardener, and it was her pride and joy. Perhaps keeping busy would help him. He had a workshop behind the double garage where he stored and maintained his racing bikes.

His best bike was clipped in a work stand, waiting for an upgrade to the pedals. Dom turned on the radio and selected tools from the bench. When the fastening bolt on the first pedal refused to budge, he threw the spanner across the workshop. It smashed into a pile of tins, sending them clattering to the floor. Rubbing away the tears in his eyes, Dom stared out of the window without seeing the view. He didn't know how long he stood there, watching the revolving video in his head.

His mother appeared in the doorway. 'Aren't you cold?'

He jolted back to the present. 'A bit. Is it teatime?'

'Soon. The police are here to talk to you.' She sounded worried. 'As if once today wasn't enough. You'd better come in.'

It was the same two detectives who had interviewed him that morning at Bethel Street. They were seated in the lounge. The coffee table in front of them was noticeably free of refreshments. The woman stood up to proffer her warrant card. The man didn't.

'I'm sorry to intrude again,' she said. 'There are a couple of things we wanted to clarify as quickly as possible. If we could have a private word?'

Dom's mother planted herself on one end of the sofa. 'I'm not going anywhere.'

'As you wish,' said the DS. She sat down next to her boss. Dom sat next to his mother. 'First of all, I would like to ask your whereabouts on Monday and Tuesday of this week.'

'Why?'

'As I said previously, it's something we ask everyone.'

Dom sighed. 'I was in work both days.'

'All day?' asked the DS. Dom nodded. 'And in the evenings?'

'Monday I went for a massage.' He smirked at the surprise in the DS's face. No doubt she was thinking of it as a euphemism for sex. 'I'm a sportsman. I use a specialist physio at the private clinic on the Watton Road. Yes, I can provide you with the man's details.'

He watched as the DS glanced at her boss, who shrugged slightly.

'Tuesday evening,' Dom continued, 'I went for a training run round the park at work.'

'Can anyone vouch for that?'

'No.' He left the bald statement stand. He was damned if he was going to justify his every action.

'Do you drive, Mr Wilkins?' asked the DI.

'Yes. It's an adapted vehicle.' Dom waved through the front window. 'You can take the licence number as you go, if you need to. Is that all?'

'I wanted to ask you about your accident,' said the DS. 'The one that left you with these injuries.'

Of all the things he had been speculating they wanted to know about, that wasn't on Dom's list. His surprise must have shown. His mother made a sound very like tutting.

'I pulled up the files,' continued the DS. 'Unfortunately, there was no corroborating evidence from witnesses or road cameras to help us identify the car that hit you. I take it that you didn't get any of the number plate.'

Dom's mother snorted. 'Ridiculous.'

'All right, Mum,' he said. 'I was hardly in a position to. Besides, it was dark, and it was raining hard.'

'And being a lane, there were no street lights,' agreed the DS. 'Would you be willing to describe what happened again to me?'

'Why? I don't see what relevance this has.'

The detective looked to her boss for support, who raised an eyebrow but didn't say anything. 'We were told you had anger management issues following the accident. I'm trying to understand about that and hope that hearing your side of the event might help us.'

'Damn right I had issues,' said Dom. 'You would have too, under the circumstances.'

'Dom went for help with all that,' interrupted his mother. 'Months of counselling sessions. They redirected his energy into his sport, thank goodness.'

The DS nodded. 'To great effect. For the sport, at least. What about your personal life?'

'I cope,' said Dom. 'Having half a leg doesn't make for romantic dates, however. Not everyone can see past the prosthetic. Or my claw of a hand.'

Except for Taryn. She had seen him for the man he still was, or so he had thought. Turns out she had preferred the whole man that was Joe Summerhill.

'You mentioned the circumstances? It was dark and raining, you said.'

'The car came out of nowhere,' said Dom. 'From the left. Hit me broadside and threw me across the road into the hedge.'

'Out of a side road?'

'No,' said Dom's mother. 'When Dom was recovering in hospital, his father and I went to look at the place. The car must have been in a field gateway. There wasn't another side road near where Dom was hit. We think it was waiting for him.'

'That wasn't what did the damage anyway,' carried on Dom. 'I managed to get upright, but the bike was unrideable, and my mobile was smashed where I must have landed on it. I heard a car and thought they might help. I tried to wave it down.'

He stopped. Dom hadn't spoken about this for years, and the memories were flooding back, threatening to overwhelm him as they combined with the image of Taryn. He began to shake.

'Did they stop?' asked the DS.

'No. I stood there like an idiot because I couldn't believe it just kept coming — that it was speeding up.'

'Did they not see you?'

'They saw me all right,' said Dom. 'I'm sure it was the same car. It was small and black, with its headlights on full. I couldn't see the number plate or the driver.'

'So how did you know it was the same car?'

'I just knew. At the last minute, I tried to get out of the way. It knocked me up into the air, over the length of the car, and I smashed into the road. That's why all my injuries are down this side.' He paused to indicate his left-hand side. 'Bizarrely, I wasn't completely out of it. I managed to look up. The car had stopped like they were checking they had hit me. Then it drove off and left me alone.'

'No one believes us. Never have,' Dom's mother added.

'That car drove straight at me,' said Dom. 'Whoever it was, they ran me down deliberately.'

CHAPTER 30

DI Edwards seemed unusually quiet as they headed back to HQ.

'What did you make of his story?' Sara asked.

Edwards simply shrugged. He parked outside the office, and Sara went to open the door.

'Hang on.' The DI tapped his fingers on the steering wheel while the engine ticked and cooled. 'Can you keep a secret?'

'Of course, sir.'

'A work secret?'

She stared at him. He was looking up at the top floor of the block.

'From top brass, sir? For you? Yes.' What on earth had he done?

Edwards shook his head. 'No. It's not fair of me to ask it of you. I have to make my own decisions.'

Sara knew he had no partner to talk to. None of them found it easy to keep personal relationships going, which was one reason, she assumed, Bowen and Aggie were terrified the bosses might find out about them.

'I'm happy to be a sounding board,' she assured him. 'You've helped me so often in the past.'

'Thank you,' he murmured. 'I'm glad someone likes working with me.'

'We all do, sir.'

He reached a decision and yanked his car keys from the ignition. 'Let's just say that things are going to be different around here very soon. I wanted to warn you to get your poker face ready in time.'

Sara trailed behind him into the office. The team had returned and were waiting for an end-of-day catch-up. Aggie was printing off yet more lists. Bowen and Noble were checking off the interviewees they had spoken to. Edwards went straight to his office and picked up the phone.

Noble glanced at the pile of lists on his desk. 'We still have all the CRU staff to interview as well.'

'Don't worry so much. The boss has asked for extra help.' Bowen turned to Sara. 'How did you get on with Dom Wilkins?'

Sara retold the story of the accident.

'Why would anyone have wanted to run him down deliberately?' asked Aggie.

'Very good question,' said Sara. 'A genuine accident involving two cars, or even road rage might account for it. There's no proof the same car came back a second time. Even so, it seems strange that this group of friends has come in for so much bad luck.'

'And all within the last five years,' said Noble. 'Is that significant?'

'Did something change five years ago?' Sara speculated. 'Or did something happen then that kicked this whole thing off?'

Edwards walked slowly out of his office, listening to their conversation. 'That seems unlikely. Who'd wait that long to take revenge?'

'Someone who had to,' said Sara.

'Anyway, we have a meeting to go to. You'd all best follow me. You too, Aggie.' The DI climbed up a floor to a large meeting room. The Drugs team was already there, as was Vice. ACC Miller stood at the front of the room while his PA tapped at a laptop to bring up a projection of the force shield and logo on the screen behind him.

'Is that everybody?' he asked. 'Okay. Thank you for coming.'

There was a general shuffling of chairs as people settled in for a lecture of some sort.

'There are two reasons for calling you together,' began the ACC. 'As you will all be aware, DI Edwards's team have a difficult case in hand. They need more manpower — sorry, officer power.'

This raised a laugh in some quarters, though Sara noticed none from the female staff. She glanced at Aggie next to her. Aggie rolled her eyes.

'I have asked for two volunteers from each of the drugs and vice squads, who have been allocated. They will be there to help with interviews or whatever else is needed from tomorrow morning.'

'Better go and clean some desks,' Aggie whispered, rising from her chair. Sara put a hand on her arm and shook her head. Whatever Edwards had been trying to warn her about, that wasn't it. Aggie sat back down.

'I have also had some good news which I felt should be shared with you all at the same time.'

Miller nodded to his PA, who brought up a slide with a diagram on it.

'For once, the force has been successful in acquiring some new funding.'

This created a murmur round the room. These meetings were usually to announce cuts.

Miller pointed to the diagram. 'Functionally, as you know, we have three separate detective teams. Drugs, Vice and Serious Crimes. Of course, at times, the work of these teams can overlap. The teams themselves are often individually understaffed and up against it, as Serious Crimes are now.'

'You can say that again,' muttered Bowen, who was sitting on the other side of Aggie. The whole team knew they were the Cinderella operation in the force. When staff retired or moved to other departments, they were rarely replaced. Extra help always came from the other teams.

'There is now funding for several new roles,' said the ACC. There was a smattering of applause. He pointed to the top of the diagram. 'The first new role is that of an operational superintendent. That person will overlook all three teams and organise help as and when necessary. They will also coordinate the work with a view to spotting links between cases. This job is currently being advertised, if any of you wish to apply.'

There was some general laughter. None of them could jump several ranks, and most of them wouldn't want to.

Another paper shuffler, thought Sara. *I doubt that will make any difference to us.*

'For the Drugs squad, there is funding for three more additional staff on the ground. Vice will have funding for one more.'

None for Serious Crimes. She sighed quietly.

'We will also be increasing our complement of Detective Chief Inspectors.' Now her blood began to surge. Vice already had a DCI, and it suited their method of operation very well.

'Each team will have their own DCI. Both of these two new posts have already been filled.'

Sara glanced at DI Powell from Drugs, then at Edwards. They both had their heads down. It dawned on her that they had both been overlooked, poor buggers. Is this what Edwards had meant? Could he face working with a new boss? The PA clicked the laptop, and a picture appeared.

'This is DCI Ranveer Chakrabarti,' said Miller. 'He will be joining us from Manchester at the end of the month to assist DI Powell and the Drugs squad.'

So, they weren't getting the Mancunian. At least that upped the other team's diversity quota, something Sara was glad to see. She held her breath.

'And this—' ACC Miller held out his hand to a woman sitting near the front of the table — 'is DCI Hayley Hudson who, I am pleased to say, will be joining Serious Crimes with immediate effect.'

CHAPTER 31

DCI Hayley Hudson was no more than five foot four inches tall. She had a light bone structure, so that although she was well-muscled, she still looked petite. Sara felt like a giant beside her, suddenly aware that too many of Aggie's cakes were giving her a bit of a permanent food baby. Hudson stood in front of the incident board and surveyed their current progress with sharp blue eyes, hands on hips. This being her first day, just like Sara had on her first morning, she had opted for a smart trouser suit in dark purple and a pristine white blouse.

'Take me through what you have,' said Hudson.

All eyes turned to DI Edwards. He looked as white as a ghost. His face was set solid, all emotion carefully hidden. As she looked at the rest of the team, Sara could see the shock clearly showing on Aggie's face. Noble's eyes were saucer-round, his hands fidgeting with a pen and notepad. Bowen looked angry, his face redder than usual. His hands were shoved so deep into his trouser pockets that Sara thought he could pull up his socks.

Edwards stepped forward to run through the photos, current actions and plan for the morning. It wasn't until he finished with, 'That's where we are, ma'am,' that it sunk in. They had a new boss.

DCI Hudson turned to face the rest of the team. One by one, Edwards introduced them and Hudson firmly shook each hand.

'Glad to be here,' she said. 'As you will undoubtedly understand, I will be senior investigating officer for this complex case from hereon in. We will look at how the team might work in the future at a later date.'

There were mumbled variations of 'Yes, ma'am.'

'I take it you were about to finish for the day?'

'We were,' said Edwards.

'Then I'll let you all get off home. Apart from you, DI Edwards. I would like to chat to you about the progress so far.'

They were being dismissed. Sara wondered what her own face looked like as she collected her handbag.

'Is this my office?' she heard Hudson say. Sara watched her sit carefully behind Edwards's desk, leaving him to use the visitors' chair. The DI's shoulders were set solid and square. Never a good sign.

The team left together. No one spoke as they passed the Drug squad office. Looking through the glass windows, it looked like they were also struggling with the news. At least they had time to get used to the idea before their new DCI arrived.

Pulling out of the car park, Sara knew she had to talk to someone about all this. The case was bad enough, but she needed to get her head around the reorganisation and its meaning for the team. It was nearly eight o'clock, and Sara's mother would already have left home with her partner Javed. They always visited the Tower Hamlets African and Caribbean Social Club on a Friday night. That left Chris, who had shouted at her the previous evening, or her Happisburgh neighbour, Gilly Barker.

Chris was nearer. It was time they had a proper talk about where their relationship was going anyway. As she drove to Norwich, Sara tried to call him. When it went to voicemail, she left a message to say she was popping in to see him tonight and to call if he was busy.

Trouble was, she mused as she pulled into the visitors' parking space behind the flats, he always seemed to pick some kind of argument with her just as they began a big new case. Perhaps he got jealous when she had to start doing all those extra hours. Sara wasn't allowed to discuss the details of any case with him, especially when it was ongoing. That sometimes upset him too. Did Chris think she excluded him deliberately?

'Does the same to me,' she said under her breath. 'All these bloody plays.'

With a rueful grin, Sara realised that she was working herself into a bad mood by dwelling on Chris's failings. Not a good place to attempt a reconciliation. She needed to focus on the times when he had been there for her, and there were many of those to be grateful for.

Letting herself into the entrance hall, she checked his mailbox. There were a couple of envelopes in there, which she pulled out and carried with her. Before she went upstairs, Sara tried his mobile again. Still no reply.

Sara knocked politely on the flat door. There was no reply, although she could hear music playing inside. A second, louder knock went unanswered, so she fished out her key. The music was clearer in the hall, although still hardly loud enough to mask her knocks. Clicking the door shut, Sara hesitated. 'Chris? Chris, are you home?'

Maybe he had popped back to his café across the road or was out for another reason. Suddenly, Sara felt like an intruder. If their relationship was in a rough patch, should she really have let herself in? If there was no reply, she'd leave a note to say she'd brought up his mail and would catch him another time. That way, Sara wouldn't feel so nosey.

'Hello?' She called more loudly this time. 'Chris? It's me. Are you in?'

When no reply came, she fished her work notepad out of her bag and began to write a quick note.

Sorry to intrude. I did try to call you first. Just wanted to see you, and—

A sudden crash made Sara jump. It was followed by a girly giggle.

'Chris?' Sara called. 'Are you there?'

'Hang on.' His voice was muffled behind a door. His bedroom door.

Chris emerged with a towel around his waist and a grin on his face. 'I was just about to get in the shower. I didn't hear you.'

'I see,' said Sara. 'Who is she?'

'What?' Chris tried to sound offended.

'Someone from the theatre, I suppose.' She pushed past him. Chris ineffectually grabbed one arm, trying to hold up his towel with the other hand. Sara looked at him, unable to hide her disgust. 'Let's get this over with, shall we?'

She opened the bedroom door. The room was lit with a romantic glow, and soft music was playing from a smart speaker. On the bed lay a blonde woman, the duvet pulled about her chest to hide her breasts. Unless Sara was very much mistaken, she had been in the last play that Chris had performed in. The woman giggled again. Chris stood in the corridor behind her.

Sara looked at the woman impassively. It had been an insanely bad day. Finding a butchered body this morning, discovering they had a new boss an hour ago, and now her so-called boyfriend was cheating on her. If she let go of her emotions, Sara had no idea if she'd be able to control herself.

'How are the lines going, Mel?' she asked.

The woman's smile looked victorious, and her tone was smug. '*Coming* on really well.'

'Good luck with your new man. You'll need it.' Sara turned to Chris and spoke with frozen calm. 'Cheating bastard. Thank God I didn't accept your proposal. You'd have done this anyway.'

She threw the key onto the carpet and strode out of the flat.

CHAPTER 32

It was blustery, as April mornings often are. Rose was having difficulty getting the garden bonfire going, and she had several things to burn, some of which were wet. To add to her problems, the stack of dry wood and leaves Aiden had left for her was depleted, leaving her with damp branches gathered from the copse behind the shed. It took several firelighters and a pile of old paper to get the incinerator up to a decent blaze.

'Here we are,' she said, feeding in a set of disposable coveralls. 'Good riddance.'

Carefully layering the wood to keep up the temperature, Rose added the other items one by one. There were goggles she had used to keep the splashes from her eyes. A paper face mask normally used for DIY projects. Shoe covers and plimsoles. She waited and built up the fire again before adding her own clothing from Thursday night, down to her bra and pants. The plastic carrier bags went in last, partly because they created a peculiar stink that she didn't like.

Rose had done her research before embarking on this project. The shower and the sinks in her home, plus the toilets, had all been doused in bleach. The front door, all the door handles, and the banister had been cleaned. Even the walls and floor of the en suite had been scrubbed. The house stank of it. Despite the chilly air, she left the sliding door to the conservatory open.

As it was Saturday, Rose had all day to clear up after herself. Of course, leaving all that other stuff in the van for a day had been very risky, especially with the police being so active. However, putting in an appearance at work yesterday had been absolutely necessary to keep suspicion at bay.

'Pulled a blinder there, I thought,' she said with a smile. 'I reckon they went straight round to interview Dominic bloody Wilkins as soon as they left.'

It had been easy enough to divert their thinking away from the department and to the parathlete. Serve him right if he was now under watch. That would add to his woes, and that made Rose even happier.

After making her ritual tea and listening to the radio, she went back down the garden to ensure that everything had burned to ash. Raking around in the embers, she checked for metal fittings, even though she had done her best to remove them before committing each item to the flames. She couldn't see anything incriminating. Besides, who was going to check up on her? And if they did, she had been careful to cover her tracks on a personal level.

Rose had changed her surname before her husband had died, wanting to distance her working life from the horrible time that had surrounded Lily's accident. They had been on the verge of losing their home, and she'd needed a well-paying, secure job, which the university had offered. Although ancient, her accountancy qualifications had enabled her to secure the position of administration assistant to Professor Chandler in the Art History department. Everyone there knew her by her maiden name.

Now, she was halfway through her project and, having come this far, Rose needed to make sure that she still had time to complete it. The police mustn't connect her or trace her activities online until it was too late. After that, she didn't care what happened.

It was starting to rain as Rose locked all the doors and windows before going into the study. She flicked on the lights and turned on the computer. There was only one necessary job this afternoon, so Rose had plenty of time to do some history cleaning. She began her usual trawl, printed out the increasingly hysterical newspaper and online news stories about the two deaths, and added them to her files. Considering that she was largely self-taught, Rose thought of herself as an expert these days. Once you got into the logic of it, many of the things she needed to do were actually simple. Rose had plenty of logic, and the mathematics were straightforward enough for someone who'd qualified as an accountant. She decided to check her stocks.

On a shelf above the computer stood four toy llamas. Two new cream-coloured ones lay on their sides, still in the plastic packaging they had come in. Two others with coloured blankets stood impaled on editor's spikes. One had a red blanket, the other a purple one. Both had blood on their faces. They were smaller than the pair in the packets.

Rose had found the spikes in a junk shop months ago, surprised to be able to buy them. She'd claimed they were for an amateur theatrical show and, being a middle-class, middle-aged female, Rose assumed she looked sufficiently unthreatening to be allowed to take them. She was getting away with a great deal by trading on people's assumptions of someone at her time of life.

Next to the llamas was a plain box. These contents had been much harder to obtain. It had taken weeks to track down a dealer prepared to supply the little glass jars with their highly illegal contents. Rose had spent hours in deep academic research to decide which drug to obtain. Not to mention the additional reading to understand the doses and strengths so that she could obtain the effect she wanted. Three bottles remained, more than ample to complete the remaining tasks.

To her frustration, her spyware was blinking a warning. Someone had been trying to track her down. The firewall had resisted the spybots, and luckily, Rose always routed out through a complex network. Whoever it was had been able to trace her a good way back up the chain, may have even identified that she was in Norfolk. With a smile, Rose knew, in that case, it pointed to the main university network. That would give someone a real headache.

'How clever are the police techs?' she asked the screen. It blinked in reply. 'Maybe just clever enough.'

Damn them. She'd been hoping to leave it a gap of a week or two before finishing her plans. If they were this close, it might be just as well to bring it all forward. The local hit was simpler to achieve, although now she would have to improvise an opportunity. The one in London was more difficult. It had always been the trickiest part.

Rose had originally intended to wait for one of the funerals, because surely the last of the Famous Four would attend. No one would question Rose being there. Now she would need another plan. The woman might have denied being involved at the time, but Rose knew better. They had all lied, or helped each other to escape justice. They all deserved to die.

Rose collected the three new plastic petrol containers she'd bought months ago and loaded them into the back of her everyday car. There was more than ample cash in her purse and, despite the rain, she needed to visit three separate garages to avoid suspicion.

She didn't need the white van anymore and calculated that three lots of fuel should be enough to dispose of the thing, which was still hidden behind the workshop. Time for it to go.

CHAPTER 33

It had been after nine o'clock when Sara had reached home last night. She didn't want to upset her neighbour so late, as Gilly Barker was a grandmother in her seventies who wouldn't welcome a knock at her front door after dark. Instead, Sara had sat on her sofa, trying to eat a microwave meal while alternately crying and becoming so angry that she had to put down her fork before she stabbed something with it.

Predictably, she didn't sleep at all. When her alarm dragged her out of bed, she felt groggy and needed a very large coffee to get her moving. Her mind worked overtime as she drove into work.

How long had Chris been seeing Mel? Had the bastard been sleeping with Mel and her at the same time, getting his jollies from two women? Mel obviously knew about Sara. Why hadn't she suspected something was going on? Call herself a detective. Too busy working, probably. Sara doubted if she would ever know the truth, because she had no intention of speaking to Chris again. She ground her teeth in frustration. Sara didn't like unsolved mysteries in her life. She'd had enough of that with her father. Well, good riddance to bad rubbish, as her mother always said. Chris was now definitely bad rubbish.

As she pulled into the car park, with an act of supreme will, her mind switched focus. Sara was comfortable considering herself a career officer. One day, she wanted to be an inspector or even a chief inspector. Having a female senior was almost like gaining a role model, especially in Norfolk, where there were fewer female officers of all ranks. What would DCI Hayley Hudson be like to work for? Time to find out. More importantly, how was DI Edwards going to react?

Please don't hand in your notice, Sara thought. *Give yourself time to get over the shock.* She had to admit that she'd come to like working with Edwards. He'd been a good boss.

Sara was shocked to find the room being rearranged. Sara's desk now faced another one in the corner nearest to the separate glass office. Her personal stuff and office equipment were scattered across the desk surface, the computer blinking, ready for her to sign in. The room she thought of as DI Edwards's inner sanctum was now the domain of DCI Hayley Hudson. The latter was already there, standing behind the desk and sorting paper into piles. Edwards's personal possessions were stacked on the desk that was now opposite Sara's own.

Two maintenance men were lifting the last of the spare desks into place at the end of two rows, which faced each other. It reminded Sara of a call centre. A grunt drew her attention to a bottom sticking out from under a desk, where a techie looked to be connecting cables to the main network in the underfloor patch point.

A single desk stood looking forlorn on the other side of Hudson's office. Aggie's workstation had been separated from the active officers, her photo frames and potted plants waiting in a jumble on it. The incident board was still fastened to the wall where it had always been, and another whiteboard now hung up next to it. The meeting table and the spare table in the corner with their coffee machine, the pile of dirty mugs and sugar bags was gone.

It wasn't looking good, in Sara's opinion. She signed herself in to the computer, wincing as she heard the techie bang his head exiting from under the desk. He shuffled on his knees under the next one.

Hudson approached her office door. 'Thank you, gentlemen.' The maintenance men left the room as quickly as they could. 'Good morning, DS Hirst.'

'Ma'am.' Sara nodded, then waved into the corner where the table used to stand. 'I'd offer you a coffee, but—'

'Filthy stuff.' Hudson turned back to her room. Sara thought about going down to the canteen to bring up morning drinks, shelving the idea in preference to waiting to see what the rest of them thought of the new office. She didn't have to wait long.

Bowen and Aggie arrived together. Bowen opened the office door as Aggie's arms were full of cake tins. They hardly seemed to be hiding the fact that they were car-sharing these days. The pair halted to survey the new layout, and Bowen instantly turned an angry red. Aggie gazed around until she spotted her own desk alone in the corner. She bit her lip as she dumped her tins on it.

'I'll get the coffee on,' she said.

'No, you won't.' Sara pointed to the empty space.

Aggie slumped into her chair.

'For fuck's sake,' exploded Bowen. 'Which one is my bloody desk?'

'I won't accept language like that in my office,' snapped Hudson, who had watched their entry from her desk. She strode into the main office and pointed at one of the end desks in the row with its back to her office. 'That one is yours. Just so you know, one warning is all you get. Keep it civil.'

When Noble appeared, he found that his desk was opposite Bowen. They all sat at their desks and waited, except Hudson, who carried on sorting through her paperwork. The tension in the air was palpable when DI Edwards walked in. He looked round blankly until he caught Sara's eye. She gestured to the desk opposite her own, and he walked over. Edwards pulled out an envelope from his coat pocket, then hung the coat over the back of his chair. Sara felt a chill run down her back.

'Good morning, team,' said Hudson. 'I realise this reorganisation will be a surprise to you.'

'Not bloody kidding,' muttered Bowen.

'DC Bowen, cut the language,' she snapped.

'Mike,' warned Edwards.

Bowen mumbled for a moment, then shut up.

'This is to accommodate the extra help we are receiving, some of which will be here this morning.' She waved to the two rows of desks. The techie's head popped up from underneath one, and he patted at Noble's legs so he could shuffle underneath another. 'I thought you might like to know a little more about me.'

No doubt she would have read all their personnel files and reports already.

'I'm joining you from Hampshire CID, where I worked as a DI. Prior to that, I was a DC and a DS in Wiltshire. You will gather from this that I am used to dealing with a mixed remit of both city and rural modes and issues. I am not expecting Norfolk to be so very different.'

The techie stood up. 'All done, ma'am.'

'Thank you.'

He scarpered even faster than the maintenance men.

Hudson moved to the new whiteboard. 'This is so we can keep track of the enormous number of tasks that are behindhand in this investigation.'

Edwards stiffened.

'Although time is of the essence in all murder cases, I feel it is exceptionally so on this occasion. Two murders, clearly linked and obviously committed by the same perpetrator. So far, we have no clue why or who it might be.'

'That's hardly true,' said Edwards. 'We have interviewed a number of possible witnesses and identified several strong leads or suspects. We just need to check their alibis.'

Hudson pursed her lips. Sara noticed then that she was wearing full make-up. She still had the smart suit on today, with a mauve roll-neck jumper under the jacket. At its edges, Sara saw that Hudson's neck was as red as her lipstick. Despite the appearance of control, their new DCI was either embarrassed or full of nervous adrenaline.

'We need to get it in order and press the suspects,' she said. 'The leads need working hard or, in my opinion, we could have another murder on our hands within days. Whatever is going on here is not random.'

'We're aware of that,' said Edwards.

'It also bears all the hallmarks of revenge.'

At this, Bowen's head came up, and Noble swung round in his chair to look at Hudson. Sara could see what the DCI meant, even though it was dangerous to make assumptions.

'And if it is revenge,' continued Hudson, 'that will automatically narrow our options. You have correctly identified the most likely routes or suspects.'

'Glad we got something right,' muttered Edwards. Sara threw him a warning glance to give the woman a chance.

'There are a number of avenues we need to close as a matter of urgency to ensure that we are concentrating on the right lines of inquiry. So, here's the plan.' She selected a marker pen. 'The extra DCs from the other teams will concentrate on fully interviewing all the staff at both these workplaces at the university. SCVA?'

'Sainsbury Centre for the Visual Arts,' said Sara. 'And the Art History department.'

'CRU?'

'Climatic Research Unit. The global warming people.'

'Good. Thank you. The extra staff will also look into the lists supplied from the Hall open days and the stolen vehicle reports.'

The additional staff had got all the dull jobs, and Sara was grateful for that. The list on the board grew.

'DC Noble?'

He nodded.

'You will liaise with Technical to find everything we can from Summerhill's laptop and the threatening email angle.

DC Bowen, you will work with the van team to follow up any likely stolen vans in the last few weeks.' Bowen grunted in disapproval. 'DS Hirst, I would like you to liaise with the FLO appointed to Summerhill's parents. They have arrived in Norwich and will view their son at the mortuary this afternoon. I want you to be with them.'

'Who is the FLO?'

Hudson checked her notepad. 'Tracey Mills. Know her?'

'Yes, ma'am. Best in the force.'

'Excellent. I also want you to look into the purposes behind the poses of the victims and the toy llamas. I believe you have already done some of this work.' Sara nodded. 'Both have to be of significance. I want you to find out what that meaning is. Mrs Hewett?'

Aggie sat upright. 'Aggie, call me Aggie. Everyone does.'

'Very well,' said Hudson with a slight smile. 'I want you to find out what is happening with Taryn Deacon's family and let me know.'

'DI Edwards?'

Everyone turned to look at the DI, who looked stony-faced.

'I'd like to have a full talk with you about current progress and interviews.'

'Good.' Edwards stood. 'Because I'd like a private chat with you too.'

'I have cakes,' said Aggie, obviously and desperately trying to relieve the tension. 'All the favourites. I didn't know what you would like DCI Hudson—'

'I don't eat cake.' Hudson looked around the team at Bowen's beer belly, Aggie's motherly shape, the thickness at Edwards's and Sara's waists. 'Bad for the figure and fitness.'

With those damning words, Hudson strode back into her office and shut the door. Through the glass wall, Sara watched Hudson slump gratefully into her chair and take a visibly deep breath.

Sara glanced at the list of jobs on the whiteboard. It was far from complete. They were concentrating on things in the wrong order. What about the CCTV around Taryn's house? What about Dom Wilkins's alibi claims? Hudson might be floundering on her first morning, but it was no excuse to make mistakes like this. Edwards was still standing, gripping the envelope.

'Boss,' said Sara. She stepped in front of his desk so that he couldn't leave. 'Don't do that. Don't be hasty. Wait and see how it works out.'

Edwards looked at his hands. 'I've been passed over, and I can't cope with that.'

Sara pulled gently at the envelope. 'And I can't work without you. Nor can the rest of the team. Please, please wait. You're not the only one who's been treated badly in the last couple of days.'

'You too?'

'Yes, except mine's personal. I'll buy you a beer some-time and tell you all about it.'

'This is personal to me.'

'No, boss. It's just work.' Sara's tone was getting more urgent. 'How many years' service?'

'Twenty-eight.'

'You can't throw that away. Think of your pension. And what would you do? You're too young to retire, for God's sake.'

'I thought about all this last night,' he said.

'Yes, when you were angry and hurt. Please wait.' Sara tugged at the envelope. 'There are things here that we need you to deal with. Or this team will cease to function. We still need you, whatever you think.'

'She's right, Will,' said Bowen. He had stepped up behind Sara without her noticing. 'Don't leave us now. We need you to lick the woman into shape.'

Sara winced at the comment but let it go. Now wasn't the time. 'Look at that board, at that list of jobs. We're going to be in an even bigger hole soon, if we don't help get the DCI up to speed.'

Edwards stared at the board, then released his grip on the envelope. Sara pulled it close to her chest. 'Thank you, boss.'

As she moved back to her chair, she noticed that both Noble and Aggie were standing by their own desks, waiting for the outcome. Everyone watched as Edwards rolled his shoulders to release the tension. Sara felt her own tension soften. He stepped to the office door and knocked. When Hudson looked up, he went in.

'Right,' he said, 'let's start with the coffee and cakes, shall we?'

CHAPTER 34

DI Edwards was with DCI Hudson for over half an hour. During that time, Aggie had done a coffee run to the canteen and surreptitiously handed round the cake tins. A couple of extra DCs had arrived from Vice, and Sara filled them in about the tasks. Noble and Bowen created a list of stolen vans of the correct type. When Edwards finally emerged, Sara could see that Hudson looked a little shell-shocked. Edwards murmured in Bowen's ear, who promptly left the office with Noble in his wake. Ten minutes later, they were jamming the coffee station behind Aggie's desk while she took a box of dirty mugs off to wash. That was sorted then.

Sara contacted Tracey Mills. The family liaison officer had already seen Joe Summerhill's parents and had arranged the visit to the mortuary. Sara would meet them all there. Aggie had obtained the name and address of Taryn's mother, who lived in the South of France. Tracey agreed to check if she had been contacted and what was happening with her.

Sara began to trawl the internet for images of Hammer horror films. It was deeply frustrating and seemed entirely pointless. There were hundreds to choose from — some even included Taryn's chair. None showed a victim strapped into it on first inspection. Sara hoped that she wouldn't have to sit through all the films to see if she could spot it. Even if the image existed, they already knew the provenance of the thing.

Hudson emerged from her office and eyed the two additional DCs from Vice. 'I had hoped there would be more of you,' she said. 'Do you have the list of the Climatic Research Unit staff?'

One of the DCs nodded.

'Then you can concentrate on them, to begin with. I want appointments made and the statements taken and entered on the system urgently.' Hudson turned to Edwards. 'I want you to chase Drugs and find out when we will get the extra staff from there. They should start with the Sainsbury Centre staff.' Edwards nodded. 'Images? DS Hirst?'

'There are hundreds of images available online.' Sara pointed to her computer screen. 'None seem similar to the victim's pose.'

'Keep looking. Aggie, any news on Taryn's parents?'

'Found her mother, ma'am, but no trace of her father.'

'Tracey Mills, our FLO, has taken that one on,' said Sara. 'She's likely to have to look after the poor woman anyway, so it seemed best.'

Hudson raised her eyebrows as if she was unused to a DS thinking for herself. 'Vans?'

Bowen stood up and held out sheets of paper. 'Yet another list. We've got dozens of the things now.'

'Best you start dealing with them, then,' snapped Hudson. Sara dropped her head forward to hide her smile. She valued Bowen's input these days, enjoyed working with the grumpy git. But she hadn't always felt this way. It seemed as though Hudson felt the same as she had on first meeting him. Sara hoped she'd learn differently. On the other hand, Bowen simply stared the DCI out before sitting back down and crossing his arms. He could wait for her to understand him. He was stubborn enough for that.

'Noble? Forensics?'

'I was helping with the list,' said the hapless DC. His willingness to help others sometimes made him an easy target. 'I'll nip down now.'

'When I ask you to do something, I expect—' Edwards cleared his throat, and Hudson switched tracks without acknowledging his intervention. 'Now would be good. Check on the laptop and crime scene information too.'

Noble was out of the office door before she could say anything else. Sara could see he had gone bright red. He was easily embarrassed and lacked confidence. They had all spent a lot of time nurturing him, because he was intelligent and diligent, a bonus to any team. She offered a silent prayer to the police gods that Hudson wouldn't undo their work.

'Good, let's get on.' The DCI went over to Aggie's desk, where she hesitated a moment. 'I'm given to understand that your cakes are highly regarded.'

Aggie nodded mutely.

'Erm, are any of them gluten-free?'

Her eyes filled with panic. 'I'm afraid not.'

'That's a shame,' said Hudson with a slight shrug. 'I'm allergic, you see.'

'O-oh, right,' stammered Aggie. 'Quite common these days, I believe.'

'Yes.' Hudson glanced at the reinstated coffee station. 'No kettle?'

Sara and Edwards were watching the exchange with interest while Bowen sat with his back to Aggie, rigidly staring at his computer screen. Aggie told Hudson that there wasn't a kettle.

'I only drink herbal teas.'

'Another allergy? Dairy?' ventured Aggie.

'No, just personal preference.'

With that, Hudson went back inside her office and closed the door. Like someone releasing the pause button on the television, everyone moved at once. The Vice DCs grabbed their lists and left, Edwards headed off to Drugs, and

Bowen picked up a phone to call the unfortunate van owners. After a few more minutes searching film images, Sara sat back in her chair with a sigh.

Aggie moved over to look at the screen. 'What are you actually looking for?' she asked. 'The DI didn't want me to put up an image of the poor young woman.'

'I think he was trying to spare your feelings.'

'I know, but I could help if I saw it.'

'You sure? It's pretty gruesome.'

Aggie nodded. Sara pulled up the image from her email files and opened it. For a moment, Aggie was taken aback. Then she looked more closely. 'That seems familiar. Hold on.'

Aggie pulled out a book from one of her desk drawers. It was titled *Masterworks of the Sainsbury Collection*.

'You are a dark horse,' Sara said.

Aggie blushed. 'I've been reading it on my lunch breaks.'

'You really like that place, don't you?'

'Once my lad went off to uni up north, I decided to do something about my own education. So, I joined this course about art appreciation.'

'Online?'

'No, here.' Aggie gestured to the logo on the book jacket. 'I did some other night classes too, before that. When I saw this course advertised, I thought it sounded good. Each week you get a talk about one of the pieces in the collection. They tell you about the artist and the techniques used. I find it fascinating. In fact . . .'

Aggie's voice trailed off.

'In fact, what?'

'Well.' Aggie seemed reluctant to share. 'You might think I'm getting above myself.'

'Why would I? What is it?'

'I've applied to join the Open University. I'm going to do a degree if I can cope with the essays and suchlike. I want to do art history. I find it fascinating.'

'That's amazing,' said Sara. 'You'll be more than capable.'

'Anyway, that pose.' Aggie pointed to the forensic photo on Sara's screen. 'There are two paintings in the collection that it might be.'

Aggie held up the book to show a smudged and dark painting of what might be a Pope in a high-backed golden chair. 'There's this one.'

Sara reached for the book.

'Hang on.' Aggie thumbed through the pages and held up a lighter-coloured portrait of a man sitting in a chair, one leg crossed over the other. He had a red scarf wrapped around his neck and hanging down his front, just as the blood had run down's Taryn's pyjama top. 'So, either the Bacon or the Giacometti, or a combination of the two. They're both in the Sainsbury Centre gallery.'

Sara snatched the book and looked for herself, flicking between the two portraits. 'Aggie, you're a bloody genius.'

CHAPTER 35

The rain was less "April showers" and more "monsoon down-pour". Dom had woken up feeling less than motivated, taken one look outside the window and decided that training was not an option today. He would hardly be able to concentrate if he tried. Instead, he had hidden inside his bike workshop to try that pedal change again. Wary of stripping the expensive cranks donated by a team sponsor, he sprayed the joint with WD40 and waited for it to soak in.

He could tell that his mother was worried about him from the way she had hovered over him at breakfast. But he couldn't burden her with the details of what he'd seen — it wouldn't be fair. His father was away on business again. Dom was grateful for that. His bluff, no-nonsense dad would soon be telling him to focus on his training or some such. Dad didn't deal in emotions.

One person needed an update about what was going on, and that person was someone he could talk to. Standing glaring out of the window at the rain, he dialled Junina, hoping that she would be in.

'Good morning, Dom,' answered a pleasant and efficient-sounding voice. 'How are you doing today?'

'Not so great, Junina.' Dom breathed out noisily, grateful to be able to say so. 'You busy? Or can we talk?'

'Sure. Dave's taken the kids to the park.'

'Park? In this weather?'

'It's a nice morning here.' He could hear the smile in her voice. 'So, apart from Joe, what's up? Why are you not so great?'

'Have you been watching the news?'

'Of course. Why?'

'Did you see that there had been a second murder here?' The line went quiet. Dom ploughed on. Tears were forming, and he couldn't keep the catch from his voice. 'It's Taryn. The bastard has killed Taryn.'

'Oh, Dom,' said Junina. 'I'm so sorry. You were much closer to her than the rest of us.'

'Not recently,' he said. 'Apparently, she and Joe had become an item. They just didn't bother to tell me about it. You?'

'Yes, I knew.'

'Fucking brilliant,' he said, his temper beginning to fray. 'Everyone knew but me. Even his housemate had guessed. Why wouldn't they tell me?'

Junina sighed. 'Listen to yourself, Dom. Why do you think none of us wanted to tell you?'

'You could have rung me. At least warned me.'

'I wanted them to be happy.' Junina's tone was becoming stern. Dom felt as if she were telling him off like one of her toddlers. 'It was always going to be difficult for you.'

'How long has it been going on?'

'I figured they were fond of each other at our reunion dinner.'

'That was months ago!' Dom's voice snapped with his temper. They'd all been lying to him.

'Take it steady,' soothed Junina. 'I think it only became official a few weeks back. You had competitions coming up. They didn't want to upset you.'

'Too late now. I am upset. And all of this makes me a suspect in the eyes of the police.'

'What?'

'They've interviewed me twice in one day.'

'Did you have anyone with you?' Junina was heading into legal mode. 'Did you record either interview?'

'They recorded the first one at the station.'

'Station! Well, at least I can officially request a copy. You want me to represent you, I take it. Is that why you rang me?'

Dom hesitated. He hadn't thought as far ahead as that. 'I guess so. I just wanted to let you know about Taryn, not for you to hear about it on the news. It was awful.'

'I'm sure it was. How did the police break the news?' Junina was scribbling on something. 'Did they manage that properly?'

'I don't know. I saw her,' said Dom, his voice broken with sobs. 'I saw Taryn sitting there. There was blood everywhere.'

There was a shocked silence at Junina's end of the conversation. 'You saw the body?'

'I sort of found it.'

'Oh my God,' muttered Junina. 'You found her? Did you touch her? Did you touch anything in the room? Dom, what happened?'

Dom searched for a piece of rag on the workbench and blew his nose on it, leaving oil marks on his face. In broken sentences, he explained about the previous morning at Taryn's house.

'At least the officer went in with you.' There were more scribbling sounds. 'Have they said anything about connections? Asked you about your past?'

'Both of the above.'

'Dom, I want you to listen carefully. I'm going to come up and see you. Under no circumstances must you make any further statements to the police without my being there. Got that?'

'Yes.' Dom felt relief wash over him.

'I'll need to sort out childcare arrangements for next week and cover for my cases. It will take time to do that. Luckily, I wasn't due in court, but there are client meetings I should be attending.'

Dom could hear Junina tapping at a computer. 'Thank you. Will you need to stay long?'

'I'm not sure.'

'Would you like to stay here? There's plenty of room, and Mum would be happy to help.'

'Better not,' she said. 'If I'm going to be representing you, I should keep a little distance. I'll find a hotel.'

'Junina,' said Dom, 'I don't know how I'm going to be able to pay.'

'Pro bono, dumbass. I'll pull in a few favours. I'll call you back tomorrow and let you know the details. If the police want to talk to you again, you answer "No comment", and that I will be with you no later than Monday lunchtime. Got that?'

'Yes.'

'One more thing, and this is the most important.'

'All right, I'm listening.'

'Do not, under any circumstances, volunteer information about the accident.'

Dom froze. 'I already have.'

'Idiot,' sighed Junina.

'They'd obviously looked it up. When they got stroppy, I told them they should have dealt with that better in the first place.'

'In other words, *you* got stroppy in return and didn't think. Great.' Junina sounded distinctly unimpressed, like she was resigned to a difficult fight. 'Hold on. Which accident?'

'When I was run down that time. When the police didn't believe me that it was deliberate.'

'I've always thought that was suspicious. But I didn't mean your accident. I meant the other one.'

'Why should I have even thought about that?'

'Because a girl was badly injured, and there was an official inquiry. You must be in the system somewhere, even after all this time. I'm surprised they haven't joined those dots.'

'No one's mentioned it. It doesn't matter anyway.'

'It does, Dom. Because we all lied about it.'

CHAPTER 36

Sara and Aggie stood in Hudson's office, barely containing their excitement.

'So, you think the positioning of the body reflects one or both of these paintings?' DCI Hudson asked. She was looking at the civilian clerk in disbelief, which annoyed Sara. Why shouldn't Aggie have an insight?

'That connects it back to the Sainsbury Centre,' Sara pointed out. She explained the significance of the ritual burial aspects involved in Joe Summerhill's murder and placement. 'Like the urn and the llamas.'

'Are you suggesting, then, that it must be someone who works there?'

'Or visits the place regularly.' Sara looked at Aggie. 'Someone who knows the collection. Perhaps someone on that course with you.'

Hudson sighed. 'Why would anyone draw attention to themselves like that? The perp is leaving these toys as a signature, surely?'

'And to make it a ritual sacrifice,' said Aggie quietly.

'It would add weight to your suggestion of revenge,' said Sara. At this, Hudson sat up straighter. 'If the victims are a sacrifice, then are they being made to pay the price?'

'How so?'

'The Incas left their child sacrifices with these silver llamas as an offering to the gods.' Sara waved a printout from her search. 'To bring on better harvests or for the health of their leader and stuff like that. What if our perp leaves them at the scene to indicate a sacrifice or a penance? I know it's a bit of a leap, but none of these choices are random, are they?'

'Agreed,' said Hudson. 'Revenge for something done to the perp, or penance for an unacknowledged sin?' She stood up and swiftly moved to the whiteboards. Sara and Aggie went after her. 'It's all a bit religious for my liking. And why this gallery? Aggie? You seem to know more about it than the rest of us.'

Aggie blushed before answering. 'It's the best in the area in my opinion. Has the largest and most varied collection. Huge selection of ethnographic items, combined with lots of modern art.'

'Lots of scope to choose from, then.' Hudson gazed at the lists both she and Edwards had created. 'You mentioned you were on a course there?'

'Yes, art history appreciation,' confirmed Aggie.

'All right. Get me a list of the participants. Let's see if there are any crossovers with our other lists.'

'Bound to be.' They hadn't noticed DI Edwards walking up behind them until he spoke. 'If they love art, odds are they may have done an open day at Barnham Parva New Hall. Worth a look, though.'

'Any luck with the extra staff?' Hudson asked him.

'From tomorrow morning, for as long as we need them.'

'Sunday,' said Hudson with a frown. 'Not helpful in reaching office staff.'

'Better than nothing,' said Edwards.

'More bloody lists,' muttered Bowen as he went back to ringing round his van list.

'Trouble is,' said Sara to Edwards once Hudson had gone into her office, 'the people who tend to like this sort of stuff also tend to be middle-class, middle-aged people who are generally law-abiding. Everything about these choices seems odd to me.'

'You're not convinced?'

Sara was always grateful that Edwards set such store by her intuition. 'No, I'm not. Yes, all this has some significance, but I think the choices are very personal. I don't think we should be going from the outside in.'

'Meaning?'

'We're spending a lot of time thinking about the external signs. Not enough thinking about the victims and their associations. My gut tells me this is something to do with this group of friends.'

'You think one of them is doing it to the others for some reason?'

'Like jealousy? Possibly.'

'You really fancy Dom Wilkins for it, don't you?'

'Maybe.' Sara wasn't at all sure. 'It's entirely possible for him to have had time to do both of these murders.'

'In which case, why the art at all? He doesn't strike me as being the art gallery type.'

Sara rolled her eyes. 'If it isn't him, it could be a confession, if our perp works or visits there.'

'Killers don't normally leave a signature like that, do they?' Edwards was leaning back in his chair, obviously enjoying the conversation. 'What if it's about art in general?'

'Rather than this gallery in particular? Or about one particular artist? Say, if they had stolen someone's precious artwork?'

'Great thought. Time to dig further back into the lives of the Famous Four, would you say?'

'I'm on it, boss,' said Sara. Then she looked over the DI's shoulder into the office and grimaced. 'I've got to go out soon, and both things are important.'

Edwards frowned in return. 'Can you get Aggie to do it? She's got time on her hands, as Hudson seems to have her down as just a typist and coffee maker. If this leads anywhere, I'll square it away with Ms DCI.'

Sara stifled a laugh and went to speak to Aggie. 'Can you do me a full-system search on each of the victims and the other members of the Famous Four? Find out if we have any previous interaction of any sort. Right back to their university days.'

Aggie nodded. 'Love to.' She had been photocopying the two paintings in her book. 'Shall I put these up too?'

'I'll do that for you. I'm not wasting any more time on Hammer horror films this morning. I think you've cracked that image thing. We just need to make sense of it now.'

She was sticking up the pictures when Noble threw open the door excitedly. Rob, the technical forensics expert, trailed in behind him, Joe Summerhill's laptop tucked under his arm. Rob's shirt flapped over his behind, and his glasses were propped on top of his head.

'Wait until you see this.' Noble strode over to Edwards and pointed at Rob, who was setting up the laptop on a spare desk. 'Sir, this might be really important.'

Noble moved to the DCI's office and knocked on the door, inviting her to join them. Even Aggie hovered at the back of the group, who crowded around Rob. He got the laptop running and flicked through various screens with the mouse.

Hudson leaned over to see better. 'What have you got?'

'Okay.' Rob drew a breath and launched into a technical explanation about running software and international searches.

Hudson folded her arms. 'Can we have that briefly and in layperson terms, please and thank you.'

'Sorry,' said Rob. He opened a screen showing Joe's emails. 'I tracked down and isolated the threatening emails into two types. The first is general nasty spam from the old keyboard warrior brigade. Climate change deniers, anti-expert fetishists, all that crap.'

Sara winced, but Hudson didn't seem to object to this use of language.

'They can all be dismissed by and large,' continued Rob. 'If you asked, I suspect most of the CRU team get stuff like this occasionally. The personal stuff is different. Whoever is sending these, I think, knows the victim directly. You can tell by some of the things they mention. There's a particularly nasty one when Summerhill's grant announcement is made. I've put them in a separate file, which I'll forward to you when I get back to the lab.'

'Have you been able to trace their origin?'

'Yes,' said Rob. 'Almost to the definitive source. The sender has a good knowledge of rerouting, even across the dark web.'

'Dark web! Bloody Hell!' exploded Bowen. That earned him a stern look from Hudson.

'Yes, they're rather good. But not as good as we are. I can't drill it down to a single computer, but I got right back to the mainframe. Of course, given the embarrassing thefts of information that have happened in the past, their firewall is superb.'

'Whose mainframe?' ground out Edwards. 'Come on, Rob.'

'The university. It goes right back to the UEA.'

CHAPTER 37

DC Noble and Rob from Technical Forensics hurried off to the university, not far in front of Sara. Her destination was the hospital. Dr Taylor's forensic post-mortem facility was part of the hospital mortuary. Murder is a rare crime anywhere in the UK, and in Norfolk is even rarer than the average. It was far easier to attach his special unit to the main mortuary at the far end of the modern hospital.

An astute and kind man, Taylor had ensured that Joe Summerhill was laid out neatly in the visiting suite with his face covered. It was possible to look in through a window from a relatives' seating area or to be in the room in private if preferred. Taylor was expecting his visitors, and Sara was ahead of Tracey Mills and Joe's parents.

'Got a minute?' he asked. He took Sara into his autopsy workspace. It was empty.

'I thought you would have Taryn here. Where is she?' asked Sara.

Taylor sat on a high stool by a workbench. 'I've finished with the physical examination,' he said. 'She's in the fridge.'

'If you've finished, why don't we have your results? Or did I miss them when I came out?'

'No, you didn't.' Taylor looked Sara up and down as if weighing her up. 'Do you like being here, Sara?'

'Yes, I do. I wasn't sure at first, now I've grown to love it.'

'Not likely to be moving on?'

'No, why?' Sara was perplexed.

'What do you think of the new DCI?'

Ah, so that was it. 'I'm giving her a chance to settle in before I decide. Either way, I'm not moving on. What makes you ask?'

'Little madam rang me up at eight this morning.' His voice sounded cold and angry. 'Demanded to know where the results were. I told her I'd go over when I had enough to tell her.'

'Have you been chatting with Edwards?'

'Last night.' The reply was fired out.

'He hasn't done it,' said Sara. 'Hasn't handed in his notice.'

'Your doing?'

'It's fair to say that we had a talk.'

'Good.' Taylor sounded genuinely relieved.

Sara wondered just how angry Taylor was with DCI Hudson. It wasn't like him to use phrases like 'little madam' or hold back information that might help. An assistant came in to say that Tracey and the Summerhill parents were here.

The three were waiting in the visitors' room. Tracey was holding Mrs Summerhill's hand as she introduced Sara. Joe's mother was a small, slight woman. She seemed shrunken sitting on the easy chair, her body folded with grief.

'DS Hirst is part of the team looking into your son's death.'

'Thank you,' Mrs Summerhill whispered.

Joe's father was in the next chair. His face was waxy and white. 'Murder, you mean. Have you caught them yet?'

'We have a large team working on this,' Sara assured him. 'If there is anything you can tell us, anything at all that was worrying Joe or worrying you, please let us know.'

'Cranks,' said Mr Summerhill. 'It has to be one of those blasted interweb cranks. Sending him hate mail like that.'

Tracey looked over at Mrs Summerhill. 'Perhaps we should go in now. Are you sure you are ready to do this?'

'Don't you get in a state, Val.' Mr Summerhill said, standing up. 'I can do the necessary.'

'No.' Val sounded determined. 'I want to be sure it's him, and if it is, I want to say goodbye properly.'

She stood up with Tracey's help, and Sara led the family into the viewing room. Dr Taylor was waiting for them. After introducing himself briefly and shaking Mr Summerhill's proffered hand, he gently drew back the sheet. He was careful to fold the sheet across Joe's neck, so they couldn't see the gaping wound.

As much to his own surprise as everyone else's, it was Joe's father who broke down and began to sob uncontrollably. 'Son! Oh, son.'

Mrs Summerhill let go of Tracey's hand and stood by her son's head. Leaning down, she kissed Joe's cheek gently before gazing at the silent figure. Tracing his face with her hand, she nodded and looked at Sara. 'Yes, this is my son.'

It took all three staff members to get Mr Summerhill back to the visitors' room, where he collapsed into an armchair.

'Sorry, I'm sorry.'

'There's no need to apologise,' said Tracey. 'Can we get you anything? A cup of tea, perhaps?'

Mrs Summerhill sat next to her husband. 'That would be kind.'

'I'll be a few minutes. I have to go up to the café.'

'Sid, why don't you help the lady?' Mr Summerhill's sobs were subsiding, and Sara handed over a box of tissues for him to clean his face. 'Stretch your legs, clear your head a bit.'

'I could do with some help,' suggested Tracey. Sara admired her quickness. Mr Summerhill nodded mutely, stuffing wet hankies into his jacket pocket. Wobbling a little, he stood up. 'Would you like DS Hirst to stay with you, Val?'

Val nodded. Tracey and Sid headed off to the nearest café.

'May I call you Sara?'

'Of course.'

'You can call me Val. Give me a minute.' Val drew a deep breath, which seemed to settle her a little. 'It's worse than you can ever imagine. Getting that knock on the door.'

Sara knew how awful it felt to be delivering such news. Receiving it must be infinitely harder. All she could do was try to empathise. Wishing she had Tracey's kind tone and generosity, she said, 'I can't imagine.'

'Sid thinks it was whoever sent these hate emails,' said Val. Sara nodded but kept her peace. 'I can see why.'

Val fell silent, her lips twisted, and she sniffed. Sara handed over the tissue box.

'My Joe was a good man,' said Val. 'He was trying to save the planet, trying to save us all.'

'It shouldn't have cost him his life.'

'No, it shouldn't,' said Val, her tone growing firmer. 'And I don't agree with Sid that it has.'

Sara waited.

'Joe was a bit wilder when he was younger.'

'Do you mean at university?' asked Sara. 'This group of friends going to gigs?'

'You know about them? Called themselves the Famous Four. You know, like the Famous Five in the books? Said it was ironic.'

'You think this has to do with something that happened back then?'

'I don't know. Maybe. It was years ago, of course.'

Sara's instincts were on full alert. 'What happened back then, Val? Do you mind telling me?'

Val sighed. 'I think someone should. There was an accident, you see. In their final year, in February. They were all sharing a house in a little village beyond the university. I always thought it was a strange choice when they could have been nearer the action. You know how young people are.'

'The gigs and concerts?'

'The pubs and nightclubs too.' Val's shoulders slumped. 'I'm not stupid. I know what they got up to.'

'This accident?'

'They wanted to go to a gig in Norwich. It was raining hard, so they decided to take one of the cars. On the way, there was an accident. A girl got knocked off her bicycle and badly injured.'

'Who was driving?'

'That's the thing. They all said Joe was driving, but I was never sure about that. He was a careful, almost nervous driver back then and wouldn't have volunteered to drive in the dark and rain. Anyway, they were all breathalysed, of course, and the others were over the limit.'

'Not Joe?'

'No. They all said it was an accident, stuck to their story. Joe was fined, and never drove again after that.'

'You didn't believe them?'

Val shook her head. 'A few years ago, Joe got depressed one time he was visiting with us. He confessed to me that he hadn't been driving that night, one of the others had, and they had been lying to the police. The driver had been really drunk. They should have seen the girl.'

'What happened to the girl, do you know?'

'That's what had really upset Joe. He'd found out that she had been left permanently disabled. Her life was in ruins. It was all their fault, and the real driver had got away with it scot-free.'

CHAPTER 38

Once Tracey had taken Val and Sid back to their hotel, Sara rang the office. Edwards wasn't in, and Aggie put her through to DCI Hudson. Sara updated her on Mrs Summerhill's story.

'Aggie is already looking into the Famous Four,' said Sara. 'This should concentrate her search.'

'It may well help,' said Hudson. 'She's tracked down this fourth member of the gang in London and will contact the woman today if she can. I think we should speak to her as soon as possible.'

'If Mrs Summerhill is right, this Junina might be in danger. So might Dominic Wilkins.'

'Let's not get ahead of ourselves. By the way, did you run into Doctor Taylor?'

'He was at the viewing,' said Sara.

'Any idea when he might have some results for me? I rang him this morning for an update, but he said he wasn't ready.'

'Some of the test results do take a long time to come through.' They both knew this was often the case. Sara also knew she was evading the real and unspoken question.

Hudson asked it anyway. 'Is he sound? Obviously, I haven't met him yet. I just wanted your opinion.'

The comment was either flattering or a trap, depending on how you looked at it. 'Best I've ever come across, even in London. Not much gets past him.'

'Given the time, I think you could head home now.' Hudson swiftly changed the subject. 'I don't think there is much you can do here at the moment.'

Sara thanked her new boss, hoping she kept the surprise out of her voice. There was still time left in the day when she could have been doing something to help. It was hard not to remember a moment in her first case when Edwards had also sent her home early from the hospital. She'd felt overlooked and dismissed then. She felt the same now. Was Hudson one of these women who didn't like to have other women around her or saw them as a challenge to her authority? She was certainly making enough errors to indicate that she felt threatened by her new responsibilities. There had been a DI like it in the Met. None of the other female detective staff had liked working with her, and it was the threat of being moved into that team that had been a minor factor in Sara's decision to relocate to Norfolk.

All the same, Sara had plenty to think about and was grateful to reach her cottage before it grew dark. The evening was sharply cold, suggesting a spring frost in the morning. She was beginning to understand the signs and signals despite having lived in the countryside for less than eighteen months. It gave her an excuse to light the open fire and have an evening in front of it. She would even ring her mum if she could summon up the courage. Her mum was very fond of Chris and might be disappointed that they had split up. Although she was sure her mum would support her when she heard about Mel, Sara didn't really know how to start so difficult a conversation when her feelings were still this raw.

The fire was crackling, and Sara was rubbing spices into a chicken breast for a traditional Jamaican recipe when there was a knock at the front door. Wiping her hands, she found her neighbour, Gilly Barker, standing outside, a smile on her face. She held out a cake tin.

'Thought you might like some flapjacks,' she said. 'I've been baking for the grandkids' visit tomorrow.'

What was it about these Norfolk women that encouraging someone to stuff their faces with cake was a gesture of caring, Sara wondered. She got this at home and at work and was going to be the size of a house soon.

She accepted the tin. 'I was just doing some fried spiced chicken,' she said. Prompted by the prospect of some company, rather than an evening on her own dwelling on her problems, she asked, 'Would you like to join me?'

'Oooh, thank you.' Gilly stepped inside. Sara knew Gilly had developed a taste for the Caribbean recipes Sara's mum had taught her. They sat in the kitchen. As Gilly chatted about her day and the visit tomorrow, Sara carried on preparing the meal. She wasn't aware that she seemed quiet until Gilly stopped talking.

'Sorry,' said Sara. 'I was miles away.' She dropped the chicken into the pan, where it sizzled aromatically.

'I can see that. Is everything all right?'

'Big case on,' replied Sara.

'The one on the news? I thought that might have landed with your team. How is that nice DI Edwards coping with double murder? Most unusual for around here, isn't it?'

'You know I can't say.'

'Of course not. Your dad used to tell me off for being nosey.'

Sara hesitated as she put a pan of rice on to boil, then carried on. 'He's not in charge anymore.'

Gilly spluttered for a moment. 'DI Edwards? Has he retired then? He didn't seem old enough.'

'He isn't,' agreed Sara. 'And he hasn't. We have a new boss. A DCI, and the team has never had one before. Our team just got bigger without any warning. They seem to be good at this sort of thing at work.'

Gilly knew about the difficulties Sara had faced when she'd first moved to Norfolk. Her appointment had been announced to the team while she was waiting in reception. 'What do you think of him so far?'

'It's a her, a woman. Not much older than me, maybe early forties. Let's just say that I'm waiting to see how she settles in. Peas or red beans in the rice?'

There was a long silence as Sara sorted out their meals, and the pair settled in front of the fire on the sofa. Gilly ate her chicken with great enthusiasm, which Sara was grateful for. Her mind hadn't really been on the job, and she had overdone the heat a little.

Enjoying another mouthful of food, Gilly looked across at Sara. 'Is there something else? Is it just the new boss?'

Wondering if the woman was a mind reader, Sara chased rice around the bottom of her bowl. Was it that obvious?

'Do you remember Chris?' she finally asked.

'We met at that barbecue you had last summer, didn't we? When your mum and stepdad visited. Handsome, I thought.'

'I caught him out the other night. I called at his flat unannounced, and he was in bed with another woman.'

Gilly held her fork suspended in mid-air, and her jaw dropped. 'That nice young man?'

'I guess he got tired of the hours and the shifts.'

Sara scrubbed angrily at the tears that began to form in her eyes, realising too late that she still had particles of chilli on her fingers. With a mild curse, she ran for the kitchen sink to rinse away the stinging as best she could. Gilly followed, dumping their bowls on the table and hunting through the drawers to find a clean tea towel. With a shaky laugh, Sara wiped carefully at her streaming eyes.

The phone coverage in Happisburgh was poor, and consequently, Sara tended to leave her mobile on the window ledge above the sink. It was the best place to pick up a signal. With typical timing, it rang now as she stood half-blinded by chilli while Gilly fussed round her trying to find an eye bath, an item Sara didn't possess. Blinking furiously, she tapped on the screen to answer her mother on speakerphone.

'My lovely,' said Teagan. She sounded excited — her Jamaican accent always came to the fore when she was happy or upset. 'How are you?'

Sara's reply was muffled by the tea towel. 'I'm good. You?'

'I have some news. Some great news I wanted to share with you, the first person we tell.'

'What is it? I'll be all right, Gilly. Please don't fuss.'

'You got company?'

'Gilly, my neighbour. You remember her from last summer?'

'Ah, lovely lady. I was hoping it might be Chris. Never mind. I'll share with you, and you can pass it on.'

'Share what, Mum?'

'Javed and me.' Teagan paused for dramatic effect. 'We're gonna get married, and I want you to be my witness.'

CHAPTER 39

Rose waited until after midnight. She had a new plan to get at Dom Wilkins. She could do it on Monday. The disposal of the van had also been carefully planned, and now it was time to carry it out. She had left her everyday car at a walkers' car park on a long-distance path about twenty miles from her home. A two-mile walk from the car park was a craft centre with a café. She had walked to the craft centre, where she had carefully shopped for some innocuous presents, had a cup of tea and ordered a taxi. The taxi had brought her back to the village but not back to her house. She'd walked the rest of the way home and had needed a nap after that.

Wearing black waterproof trousers, a hooded jacket, gloves and a mask that almost entirely covered her face, Rose placed a small rucksack on the van's passenger seat. Inside there was a torch with fresh batteries and a box of long cook's matches. The final items were the two Molotov cocktails she had carefully prepared from a recipe she'd found on the internet. It hadn't even been hard to track down. A glass bottle filled with fuel and a rag wick soaked in the same fuel poking out of the top.

The van bumped out of its hiding place behind the shed, down the wide path in the copse to the farmer's field behind.

The rain had meant that the van's passages over the last few days were marked in the dark soil. She knew the farmer had planted spring barley early in March, and the green shoots of the crop were already showing above ground. In a few days, the green shoots of the young plants would have filled in the ruts. There was no reason for the farmer to be checking the field for the next few weeks, especially at the back of her house. The crop could be left to get on with its growing for weeks at a time.

Rose didn't turn on her headlights until she had gone a couple of miles down the lane. This was a difficult moment. She couldn't see all that clearly. Mercifully, weaving her way to the main road, she didn't pass a single vehicle. There were bound to be traffic cameras on the A11, but Rose only followed it for a few miles before turning off through the lane network again. She kept her face covered.

She had hired the van online and had picked it up from the hire firm's desk at Norwich Airport. This was the only major flaw in her plan, and Rose knew it. She had booked the van for eight weeks, giving no reason to the woman who handed over the keys. It was an unusually long booking, and Rose had only used it for three of those weeks so far. With luck, no one would miss it until she failed to return it at the end of the hire period. By then, it would be too late.

Her chosen burn site was a derelict piece of waste ground that had once been part of the war effort. Being close to the continent, Norfolk had been covered in airbases during the war. In an attempt to confuse the Luftwaffe bombers, a number of fake bases had also been built. These had runways and temporary buildings on them. Some, the historians claimed, even had pretend bombers on the grass, made of wood and canvas, like scenery in the theatre. This piece of land was one of those fake sites.

It didn't seem to be used for anything at all now. The old site was truly abandoned in the middle of nowhere and miles from any towns or villages. The old chain-link fence was falling down. The concrete runway was breaking up, weeds and brambles forcing their way up from the soil beneath. A gate that should have protected the site was falling off its hinges. A sign at the entrance claimed that a new housing estate would be built there imminently. But the board was weather-beaten, and the dates indicated that it had been acquired before the financial crash in the noughties.

It was perfect for Rose's needs. She pushed aside the gate and drove down the decaying runway to the end farthest from the road. Little hills of bricks and timber stood guard, presumably where the old buildings had been demolished at some time. Choosing the largest pile, she parked behind it and climbed out.

Taking the three full petrol cans from the back of the van, she threw the contents all over the vehicle as best she could, making sure there was a concentration of it underneath what she thought was the fuel tank. Ensuring she had her mobile in her pocket, Rose emptied the rucksack onto the floor twenty yards away and put the three empty petrol cans in the back with the museum ladder. To stop them rattling, she had padded the steps with the blankets Joe Summerhill had been using in the shed. The old mattress lay on the van floor beside the ladders. She upended one of the petrol cans and splashed a few dribbles on the dirty fabric.

Standing a few yards back, Rose took the box of matches and lit the first cocktail. There would only be a few seconds' grace before it went off. She lobbed it at the van, where it smashed satisfyingly against the tall side.

It felt as if time slowed down. Rose watched as the rag's flame caught the bottle's contents. Fire raced across the side of the van, catching more and more fuel as it moved. She lit and threw the second cocktail. It smashed on the ground by the van's back wheel. The van itself was already burning in earnest, the heat from it rising rapidly. Stepping further back, Rose stripped off her coverings. Underneath, she was wearing jeans and a chunky jumper, looking as near to a rambler as she could manage. The broken-down walking boots were a nice touch.

The torch would guide her off the site. About three hundred yards down the lane, she would get to the place where the long-distance footpath crossed the road. It might be tricky, as there wasn't much moonlight, but at least it wasn't raining. Should she meet some insomniac dog walker or hiker, Rose already had a story worked out — a night walk challenge for charity.

The black leggings, coat and mask stank of fuel and needed to be burned with the rest. The van was blazing well. It wouldn't be a problem. Rose walked cautiously closer, bundling the clothes into the rucksack to burn everything that might leave a trace.

As her arm windmilled the bag towards the van, the fire reached the fuel tank. With a huge bang, the van exploded in all directions. Flames, heat, burning fuel, noise blasted Rose, lifting her off her feet and flinging her backwards. When she hit the floor, the air was forced from her lungs. Her head rattled on an old piece of concrete, her eyes swimming.

Pain shot down her arm. Lifting her hand between her face and the starry sky above, she could see it was red raw and dripping with blood. Then everything vanished.

CHAPTER 40

Unsure how long she had been passed out, the flames from the van were still reaching high into the sky when Rose regained consciousness. Rolling onto her side, her hand protested in agony as she tried to lever herself upright. She shuffled on her knees towards the pile of rubbish where she had left her torch. Blood was dripping in rapid, uncontrolled globules onto her jeans and the floor. Stretching with her left hand, she pulled the mobile from her pocket. It was smashed. The glass was in fragments, and the screen was black. She didn't even know what time it was.

Somewhere, in the very far distance, there came the sound of sirens wailing.

'Shit.' Pulling the woolly hat from her head, Rose tried to stem the bleeding. It only partly helped. She dragged the sleeve of her jumper down and tied it in a ragged knot to cover the damaged hand. Grabbing at the torch, she managed to turn it on and scrambled to her feet.

Almost blinded by the pain, she stumbled away from the burning vehicle and behind an adjacent pile of rubble. Her head was spinning, and she was dripping a trail of blood. The sirens were getting nearer.

Who the hell had seen this? Who had called for the fire brigade? Or was it just a coincidence?

'Fucking move,' she demanded of herself. 'Not a coincidence.'

Rose staggered as quickly as she could from behind one pile to the next, all the time wanting to scream in pain. The piles were all at this end of the old runway. All she could think to do was use them to get as far away from the van as possible. The last pile on this side was almost in the hedge. She scrambled behind it as the fire engine jolted through the gate and headed past her. She ducked between the pile and the high thorny bushes. The pain was excruciating. Cursing and crying, she managed to turn off the torch, then forced herself to be silent.

Suddenly there was light and noise of a different kind. She heard voices shouting instructions, the sound of feet pounding about, the engine running as the officers laid out pipes, followed by an increased whine as they pumped water onto the burning van.

Rose lay among the weeds and broken bricks, gripping her jumper over her damaged hand, teeth clamped on her lower lip to stop them chattering, biting a raw hole with the effort. She had managed to get about two hundred yards away from the blaze. The fire crew hadn't trained their working lights in this direction. The sight of them terrified her, but the veteran planner in her brain told her to stay put and stay quiet.

It was possible that she actually passed out again. Certainly, she lost all track of time. The noise became a blur. At some point, a police car turned up. The fire was almost out, and the two officers stood looking at the burned-out vehicle and chatting to a couple of the fire crew. Rose was too far away to hear what they were saying. At least her hand seemed to have stopped bleeding, although the sleeve of the jumper was matted and soaking. The pain had subsided to a deep throb.

With a breezy goodbye between the officers, the police car went back where it had come from. At least that suggested that no one was expecting whoever had started the fire to be hanging around. Propping her back against a block of concrete, she tried to get her bearings. From the shouts between the fire crew, it sounded as if they were packing up too. All she had to do was wait and try not to pass out again.

Eventually, the fire engine bounced back to the road and off to its base. Rose was grateful after all that noise, heat and light that the silence and darkness enveloped her. No, she hadn't passed out. There were stars and a sliver of moon. Thin, grey clouds scudded high up. It was cold. The frost was descending. Despite all that had gone wrong, Rose still needed to finish her plan, or she could lie here and die of exposure. Having no idea how much time had passed, she knew that she risked being seen in daylight if she rested for too long.

With a cry of pain and another very unladylike curse, she managed to stand up. As she limped along, Rose could feel the reassuring dig of her car keys in her jeans pocket.

'Thank God for that,' she said. Her voice sounded loud in the shadow of the hedge.

At the gate, Rose checked up and down the minor road. When she felt sure that there was no engine in the distance, she staggered the three hundred or so yards to the walking track. Her head was woozy, and her hand was beating a tattoo of pain, which confused her. For several seconds, she couldn't make her mind up which way she should turn or which direction the car park was in. The sudden hoot of a nearby owl made her jump.

'Stupid bird.' Her voice rang out in the stillness, and with a complaining screech, the owl bustled out of the tree above her and flew off into the night. The fright had cleared her head, and she chose a path. It was at least three miles, and Rose wasn't keen on exercise. She'd already done a lot of walking that afternoon. Now she was left with just her own determination to get away from the scene, to reach her home.

The track was an old railway line, converted to a long-distance footpath. Some sections were well made, with light-coloured gravel rolled flat for ease of use. Other sections were narrow, muddy ridges, deepened by the tyres of mountain bikers. All were littered with piles of dog faeces at the edges. Beside the track, mature trees stood in two single-file battalions. Perhaps they had been planted by the railway company. Rose issued a silent vote of thanks to the Victorian businessman who had conceived the idea.

She lost count of how many times she stopped to rest. Five, ten, more? It was the trees that kept her going. Counting them down, Rose kept moving on the promise of numbers.

'Ten more trees, and I'll have a rest.'

She was desperate for something to drink. If there had been a stream, she would have risked the water in it. There wasn't.

'Eight more trees, and you can stop.'

'Count to fifty, then move on.'

At one fallen tree, Rose sat on the mangled trunk and began to count the rest aloud. The words trailed off as her head nodded sleepily to her chest. The gentle momentum dragged her forward from her seat, and she slumped onto the dirty floor. Automatically putting out her hands to save herself, Rose screamed as her damaged hand tried to take her weight.

Her torch was beginning to grow dim, and the sky was starting to lighten when she reached the car park. Weeping with relief, Rose managed to unlock the door and climb in. Now all she had to do was drive home, with her right-hand bleeding freely again.

Cursing the day she had turned down the chance of an automatic gearbox, Rose started the engine and pulled away.

CHAPTER 41

Naturally, Sara had congratulated her mother and agreed to be her witness at the wedding. Not wanting to spoil the moment for her mum, she had kept the news about Chris to herself. She had pulled on a fluffy cardigan and wandered down the garden for the conversation. It was the best place to get a full mobile signal. When she'd returned to the kitchen, Gilly had washed up, left a fresh cup of tea on the table for Sara and let herself out.

Making up the fire, Sara had stared at the flames absently until thoughts of work overtook her own problems. The trouble was that people didn't really like change. Everyone liked "a change" when they went on holiday, but fundamental change like an unexpected new boss at work who threatened the status quo was another matter. Most people preferred a solid base of boring old routines in their daily lives. There'd been a gutful of change these last few days for Sara. The case needed to come first.

She went into work the next morning at her usual time. As it was Sunday, the roads were clear, and the run took less time than normal. Like other routines, Sara had become used to the commute from the cottage. It gave her valuable thinking time. Coffee on, she got a notepad and began to get her thoughts in order, deciding to weigh up the two options.

Heading one column *Dom Wilkins*, she wrote the things that stood against him — trouble with his temper, jealousy of the Summerhill/Deacon relationship, alibis not checked, which appeared to give him time to commit both murders. Why had he taken the keys to Deacon's house? To let himself in to kill her? He'd had access to the open bottle of wine to drug it, just as much as Rhys had. None of them knew where Summerhill had been for two days. Could Wilkins have held him captive somewhere?

In the other column, she made notes about this group of friends. What was this accident that Val had talked of? What had become of the victim? What was the connection to the SCVA? Or the artworks there? Or the artworks at Barnham Parva New Hall? Her list of questions grew, and her confusion grew with it. Something bound all this together, if only she could see it.

Sara looked again at the list of jobs on the whiteboard. If she could see that DCI Hudson was missing a couple of major things, surely the others could too. Should she mention this, or wait for one of the others to do it? The woman was new, trying to catch up. She didn't want to be seen to be taking sides. She slammed her notebook shut and went down to the canteen.

Whatever DCI Hudson's opinion of cake, Sara had brought enough bacon rolls for the expanded team by the time the rows of desks were filled. Hudson was looking at them longingly, she noticed. DC Adebayo, seconded from the Drugs team, saw Sara watching and winked at her conspiratorially. Sara couldn't help but grin. Both teams were in the same precarious boat at the moment.

'Not disturbing you, am I?' Dr Taylor pushed through the office door, his hands full with bags. Aggie twittered around him as he set up his laptop and pulled out files of notes. DI Edwards introduced Taylor to Hudson.

'Any cake, Mrs Hewett?' asked Taylor.

Glancing shyly at Hudson, Aggie nodded.

'Good. It always makes my visits here so much more pleasant. Got something to project with? Ian?'

The fact that Taylor obviously knew the team better than their new boss wasn't going down well.

'What have you got for us?' Hudson demanded. Edwards turned away to hide a smile.

'Shame,' said Taylor to Ian, who had said there was no projector. He ignored the DCI. 'Got a lot to show you all. Shall we get started?'

The team and the extra staff settled in their seats, leaving Hudson standing at her office door. Whatever she'd actually said, Hudson had clearly annoyed the pathologist, who was being rude to her in the politest of ways.

'Are you up to date with the death of Joe Summerhill?' he asked. If anyone didn't know, they didn't say. 'Further tests have given us some new data. We assumed he had been drugged in some way, but there was nothing in his blood tox screen. So, I sent off a hair sample. Lo and behold, our old friend gamma-hydroxybutyric acid.'

DC Adebayo frowned. 'Liquid ecstasy? Why?'

Sara glanced at DCI Hudson, who looked equally surprised. GHB had once been fashionable in the rave scene but had fallen out of favour recently.

'Good question,' said Taylor. 'For one thing, it's colourless and odourless. You can put it in any drink as a spike, and no one notices.'

'The date-rape drug?' said Hudson. 'I thought it was hard to get hold of these days.'

'Can be,' agreed Taylor. 'Available if you know who to ask. I don't think it's being used as a date-rape drug in this case, though. Although it can be hard to control the doses in a casual situation, if you're careful, it can have other effects, which might have been useful to our perpetrator.'

'Such as?'

'Confusion, blurred vision, loss of consciousness or death. If a victim does pass out, they often cannot recall anything they did when under the influence. However, they may have felt good about it!'

'GHB makes it possible for someone to feel euphoric and yet be unaware of what they're doing?' asked Sara. Taylor nodded and waited. 'Unaware of danger?'

Taylor smiled at her. 'That's the one. Whoever administered this to Joe could have kept him sleeping for hours, then when he did come around, he may not have had any sense of danger. His coordination might have been shot too.'

'And if he knew and trusted whoever was giving it to him, he might have gone along with what they asked him to do?' asked Sara.

'Like walking up a set of ladders for a joke?' asked Bowen. For once, he looked surprised, something he rarely was. 'Or because he had been persuaded he was being helpful?'

'Exactly.' Taylor sounded triumphant. He looked at Hudson, who was nodding thoughtfully. 'The same drug was used on Rhys Davies. I took a hair sample from him, and the young chap is lucky to be alive. He'd drunk a very high dose, which is why he was so uncoordinated when we found him at Taryn Deacon's house.'

'Could he have slept through the murder?' asked Edwards.

'Easily.'

'Had Deacon had some too?' asked Sara.

'I can't find it. She was dosed up on sleeping tablets, however. A prescription, I understand.'

'They got the doctor to prescribe them because she was so hysterical about Joe,' Sara confirmed. 'I didn't get the impression that she normally took them.'

'The sleeping tablets were on her bedside table,' said Taylor. 'A match for the contents of her stomach. She would either have been asleep or disorientated after taking them.'

'Could someone have persuaded her to go downstairs without waking Rhys up? Especially if she knew them?'

'Possibly. Speculation is your province, not mine. Unfortunately, we haven't found the murder weapon at the scene.'

'What do you think it was?' asked Edwards.

'My best guess is still a cut-throat razor,' said Taylor. There was a rustle among the team. It was an unusual choice. 'Rather in keeping, I felt, given the young lady's lifestyle. It's a very gothic choice. Also used on Joe Summerhill, of course. Can be used by anyone, no strength required.'

'Do we know who was in the house apart from the victim?' Edwards leaned over his desk towards Sara. 'Have we screened for DNA on visitors?'

'We've done various swabs in the house,' confirmed Taylor.

'We know the two men were there,' replied Sara. 'And Rose Crawford from the university, who had looked after her all afternoon.'

'Let's get those samples done then.'

'Where did this Rhys Davies get his dose from?' Hudson suddenly asked.

'Wine.' Taylor held up a sheaf of papers. 'These are my reports. I'll email them all over to you later on this morning.'

'Wine? At Taryn's house?' Sara thought of the empty glasses in the living room that Dom Wilkins had been so keen to clear away. 'The bottle on the coffee table?'

'Indeed.'

Sara turned to look at Edwards out of habit. 'Wilkins said that he'd had some of the same wine, but only half a glass because he was driving. Would that have made him incapable as well?'

'More likely to have made him rave-ready at half a glass,' said Taylor.

'Didn't you tell me this Wilkins is an Olympic hopeful? A parathlete?' Hudson asked.

Sara nodded.

'Then it might not have had any effect on him at all.'

'There's no evidence that it enhances athletic performance.' Taylor looked at Hudson with rather more respect.

'Street rumours say that it does,' said DC Adebayo from the back of the room. 'He could be taking it to gain an edge.'

CHAPTER 42

How she made it home, Rose would never be sure. The pain and confusion blocked any memories of practical actions. All Rose knew when she woke up on Sunday morning was that she hurt. Blinking, she could see she had made it to her own bedroom. By the feel of it, she was still dressed in the same clothes she had been wearing last night. There was a lump in the back pocket of her jeans. Was it her smashed mobile? She could only hope that she hadn't left it at the deserted airfield.

As she tried to sit up, Rose realised that her face was stuck to her pillow. Her right arm and hand were still wrapped in the jumper sleeve. The blood on it had dried onto her wounds and crackled as she pulled at the knot. She yelped with pain. Her arm began to shake uncontrollably. She lay there for some minutes waiting for the agony to subside, trying to decide what to do.

Using her undamaged hand, Rose peeled gently at the cotton pillowslip. She felt like a child pulling off a sticking plaster very carefully. It was taking ages, and there was so much to do.

'Get it over with,' she said in a tone her mother would have recognised. She sat up abruptly, ripping away any remaining dried scabs. It made her cry out, but it was done. Panting with effort, she headed for the bathroom.

She moaned with self-pity at the sight of her face in the mirror. The blast from the van had not only caught her throwing arm and hand. The bridge of her nose, her cheeks and forehead all looked bright red. Her eyebrows had been singed, although they hadn't completely vanished.

'Woman up,' she scolded her reflection. 'It's not as bad as it looks. Just needs cleaning and some burn cream.'

Reaching round with difficulty, Rose pulled out the lump in her back pocket. As she had hoped, it was her dead mobile. *Thank God!*

Her arm was another matter. The warm woolly jumper she had worn to make herself look more like a hiker was caked in blood and covered in dirt, as were her jeans. Picking gently at the dried-up sleeve was getting her nowhere. Running warm water into the basin, Rose lowered in her arm, hoping to soak the fabric free. The water instantly turned dark red, and even that gentle sensation was almost unbearable. Slowly, she was able to separate the wool from her flesh.

Rose lifted her arm out of the water. The knot was so wet it was impossible to pull open. Instead, she wriggled out of the jumper and dropped the whole sopping mess into the bath. The back of her hand and her forearm were in a worse state than her face. The skin was raw. In a couple of places, protective blisters had formed, which had been pulled open as she'd removed her clothes. They were weeping pus-filled water and blood.

'Stupid, you're so stupid,' she berated herself. Shaking with cold, Rose went back to the bedroom and pulled on her dressing gown. At some point, she had at least managed to remove the walking boots, which she spotted lying in the hall. Stiff with shock and unexpected exercise, Rose went down the stairs one at a time. It made her feel like a little old lady.

Equally unwelcome were the bloody smears and handprints that seemed to be everywhere. On the doors, the banisters, even the walls. At least it could only be her own blood.

Everything else had been burned — she was sure of that. A glance into the drive told her that the car was there. Not parked in its usual neat way, but slewed across the gravel. There would be blood in there too, no doubt. It would have to wait.

Rose went into her daughter's room. Carefully hidden since the time of Lily's death, she had retained the various morphine-based painkillers. From oxycodone to oramorph, Lily had been through every prescription painkiller available. Some of them might be out of date, but they should still do the job. Rose opened a bottle and swallowed three or four of the tablets with considerable difficulty. The side effects didn't matter, so long as she could numb the pain long enough to clean up.

There was no sense in making a ritual cup of tea in this state. A teabag in a mug would have to do. The warm liquid in her stomach soothed her as she waited for the pain to subside. She might even be able to eat something soon. Rose knew she needed to get organised, needed a plan.

Firstly, she had to cover her tracks from last night. Clean up all the blood and marks. Get rid of the clothes she had been wearing and any mess on the inside of her car. Then she needed to treat her wounds. Or did she need to do that first? Either way, there was burn cream for her face in her first aid kit. The deeper burns on her arm would need to be bandaged. She couldn't take the risk of going to the hospital. Somehow, Rose would have to do that herself.

Finally, she had to work out the implications of last night's failure on the rest of her plans. At the very least, she would have to go to work on Monday, because that was where she planned to get at Dom Wilkins. God knows, there were enough drugs of all types in Lily's room to get her through that.

The temptation to rest her head on her arms and doze off was enormous. The ticking of the kitchen clock seemed to get louder. *There's no time to sleep*, it warned her. *It's after ten o'clock*, it reminded her.

'Got to get clean,' she said. The mug went into the kitchen sink, Rose into the shower. The cool water seemed to soothe her burns, especially her face. She just wanted to stand there for ever and let it work its magic. But there was too much to do. The shampoo got into her burns, making her yelp. Eventually, Rose climbed out.

She wrapped herself in the largest bath towel she possessed and sank onto the bed again. Her blood-soaked clothes lay on the floor.

'Must burn them too,' she murmured. Sleep was forcing her to lie down. Fighting the urge, Rose focused on the pile of dirty clothes. Something was missing.

The bloody hat, the one she had first put over her injured hand. It had been tied under the sleeve of the jumper to help stem the flow of the blood, hadn't it? Where had she lost that? Was it in the house or in the car? Somewhere on the long-distance footpath that had cost her so much effort to walk along last night?

'Fuck my life,' she sighed. Then she curled up on the bed to sleep.

CHAPTER 43

It seemed that DCI Hudson had suddenly decided that Dom Wilkins was top of their list of suspects for pretty much the same reasons as Sara. It still hadn't made Hudson change her list of jobs.

'He was well known to both the victims,' she said. 'They would have trusted him.'

Sara looked at DI Edwards. His face was impassive, which she suspected meant that he was noticing the same things Sara was. If he was, he was going to give the woman enough rope to hang herself by allowing her to pile up the mistakes. The whole situation was making Sara deeply uncomfortable. She didn't like to think of her boss as being so petty. Perhaps another day or two might improve his temper, and if Hudson hadn't picked up on her errors by then, Sara could have a quiet word.

'He had easy access to both homes. He has anger management problems, and Mrs Crawford claims Taryn was afraid of him finding out about her new relationship with Joe Summerhill.'

'Then what's the point of all these art references?' asked Edwards.

Hudson looked annoyed and ignored him. 'From what you've told me, the standard of his sporting performances has improved exponentially in the last two or three years. Is he taking drugs to help with this?' She turned to DC Adebayo. 'Do you think we have enough on the drugs front for a search warrant?'

Sara sucked in a breath. Adebayo might be on loan from the Drugs team, but he was hardly an expert. His eyes widened a little, and he shrugged.

'You might get lucky,' said Edwards. 'Not least if he is a murder suspect.'

'Let's get some paperwork done, then,' snapped Hudson. 'Home, outbuildings and his office at work.' She stomped into her office, slamming the door as she went.

The team got on with other tasks. The spare DCs knuckled down to arranging statements from the victims' co-workers. Noble and Bowen worked on the van lists while Aggie typed up the warrant request. Sara helped Dr Taylor take his laptop and files back to his car.

'Get those DNA tests organised, could you?' he asked before he left. 'From anyone we know might have been in those houses.'

She nodded and picked up a kit on the way back to the office. If she did nothing else useful today, she could get Rose Crawford's DNA sample, if the woman would volunteer it. She just needed to check her address.

'When that warrant gets signed off,' said the DI when Sara returned, 'I think I'd better make sure I go with her.'

Sara smiled grimly as she typed up her notes. The combination of blunt northerner and newbie DCI out to prove herself would be interesting. 'What's your feeling on all this, boss?'

'I think you should look at the evidence to find the murderer, not make it fit someone you fancy for it. Or, indeed, to fit your own bloody theory.'

'I agree,' said Sara. 'Other people might fit these criteria. Known to both perpetrators and trusted by them. It doesn't

200

have to be as simple as jealousy, does it? I hate to admit it, but holding a grudge or seeking revenge works just as well.'

'You were up for jealousy and Dom Wilkins the other day.'

'I know.'

'What's changed your mind?'

'These car accidents. We'll never prove anything about Wilkins's claims because there isn't any evidence. But is it linked to the first accident?'

'What do you mean?' Edwards looked at her sharply.

Sara glanced over at their admin support. 'Aggie's busy, so I'm going to dig up those old reports. Mrs Summerhill says they knocked some student off her bike. Then Dom Wilkins gets knocked off his bike, also in the dark and the rain. We don't do coincidences, do we?'

'No. And what about these bloody art references? Toy llamas and ritual sacrifices? If you ask me, Dom Wilkins doesn't know the first thing about all that and wouldn't be interested if he did.'

'You think it's someone connected to the Sainsbury Centre, then?'

'Or even the people at Barnham Parva.'

Sara hunted around on the various police databases. The case of the girl on the bike was old enough to have a number and a mention on the system, but the main file was still held in the manual archive.

'Found it,' she said to Edwards.

He moved round to look at her screen.

'The girl was called Lily Kerr. She was a student at the Art School, not the UEA.' She exchanged a glance with Edwards. 'Was seriously injured and in hospital afterwards.'

'I think you need to order up that file asap,' said Edwards. 'What if this is Lily Kerr getting her revenge after all these years?'

Sara typed up the request as top priority. She doubted if there were many staff in the archive on a Sunday. With luck, it would arrive tomorrow morning. It was a paperwork sort of day, it seemed. Sara's least favourite kind.

Aggie's printer rattled out the search warrant request, and DCI Hudson reappeared from her office. 'Magistrate?'

Aggie held out a piece of paper with an address on it.

'Right. Let's get this signed off.'

'If you don't mind, I'd like to be with you on this one,' said Edwards. 'Most of the magistrates know me. It might help.'

Hudson blushed before she considered this, then nodded. 'Hirst, get on with organising the teams to go in.'

There was a sense of relief as the pair left the office.

Aggie slumped back in her chair. 'Is it always going to be like this?'

'She's just settling in,' said Sara. 'And what a case to be landed with before you even know where anything is.'

'Career-making,' said Bowen. He sounded as cynical as Sara had ever heard him be. He threw Sara an old-fashioned look. 'You be careful.'

'Me?' Sara was surprised.

Bowen motioned her over, and the old team gathered at Aggie's desk.

'We were talking about this last night.' Aggie kept her voice low as she looked at Bowen.

'You see the big picture,' he said. 'We've all seen how the boss knows that and leans on your opinions. Surprised you haven't gone for your inspectors' exams.'

'You see things the rest of us don't,' said Aggie. 'She's new, can't wait to make a big splash.'

'Don't get between her and the boss either,' hissed Bowen in a half-whisper.

Sara wasn't used to Bowen showing this much concern for her. Noble was nodding vigorously.

'Whatever you dig up,' Bowen said, 'I reckon she'll take credit for.'

Sara couldn't believe what she was hearing. 'You lot are winding me up, right? Why would the woman do that?'

'Don't give me that all-sisters-together crap,' scoffed Bowen. 'This one doesn't have your back just because she's a high-ranking female. She didn't get there without trampling on a few people on the way up.'

'We've got your back.' Aggie smiled.

'You're one of us, after all,' said Noble.

Sara didn't know whether to thank them or laugh at the joke. Before she could decide, Noble's phone rang, and he swung back to his desk to answer it. Aggie bustled off to make more coffee while Bowen treated Sara to a broad grin. That made her even more uncertain.

Noble put the phone down. 'You're going to love this,' he said. 'My flag on the missing vehicles system has just been seen by Traffic. Guess what they've got?'

'Oh, get on with it,' said Bowen.

'A vehicle matching our description was burned out on a disused airfield last night.'

'And the top brass are all out.' Bowen smiled. 'Guess we'll have to deal with it ourselves then. Get your coats.'

CHAPTER 44

They left Aggie to organise the search teams.

'You get off,' she said, phone already in her hand. 'I'll set this up for two this afternoon.'

It was quite a long drive, although, at the speed Bowen drove, it was hair-raisingly fast. He took the A11 south before turning off into the maze of small lanes and back roads typical of Norfolk, whichever part of the county you were in.

They knew they had arrived when they saw blue-and-white police tape fluttering between a pair of rusting metal gates. A car was waiting for them just inside. Bowen jumped out and spoke to the driver, then they drove behind them down the field.

Tall piles of demolition debris stood on either side of the broken-up concrete airstrip. Beyond them was a strip of derelict scrubland. The burned-out van stood behind one of the piles of building rubbish. The ground around it was darkly hued with burning and soot.

'Quite a big fire,' said the officer who had led them to it.

'How was it seen?' asked Sara. Looking round the site, it was obvious that the driver had chosen the position carefully. She waved at the piles. 'It's about as far from the road as it can be and hidden behind these.'

'Chance,' said the officer with a shrug. 'It was late. There shouldn't have been any traffic along here at that time of night.'

Sara knew that many things went unseen in these rural spots simply because the road network, though often of poor quality, was extensive and little used.

'It was an older couple,' continued the officer. 'They'd been to the theatre in Norwich and stayed for a drink with friends afterwards.'

'You've spoken to them?'

'We went there this morning,' he waved to his partner, who was chatting with DC Noble on the far side of the car. 'They were rather shocked, I thought. They live in the village about three miles that way and were heading home when they saw an explosion.'

'Fuel tank going up?'

'That seems most likely. They didn't stop, in case it was "hardened criminals", as the wife put it.'

They shared a smile. 'Does she mean drug dealers?'

'That's what I assumed.' The officer pulled out a packet of cigarettes and offered one to Sara. When she shook her head, he asked, 'Do you mind if I do?'

'Not at all.' According to official police policy, smoking affected your fitness, and it was frowned upon. But Sara wasn't surprised that so many officers did smoke when the job was so stressful. Eating too much cake could also adversely affect your annual medical. She shook her head to clear the tangent of thoughts away. 'So, what did they do?'

'The husband was driving, so the wife rang for the fire brigade as they carried on. They know the area well, so they could easily describe where they thought it was. The call was logged with control at 12.50 a.m.'

'What made you think it might be our vehicle?'

'I don't, necessarily.' He pulled on his cigarette before gesturing at the van. 'Just seemed too much of a coincidence. We don't get much of this sort of thing out here, and it would be a good place to dispose of evidence.'

'Have you looked more closely at the vehicle?'

'Just a quick scan,' he admitted. 'Number plates are gone, of course. But the vehicle ID number on the chassis might still be readable. There were metal objects in the back of the vehicle as well. Didn't know if they were important.'

'Can you show me?'

The officer led Sara to the perimeter of the burned area. He pointed at the rear of the van. Despite the heat and the explosion, the shape of the vehicle was still recognisable. All the doors were open, the windows shattered, and the metal structure had a variety of acrid colours along its length.

'Whoever did this wanted to make sure the thing went up properly. Probably poured fuel all over the place before lighting it,' the officer said.

He was right that a simple engine fire wouldn't necessarily have destroyed the whole vehicle. Sara walked further around the back of the van to get a better view inside. A twisted heap of metal lay contorted on the floor of the carrying space.

'What do you think that is?' she asked.

The officer drew on his smoke again before answering. 'Not sure, but it could be ladders. It wouldn't be unusual in a workman's van. Was it stolen?'

'We've been working on that assumption,' said Sara. Her heart was racing. If, as they thought, the murderer had got Joe Summerhill into the Clifton urn using museum ladders, this could be what they were looking for. It was too good an opportunity to miss. 'Thank you for contacting us. I think this could be very useful.'

'My pleasure.' The officer pulled a metal tin from his jacket pocket and stubbed out his cigarette carefully in it before putting the lid back on.

'Have you searched the area?'

'No. Didn't know if it was necessary. Would you like us to hang around to stop people coming into the site?'

'That would be great. I'll get onto my boss immediately.'

Pulling out her mobile, Sara realised that she didn't have a number for DCI Hudson, who should be the first to know by rights. She rang DI Edwards, who quickly answered. Before she could outline their find, Hudson had snatched the phone.

'Why didn't you ring me directly?' she demanded. 'Or haven't you got used to having a proper boss yet?'

Sara winced, knowing that Edwards must be hearing the other end of the conversation. She could imagine him standing there grumpily, arms crossed and that sour look on his face. 'It's not that, ma'am. I don't have your direct number yet, and I thought you were together on the warrant.'

There was a pause as Hudson backtracked. 'I must rectify that when you get back in. What have you got?'

Sara outlined the finding of the van and her hope that it could be the murderer's vehicle. 'Worth a forensic investigation, ma'am?'

'Yes. Can you stay there until the team arrive?'

'Aggie can request them,' said Sara. 'We can do a preliminary sweep away from the vehicle while we wait.'

'We?'

Sara felt heat rising at her embarrassment. Damn, she hadn't meant to drop them all in it. 'DCs Noble and Bowen are with me.'

'Why?' exploded Hudson. 'I gave them things to be doing, important things. You could have dealt with this on your own.'

Sara heard Edwards speaking, none too gently, though she didn't catch the words. Then Hudson's cold reply. 'I am aware, DI Edwards, that this has all happened very suddenly for the team. However, there needs to be respect for the correct way of doing things, and an order from a superior officer is still an order, as you are very well aware.'

CHAPTER 45

Dom's father had arrived in a taxi about ten minutes before the Sunday roast was due to be put on the table. That was why his mum had been making such a fuss about the meal. It was his father's favourite. Beef, dripping red with blood in the middle, just how Dad liked it. The sight made Dom's stomach heave, and he ran from the room to vomit in the downstairs toilet. When he tried to return to the dining room, he could hear his mother telling the tale of the last few days. His father's gruff replies were exactly what Dom had feared they would be.

'No reason to consider it a problem.' He dismissed his wife's worries. 'If necessary, I'll get him some legal representation. He should just tell the truth and get on with his life.'

'I think he was rather fond of this girl,' said his mother.

'Too late now.'

Dom felt his shoulders sagging. Of course his father wouldn't understand. When Dom had been coming to terms with his disability after the accident, his father was happy to pay for private physiotherapy while declining to pay for counselling. Deal with the practical, ignore the emotional. That was Dad. Dom felt that he ought to go back into the room, but the scraping of cutlery on china reminded him of the bloody joint, and his stomach rebelled again.

He flushed the toilet and was splashing his face with cold water when he heard the front doorbell ring. His father must have answered the summons because Dom could hear his voice rising rapidly and angrily. When he joined his mother, who was hovering in the hallway, he couldn't see who was standing outside.

'This is absolutely ridiculous,' his father was saying. 'You have no grounds whatsoever to come into my home and do this.'

'We have a search warrant, sir,' said a woman's voice. Her tone was steel-hard. 'If you do not allow us in of your own volition, then I will ask one of my officers to break down the door.'

Dom could see that his father was almost hopping from foot to foot with pent-up anger. 'You have no right.'

'Inspector,' the woman called behind her. 'Do you have the enforcer?'

'Yes, ma'am.'

'Fetch it, if you please.'

Dom recognised the male voice, even if he didn't know the female one. It was the DI who had questioned him before. He stepped up to his father's shoulder.

'Dad, I think this must be something to do with the murder of my friends.'

His father turned on him. 'This is all your fault. Invasion of my bloody privacy. You can damn well deal with it, then.'

He stalked away to the kitchen, catching Dom's mother by the arm and forcibly escorting her with him. Dom looked outside. The woman held up her warrant card and an official-looking piece of paper.

'DCI Hudson,' she snapped. She thrust the paper into his hand. 'Your copy of the search warrant. Shall we get on with this?'

Dom nodded and opened the door wide. He watched the DI put a piece of heavy equipment back in the boot of a car while a stream of officers, plainclothes and uniformed, headed past him.

'What outbuildings are there and where?' asked Hudson.

'In the back garden.' Dom indicated a side gate. 'I'll show you.'

The two senior officers followed him. Dom took them to his workshop first. His racing bike was still in its maintenance stand while others were leaning against the wall. He watched as the pair began to turn over or open every piece of moveable equipment on his workbench. There was a scrabbling at the door. Dom turned to look.

'Shall we start in here, ma'am?' asked an officer in a dark uniform. He held the lead of an already overexcited Springer Spaniel.

'Thank you.' The DCI guided Dom outside. 'Any other outside buildings?'

'The greenhouse and garden shed are behind that fence.' He pointed to the back of the garden. The pair of roofs could be seen peeking above the high panels. 'Can I ask what you are looking for? Am I allowed to know?'

'Read the warrant.' The woman grimaced and went back inside the workshop. Dom looked down at the document. It stated that they were searching under the Misuse of Drugs Act. Then something about Class C drugs.

The French windows at the back of the house slid open, and Dom's parents stepped outside, both holding coffee cups and wearing shocked expressions, which they directed at their son. The DI moved to stand next to Dom.

'DI Edwards,' the man said. He pointed to the warrant. 'We have reason to believe that your friend was drugged with a Class C drug. Something that might also be used to enhance an athlete's performance. I'm afraid we want to look in your office at work as well.'

'I have nothing to hide.' Dom was absolutely furious. 'I train damn hard. My success has nothing to do with cheating. Besides, I've already said that I will do anything to help you find this killer.'

His voice must have carried as he heard his father snort derisively.

'This may take a while,' said Edwards. 'We can give you a lift up to the university afterwards. In the meantime, I would appreciate it if you refrained from using your mobile phone.'

'Never answers it anyway,' interrupted his father. 'Damn thing has been ringing out all morning, your mother says.'

'Mum?'

'You left it in the kitchen when you went up to shower.'

The DCI appeared from the workshop. 'We'll do the other outside buildings next. Got the keys?'

'They're in the key rack, in the kitchen,' said Dom. 'I'll fetch them.'

'I'll go with you.'

Edwards followed Dom inside. His mother had dumped his mobile next to the kettle while she'd made the lunch. Not somewhere he would usually leave it, which may have been why Dom hadn't missed it. Selecting two padlock keys, he pointed to the phone. 'Can I find out who's been trying to contact me?'

Edwards held out his hand, and Dom passed the phone over. After swiping the screen, the DI said, 'Junina. Isn't that your lawyer friend?'

'Yes.' Dom didn't want to elaborate. Edwards left the mobile on a work surface, and they went outside with the keys.

The officer with the sniffer dog seemed to have finished with the workshop. Hudson claimed the keys and set off across the lawn. As the handler passed Dom's dad, the dog barked and wagged its tail furiously. Then it jumped up and down, trying to shove his nose into his father's trouser pockets.

'Need to check that, sir,' said the officer. 'The dog isn't usually wrong.'

Dom's dad began to splutter.

'Search him. Properly,' Hudson called. 'Could be covering for his son.'

Edwards patted at the man's arms and legs as Mr Wilkins protested vigorously. 'This is an infringement of my civil liberties — you can't do this to me in my own home.'

The side gate swung open and closed with a loud click. To Dom's relief, Junina was walking towards them, one eyebrow raised haughtily.

'Been trying to reach you all morning,' she said. 'Got away early. What's going on?'

'Who are you?' demanded the DCI.

'Junina Kaur Nagra.' Junina reached out a card from her jacket pocket. 'I'm Dom's legal representative. I repeat, what is going on here?'

'We have a properly signed-off warrant, Ms Kaur Nagra,' said DCI Hudson, reading the name from the card.

'Then you can give me a copy immediately.' Dom handed over the paper he was clutching. They were interrupted by Edwards.

'Ma'am, I think you ought to see this.'

The dog was getting frantic, almost wrapping itself in a knot, evidently pleased with what it had done. The handler gave it a treat.

Edwards held out a small plastic packet.

'Well?'

'Cannabis, ma'am.'

Dom looked at his red-faced, spluttering father in horror. His father was a stoner? And he had just come back from a business trip to Amsterdam, hadn't he?

With a wry smile, Junina said, 'Make that the family legal representative.'

Dom's mother began to laugh hysterically.

CHAPTER 46

The afternoon dragged on. As they'd all travelled in one car, Bowen and Noble had to stay with Sara, despite DCI Hudson's anger with them for being there. A couple of hours passed before the forensic team got to them, while the helpful officer at the gate was replaced and got to go home. Unwilling to waste time, they had walked slowly out in quadrants away from the burned vehicle.

'I'd swear this is blood.' Bowen pointed at a small dark patch he found behind one of the piles of building debris. 'I'll make sure they take samples.'

They continued to search the floor until Sara found what she thought might be a trail of drops. It led to the pile of debris furthest away from the burn site. Calling the others over, she ensured they kept out of the area.

'What do you reckon?' she asked.

Bowen squinted as the light was beginning to fade. 'Looks trampled down, doesn't it?'

'Could someone have been lying there?' asked Noble. 'Hiding from the emergency teams?'

'That's what I wondered,' agreed Sara. 'And what do you make of this?' She led them around the pile close to the perimeter hedge. 'Looks like someone came out from here, maybe?'

Noble walked parallel to the trail of flattened grass, far enough away from it not to disturb anything. He stopped. 'Sarge?'

The others caught up with him. What appeared to be a small, blood-soaked piece of dark fabric lay close to the hedge.

Sara stepped a little closer and tried to focus on it. 'Some kind of hat? The sort you might use if you were hiking? It's got a label of some sort. I don't want to touch it. Well done, Noble.'

When the forensic team arrived, they showed the team leader all their finds as the rest of the investigators set up working lights.

'Can we make a stop-off on the way back?' asked Sara. Although Bowen grumbled, they did it anyway. 'I've got the home address for Rose Crawford. We could do with a DNA sample from her, as she was at Taryn Deacon's house.'

It was down another minor country road. At first, they thought they had got it wrong until Sara realised that the cottage was at the end of an overgrown track that opened out into a parking area in front of a pair of semi-detached homes. A small car was parked to one side of the space. There were lights on inside, and a radio was playing. Polite knocking didn't bring an answer.

'Let's get back to the office,' said Bowen. 'Lots of people leave stuff on like that when they go out for the evening. She's probably not there. We might as well face the bloody music tonight.'

Sara agreed, and Noble didn't disagree. They knew they shouldn't have all gone out, leaving Aggie alone. Gloom settled in the car before they reached the HQ car park.

'Bloody woman is proving high-handed,' muttered Bowen, as if that justified their disobedience of orders.

'Let's see how she handles it, then,' replied Sara. She opened their office door.

None of them expected to be greeted with the sight of Hudson and Edwards sitting in the corner office, laughing so hard that tears were rolling down the DCI's face. Aggie's desk was tidy, and her computer off. For a moment, Sara feared the worst until Edwards saw them and bowled out to share the joke.

There was rarely anything to laugh about in their line of investigation. The story of their suspect's crusty middle-class father being caught with Amsterdam weed in his trouser pocket by the sniffer dog would be round the canteen in milliseconds. Sara didn't find it as funny as her bosses did. Perhaps it was one of those moments when you needed to be there. Even so, it seemed to have broken the atmosphere that had been brewing. At least for now.

After exchanging their news, Hudson dismissed them for the night. 'We couldn't find any drugs in Dom Wilkins's possession, despite his father's cock-up. Let's have a recap tomorrow and see what the forensic team comes up with at your van.'

'Where's Aggie?' Bowen asked Edwards when Hudson went for her coat.

'She finished and went home early. Got a taxi.'

Sara breathed a sigh of relief as she got into her own car to head back to Happisburgh. She couldn't wait to get inside, thinking about how warm and welcoming her sitting room would be once she had lit the fire. Perhaps that was all she needed, and maybe a sandwich and a mug of hot chocolate.

The route might have been convoluted, but the traffic was light, and it took less than the usual hour before she was pulling into the parking space in front of her home. Of all the things she could have envisaged to welcome her, the one she wasn't expecting was the voice that called to her as she unlocked the front door.

'Sara. Don't slam the door. Sara, please.'

It was Chris. His car must have been parked further down the road because she hadn't noticed it.

'What are you doing here?' How long had he been waiting there for her?

Chris approached her hesitantly. 'I want to talk to you. About the other night. It's not what you think.'

'What I *think* had little to do with it. It's what I saw that gave me all the information I need.'

'I can explain. I love you. I don't want to throw away the last two years.'

Sara almost laughed in his face. Instead, she started to close the door. 'Come any closer, and I'll call for backup. Stalking charges would do for a start.'

Chris flinched. 'I'm sorry. I was stupid. Please let me in, so we can talk.'

'Fuck off, Chris. I don't want to know. I don't want to hear your excuses. No, you can't come in. Go home. Go back to Mel and your am-dram mates.'

Sara slammed the door and leaned against it, waiting for the frantic knocking to stop.

CHAPTER 47

The manual file was on Sara's desk when she got in on Monday morning. It was quite thick and had been sent to the Crown Prosecution Service at the time. Sara turned to the back of the file and began to work her way forwards.

On a dark and rainy Wednesday evening in early February, the emergency services logged an accident at 8.22 p.m. The victim had been cycling along a minor road in dark clothing with no lights on her bicycle. She must have been carrying artwork in some kind of holder, as the attending officers had cleared it off the road and left it in the evidence store. The car that hit her had been occupied by three people.

'Three?' Sara made a note. *Dom Wilkins, Joe Summerhill and Taryn Deacon.* Three of the Famous Four. Where was Junina Kaur Nagra, then?

Resisting the temptation to flick through to find an answer, she carried on reading methodically. The cyclist was Lily Kerr, aged twenty. Her injuries were severe, and she was taken to hospital. The three had been breathalysed, with only Joe Summerhill being sober. With his aggressive and confrontational behaviour, Dom Wilkins seemed suspicious to the officers.

Accident investigations the following morning suggested that the driver had never seen the cyclist. Instead, they'd ploughed into her from behind, knocking her forward, before the car ran over her as it braked. She was lucky to be alive. If lucky was the word. She had back and brain injuries. After months of help, mainly at Stoke Mandeville Hospital, Lily was released into the care of her grandmother in Leicester.

Despite repeated interviews, the three stuck to their story, which essentially blamed Lily herself for riding without lights and put Joe behind the wheel. There were holes in their narratives, small details that varied from person to person. When interviewed under caution, Joe had stopped talking entirely. The investigating officer noted that he felt the other two were being coached in what to say or leave out. He didn't believe that Joe was driving, but couldn't prove otherwise.

Sara sighed. If ever an accident could have been described as a tragedy, this was it. These days, they would definitely charge Summerhill with dangerous driving. But the law on accidents had been different twelve years ago. Joe had been charged with careless driving and, after an emotional appeal by his lawyer, given points on his licence and a fine.

The team was waiting for DCI Hudson to allocate their tasks for the day. Aggie was delivering coffee mugs.

'Anything I can do?'

Sara pulled a report from the file. 'See if you can track down what happened to Lily Kerr. Is she still alive? Who is her grandmother? Where do they live?'

'Sure.' Aggie took the page with a glance at Hudson's office. 'She seems a bit more relaxed this morning.'

It was true. Hudson was sitting on her office chair, swinging it gently from side to side as she spoke with DI Edwards. She was still wearing her smart suit, though its jacket now hung on a hook behind the door and her top was a practical woolly jumper. The body language of both seemed to suggest that they were more at ease with each other. Sara felt a sudden pang of jealousy. She enjoyed being necessary to DI Edwards's working life. Was she going to lose that as well as everything else? What a godawful week.

'Updates,' Hudson called. She stood in front of the whiteboard.

'Forensics are having a grand time with the van,' said Bowen. 'They've found the chassis ID number and are emailing it over. They've also sent off various samples for DNA testing. A couple of days for those, probably.'

'Let's get that vehicle traced as soon as,' said Hudson. Bowen nodded.

'No luck at the university with the computer, I'm afraid,' reported Noble. 'The routing went into their system, rather than out. Not much chance of finding a final destination, I'm afraid.'

Hudson surveyed the list of tasks on the board. 'I'm going to interview Wilkins again this morning. Did we check his alibis?'

Sara felt a release of tension. Hudson was catching up at last. The DCI surveyed the room. When no one answered, she looked at Noble. 'Start that next, Noble. Let me know anything you find.'

Sara was up next and explained about the older accident. 'If Mrs Summerhill is correct, that puts Dom Wilkins in the frame as a potential victim, as well as a suspect.'

'Why not this lawyer lady?'

'They never took a statement. She wasn't logged as being in the vehicle.'

'We can ask her this morning,' said Hudson with a smile. 'When she comes in with Mr Wilkins senior about his stash of weed.'

This raised a laugh in the team, all of whom had enjoyed hearing the story that morning.

'If they were on their way to a gig,' said Edwards, 'what I don't understand is why two of them were already drunk.'

'Preloading,' said Sara. 'At least, that's what I think they used to call it. Drinks can be expensive, even in a subsidised student bar. Back then, the idea was to have a bottle of something like vodka before you went out. You were already drunk and just topped up as the night went on.'

'Could it be as simple as it sounds? Was it just an accident?' asked Hudson.

'The attending officers didn't think so. They tried hard to put one of the two who had been drinking in the driver's seat without success. Summerhill was let off on the minor charge.'

'It doesn't follow that the victim's family felt satisfied, does it?'

'No, ma'am,' agreed Sara. 'We'll see if we can trace where Lily and her family are now.'

'And why the art connection?'

'Lily was at the art college, not the UEA. That might be important.'

'See if you can track down anyone there who remembers her,' said Hudson. 'Let's see what kind of student she was. DI Edwards can go with you.'

Sara looked at her boss, who shrugged. Maybe she could get some low-down on the DCI while no one was listening. Given that he'd been incensed enough to hand in his notice two days ago, she was curious to know what he thought of her now.

The extra officers were despatched to take more official statements at the university. Sara waylaid DC Adebayo as he set off with his partner. 'You got the Sainsbury Centre?'

'Yes,' said Adebayo. 'Why?'

Sara held up a DNA-sampling kit. 'If you see Rose Crawford, could you get a voluntary swab? She was in Taryn Deacon's house, and we need to eliminate her from the traces found there.'

'Sure thing.'

'Thank you, DC Adebayo.'

'Dante,' he said. He took the proffered kit with a smile. 'You can use my first name if you like. The rest of the other team do.'

'Oh, okay.' Sara had never been comfortable with the whole 'first names versus status' thing at work. She still tended to call the rest of the SCU by their surnames or, in Edwards's case, simply 'boss'. Aggie was the exception. Perhaps it was time to unbend a little. She smiled back. 'Sara. Thanks again.'

'No problem, Sara.' Adebayo left.

'Oooooh, call me Sara,' came the mocking voice of Bowen from behind his computer. 'Fancy our tall, handsome newcomer, do you? Well, don't think you can call me Mike. I would faint from the shock.'

'You weren't invited to call me anything but Sarge,' she said. Her tone was sharp until she laughed in turn. 'And no, I don't fancy him, thank you. Besides, I couldn't call you Mike. It just doesn't seem right.'

She looked up the number for the Norwich University of the Arts and tried their switchboard. She was passed from extension to extension without success.

Noble waved to catch her attention. 'Sarge?' His tone sounded serious. 'That number came through, and I rang the DVLA.'

'And? Is it on our stolen list?'

'It's quite a new vehicle. Registered to a van hire company out at the airport. I just spoke to them, and they said it wasn't due back to them for several weeks. It was out on long-term hire to a woman.'

CHAPTER 48

Rose had spent much of Sunday cleaning up her mess in between long hours of sleep. Around teatime, a car had pulled up in the parking area in front of the cottages, and someone had knocked on the door. Recognising one of the voices outside as the detective she'd spoken to during the week, Rose had lain silent and still under her duvet until they'd given in and gone away again.

The more superficial burns on her face were still red when Rose got ready for work on Monday morning. Her arm was in poor shape. She plastered burn cream everywhere she could bear before re-dressing the bandages. She took a random fistful of Lily's painkillers, shoved the container in her handbag and drove hesitantly into the university. If ever she was due a day off sick, this was that day.

Professor Chandler took one look at her moving slowly through the department and shot out to meet her.

'My God, Rose. What happened?' He held out his hands as if trying to steer her to a nearby chair.

She had already thought through her answer, knowing this question would be asked. 'I was burning some rubbish on the garden bonfire.' She ran her free hand through her hair. 'There must have been a bottle of something I had forgotten about. It went up in my face.'

'You poor thing. Did you go to the hospital?'

'Yes, A & E,' she lied and carried on into her own office.

Chandler followed her. 'You shouldn't be here. I insist that you go home to rest.'

'There are some urgent things I need to do for the next Barnham Parva visit.' Rose eased herself into her chair.

'That's not until Friday. Can't it wait for a day or two?'

Rose hadn't anticipated that Chandler would remember the date. 'It won't take that long. I was worried about it.'

'As soon as you've done that, please finish for the day. Can I fetch you a coffee?'

She nodded and turned on her computer. There wasn't really much to do. Just a couple of emails to chase if acceptances hadn't come in yet and a list to complete for Stuart at the Hall. It could have waited, but that wasn't why she was here.

Rose closed the blinds next to her desk and turned on her desk lamp. Once the professor had returned with her drink, she slumped back into her chair and waited, knowing that she couldn't easily be seen.

Chandler had a study group due at nine. The four students drifted in, and before long, the professor's door was shut. She could hear their voices rise and fall with debate while several of the adjoining offices remained unoccupied. Safe from observation, Rose took a washbag from her capacious handbag, put it in her desk drawer and locked it. Then she made her way steadily through the gallery to the entrance.

Waving her pass card at the lady on the desk, Rose went down in the accessibility lift to the bunker level. Part of this area contained visiting exhibitions. Today it was closed, as the previous show was being packed up in readiness for the new one, which Taryn had been organising. There were specialist workmen down here, moving the valuable artworks either into their own store or, if they had been on loan, crating them ready for transport back to their home gallery. She nodded to the pair that she recognised, then went through a hidden door. This morning it was propped open, where usually it was locked. Rose's pass would have given her access in any case.

Behind the door was a wide corridor, leading progressively past the restoration workshops and the storage galleries with their specially controlled climate conditions to the hidden loading bay, which was accessed under the restaurant at the far end of the building. There were a couple of storage rooms among all this specialist activity used to keep stock for the gift shop and general office supplies. Rose unlocked one. Selecting a blue plastic packing box, she went slowly back upstairs.

Even that much effort meant that she needed a rest before she carried on. Taryn's office was unoccupied. Her fellow curator was out on a visit this morning. Taking her time, Rose loaded Taryn's personal effects into the blue crate. The books would have to wait. She couldn't manage them as well. Even so, the box was too heavy for her to carry. She went in search of a trolley, cursing herself for not thinking of it before, returning with a rattling thing that weaved its own path on tiny castors.

'Good morning,' said a polite voice.

Rose looked up from trying to steer the trolley around the corner with one hand. A tall, well-set young man held out a police warrant card.

'I'm DC Adebayo,' he said with a smile. He indicated a blonde woman standing next to him. 'My colleague and I are here to take official statements from Taryn Deacon's colleagues. Can you help us?'

Rose was flustered. Chandler had asked her to deal with this, and because of her injuries, she had forgotten all about it.

'I'm afraid you've chosen a rather poor day,' she said. 'There aren't many of us here. The professor will be teaching until eleven. I'm Rose Crawford, Professor Chandler's PA.'

'Lovely. DS Hirst said you were really helpful when they were here before.'

Rose glanced at the offices and saw that one or two people were now purporting to be working at their desks.

'We set aside a meeting room for your use.' She pointed with her free hand. 'I'll get you settled in.'

'Can I help you with that trolley?' he asked. 'It looks as if it has a mind of its own.'

'It does rather,' she said. Her voice was shaking. 'I was taking it to my office.'

The DC followed her, also struggling with the wayward trolley. 'Perhaps I can help you with whatever you are moving, especially with your injuries. It might be easier than this.'

Rose blushed. 'Just a silly gardening accident. That's okay. I'll manage. Now let's get you set up. Do you have the list I provided, or do you need copies?'

The blonde woman waggled a clipboard. 'All here, thank you.'

Rose did her best to stay calm as she sorted some drinks from catering and left the two police officers to get on. She could have done without the pressure of having them there all day.

With difficulty, she got the blue crate onto the trolley. Taking the washbag from her drawer, she tucked it under some of Taryn's office stationery. Then Rose took a new toy llama from her handbag and placed it in the crate next to the washbag. It was a pity that she wouldn't be able to retrieve the trophy one.

Luckily, the trolley seemed to behave better with some weight on it. Rose took the box back to the storeroom. There were internal phones in every area. She could ring Wilkins's welfare office from down there.

She was ready. The trap was baited. Dom answered after three rings, and they exchanged pleasantries.

'I'm so sorry to ask this of you,' she said, keeping her voice as motherly as possible. 'Now the police have finished in Taryn's office, I thought it wasn't right that her personal things should just be left there. So, I've brought them down to the storeroom for safekeeping.'

'That's kind of you.'

'Would you be happy to pick them up?'

Dom was silent for a minute. 'I suppose so. Her mother is coming over here, you know.'

Rose couldn't cope with this complication. She improvised. 'My boss has asked that we get rid of them urgently. Says he doesn't like the reminders. Couldn't you pop down and collect them at the end of the day? I'd be really grateful.'

'You were so helpful to Taryn, I don't want to get you in any trouble.' Dom seemed to still be considering what to do. 'I only popped in to pick up some paperwork. I was going out for the rest of the day. But they've already searched my bloody house, so I could leave them in my workshop.'

Rose couldn't keep the broad grin from her face. The police had searched his house. That must mean he was the prime suspect. Wonderful.

'I'll pop down at five,' he said. 'Then I can take it straight home. Would that be all right?'

'Perfect,' said Rose. 'See you then.'

CHAPTER 49

Bowen headed off to the car hire booth at the airport, while Noble checked up on Dom Wilkins's alibis. Sara and Edwards went to the old art college.

Sara glanced at the DI. 'You seem to be getting on with Ms DCI now,' she said.

He manoeuvred the car into a tight space in the multi-storey car park in the city centre. 'What happened yesterday was rather funny.' He smiled. 'Thank you for your advice, by the way.'

'You're welcome. Which advice in particular?'

'To wait and see how it pans out. I'm giving her the benefit of the doubt for now.'

'Me too.'

After being transferred round the houses, Sara found an administrator at the University of the Arts who remembered Lily Kerr.

'I've been here for twenty-five years,' said Mrs Frost, who had welcomed them into the plush new building on Duke Street. 'We were Norwich Art School when I joined, became the Norwich University of the Arts back in 2013.'

'You remember the accident involving Lily Kerr?' asked Sara. She and DI Edwards followed the slim, middle-aged woman up some stairs and into an office with two desks. Mrs Frost invited them to sit down.

'I do,' she said. 'After you rang, I went over to the archive building and dug this out for you.' She lifted a buff folder and handed it to Sara. 'It stuck in my mind because it was such a terrible thing to happen.'

'Being run down like that?'

'Well, that and how it worked out afterwards.'

'She was badly injured, we understand.'

'Terrible injuries.' Mrs Frost shook her head slowly. 'We all thought she would die. I know it's cruel to say it, but perhaps it might have been better if she had.'

'Can you tell us more about Lily?'

'She was a local girl, you know. Back in the noughties, there were more local students than those from away. We didn't have any accommodation to offer then, unlike the UEA. These days, competition is fierce to get a place here, with all our specialised courses.'

'She was from Norwich?'

'If you look in the file, you'll see all her details. She was from Old Buckenham way.'

'Long way to cycle each day.' Edwards was flipping pages in the file. 'Says her home address was Stoke Holy Cross.'

'I believe that she stayed there with a relative during the week.' Mrs Frost sounded defensive at Edwards's tone. 'Hence it would be her next-of-kin address. Her application form has her home address.'

Sara fell into her usual role of stopping her boss from blundering with his bluntness. 'You seem to remember her well. Did you take a special interest in the case?'

'I looked after some pastoral matters in those days.' Mrs Frost's smile became sarcastic. 'Before they promoted me up here out of the way. Now I look after all the front end of the system — applications, interviews, admissions, that sort of thing. I worried about Lily and her family. Things were already tough for them before this.'

'How so?'

'Her father was disabled. Lily's mother was his full-time carer. Lily got the financial and personal support from us that her family couldn't really give her. She was a scholarship student.'

'Was that why she went to live with her grandparents later, then?'

'It was just her grandmother. The specialists felt that she was fit enough to look after Lily. After that, we lost touch. There was no way that Lily was ever coming back to us. Her injuries were too severe, as was the impairment to her faculties.'

'Was she a talented artist?'

'I couldn't say. However, I spoke to Jo Peters.' Mrs Frost tapped a box on the form at the front of the file. 'Jo was Lily's main tutor. She remembers Lily too. Would you like to speak to her? I checked that she would be free and willing to help.'

It sounded like a very good idea. Edwards brandished the folder. 'Can we take this with us?'

'So long as it comes back to me,' said Mrs Frost. 'Jo's office is in St George's. I'll take you over there.'

The university was based in the very centre of Norwich. It had taken over a growing number of buildings in and around the various lanes that defined the old city. As they walked from Mrs Frost's office in the Duke Street building, Sara recognised the next pedestrianised street. They passed the Playhouse, where she and Chris had often gone for a drink when she had lived here.

They went over a small metal bridge flanked by buildings on either side which belonged to the NUA. Mrs Frost turned under an archway into a garden quadrangle, which they crossed to enter a building on the far side. The place was a maze.

Jo Peters' office was up some incongruous modernist metal stairs inside a Victorian building. Mrs Frost introduced them and left them to it. Sara could only hope that they would be able to find their way out again afterwards.

'Call me Jo.' The woman held out her hand. She was tiny, on the plump side, with round reading glasses hanging on a plait of multicoloured ribbon around her neck. Her hair was bright magenta, pulled up into spikes. Her clothes were ethnically hippy as if she bought all of them from music festivals. All the same, Sara decided that the woman was sixty if she was a day. 'You want to know about Lily Kerr?'

'We're reassessing her accident,' said Edwards. It was a good cover, Sara thought. What surprised her was the warm smile Edwards was giving the tutor.

'Cold cases, eh?'

'Something like that.' Edwards nodded encouragingly. 'We believe you're the best person to talk to about her.'

Was Edwards actually flirting? Sara wondered in horror. She was so used to her boss being borderline angry all the time that this geniality was coming as a shock. Jo Peters was smiling back at him. Sara might as well not have been in the room.

'I was her personal tutor,' said Jo. She led them to an artist's drawing board, which stood under a tall window. Edwards pushed next to the tutor. Sara was left to peer over Jo's head, which she was tall enough to do.

'I got out some of her work.' She pulled at various pieces of paper. 'These are just some samples of her first-year work. Watercolours, acrylics, collage, even frottage. We teach lots of different techniques to begin with, until the student finds the best one for them and begins to specialise.'

'You kept these examples all these years?' asked Edwards.

'I rated it highly. After the accident, I could never bring myself to throw it away. There didn't seem to be any medium Lily couldn't conquer. She was as good in the plastic arts as the traditional.'

'Plastic arts?'

'Sorry. Jargon term.' Jo pouted a little. 'Things that require the manipulation of a physical medium.'

'Like ceramics or sculpture?' asked Sara.

Jo jumped as if she had forgotten that Sara was standing behind her. 'Yes. She could do all of that too.' Jo swivelled on her colourful Doc Marten boots to look at Sara for the first time. 'None of us was quite sure where she would specialise, though we all hoped she would come into our fields. She would have been an asset whatever she would have chosen to do.'

'Multifaceted,' said Sara. 'Huge amount of potential?'

'Amazingly so.' Jo's eyes began to film over with tears. 'I mean, she could have been as famous as Damien Hirst or Tracey Emin. The Turner Prize would have been a given, almost. As a tutor, you wait years for someone as good as that to come along.'

'So the accident was doubly cruel,' said Edwards.

'Oh yes,' agreed Jo. 'Lily Kerr was one of the most talented artists it has ever been my privilege to teach.'

CHAPTER 50

After the Springer Spaniel incident on Sunday afternoon, the DCI had asked to see Dom's father at HQ on Monday morning. The search team had taken Dom to his university office too. Whatever they had been looking for, they didn't find it. Dom had also been asked to go in to make a formal statement.

'I assumed this would be done in Norwich,' said his father.

'Depends on the case and who has requested the interview, sir,' said the genial-looking desk sergeant. 'I'll call up to the office. Please take a seat.'

Dom watched his father's fingers twisting nervously on his knees. He didn't often see his father so far out of his comfort zone. What on earth had he been doing with a bag of weed, anyway? He didn't know that his father indulged in it.

'Dad?' he asked. 'I didn't know that you . . . you know . . . that you ever smoked.'

His dad's gaze remained focused on the floor.

Junina leaned forward and spoke in a low voice. 'Your father has assured me that this was for personal use.'

'So? I still didn't know he smoked.'

'I don't,' mumbled his father. 'It's for your mum.'

Dom felt himself stiffen. Was his father going to try and blame Dom's mother for this? The strictness and lack of emotion, Dom was used to. Pushing the blame onto others, he was not.

'Mum?' he hissed.

'She's found it beneficial for her menopause symptoms,' explained his father. 'Bakes it in brownies. Sort of got into the habit of it. Asked me to bring a bit back, as I was going to Amsterdam. You know how flaky the customs people can be at Norwich Airport.'

'You're going to blame her?'

'No, son. Why would I do that? I bought it. They found it on me.'

'There's no previous,' said Junina. 'And it was a small amount for personal use. They should just give your father a caution.'

They were all led up a floor to an interview suite. Junina and Dom's father went in first, while Dom waited on a chair in the corridor. His dad wasn't in there for more than ten minutes. DCI Hudson escorted him out, followed by a uniformed officer.

'Don't let us catch you again,' she said.

It was Dom's turn next. Junina was sitting opposite a detective Dom didn't recognise, DS Ellie James. They started recording, and Hudson turned her full attention onto Dom. The suspicion in her face intimidated him. He looked to Junina for support. She had explained what was likely to happen the previous evening. Now she nodded for him to begin.

'Let's start with the discovery of Taryn Deacon's body,' said DCI Hudson. 'Tell me in your own words what happened that morning.'

Start by going for the jugular, he thought. The image of Taryn tied to her golden gothic throne, her head tipped forward, blood everywhere, and that goddamn llama on her lap was seared onto his brain. He shuddered. When he opened his mouth, no words emerged.

'All right,' said Hudson. 'Let's keep it simple. Why did you go back to the house that morning?'

'I'd arranged to meet DS Hirst so Taryn and I could make official statements about Joe,' he stuttered. 'I called in on my way to work.'

'Meeting DS Hirst when you got there?'

'Yes. I thought that Rhys would be up, even if Taryn wasn't. When no one answered the door, I let us in.'

'You have keys for Doctor Deacon's property?'

'I borrowed them. In case of emergency.'

'What kind of emergency did you envisage, Mr Wilkins?' The DCI's voice was icy. 'After all, Rhys Davies was spending the night in the spare bedroom to take care of Doctor Deacon. Why did you need the keys?'

'May I remind you that my client is giving this statement voluntarily,' said Junina. She was speaking as much to Dom as to the DCI. 'If he doesn't wish to answer a question, he is not obliged to.'

Hudson changed tack. 'When there was no answer to your calls, DS Hirst asked you to stay in the hallway, didn't she?'

'Yes.' Dom guessed what was coming next.

'So why did you leave it?'

'I was worried about Taryn.'

'You went into the living room?'

'I just opened the door. I didn't go in.'

'DS Hirst joined you almost immediately.' Hudson hadn't taken her eyes off Dom's face.

He shuffled uncomfortably. 'Yes.'

'What did you see?'

'Enough. Too much.' Dom looked to Junina.

Before Junina could interrupt again, Hudson changed the line of questioning. 'Can you tell me about the day before?'

'After we found out that it was Joe who had been killed?'

'Yes.'

'Taryn was in a state,' said Dom. 'We had to take care of her.'

'Why didn't you call her parents?'

'They're divorced. Taryn doesn't see her dad anymore, and her mother lives in the South of France. We thought we could take care of her, at least until we could contact her mum.'

'Who called the doctor?'

'Rhys did.'

'Why did you think it necessary?'

'We needed some help. She was getting hysterical. Kept saying she didn't want to be alone. The doctor prescribed some sleeping pills, which Rhys went off to the pharmacy to get. When he got back, Taryn took some, and they knocked her out pretty quickly. We helped her to bed.'

'Did you leave straight after that?'

'No. Rhys had found a half-bottle of red wine in the kitchen and asked me if I wanted a drink. I only had half a glass because I was driving.'

'He found the bottle? You hadn't noticed it before that?'

'Definitely not.'

'Did the drink affect you at all?'

'Not really. I only had a few sips.'

'Not really?' The DCI looked even more attentive.

Dom looked at Junina, who shrugged. 'I felt a bit odd when I got home. Tired. Happy too, which was strange under the circumstances. I went straight to bed.'

'Why did Rhys Davies stay the night and not you?'

Dom looked over at Junina.

'You don't have to answer,' Junina reminded him.

'No comment.'

'After all, you knew her much better than Davies. Could it be that Doctor Deacon specifically didn't want to be left alone with you?'

'No comment.'

'You needed anger management counselling after your accident, Mr Wilkins. What did the others think of that?'

'No comment.' Dom's voice cracked with pent-up emotion.

'I think we've had enough of this,' said Junina. She rose from her seat. 'Unless you wish to charge my client with something, I think it's time to go.'

Dom stood to leave.

'I haven't quite finished, I'm afraid,' said Hudson.

'My client has said all he is willing to say about this matter at this juncture.' Junina was using her best London-lawyer accents. They dripped with just enough threat to be intimidating.

'I have some questions about another incident. An accident some years ago, when your client was in a vehicle that ran down and severely injured a young art student.'

Dom slumped back into his chair in defeat. He should have known they would find it.

CHAPTER 51

DI Edwards gave Jo Peters his card before leaving the NUA. She declared herself happy to make any statement they required and suggested that a coffee date might be in order. Sara bolted out of the office and down the stairs before being forced to listen to any more. It seemed that everyone was on the brink of or fully invested in some kind of relationship — even her mother was finally marrying Javed after years of living together — while Sara's scummy boyfriend had been sleeping around for God knows how long with actresses at the bloody theatre.

When they got back to HQ, DCI Hudson was in the interview room with Dom Wilkins and his legal friend, Junina Kaur Nagra. Sara and Edwards stood in the observation room for a few minutes until it was clear that Hudson was making little progress with Wilkins. She was alienating him, and once the old accident was mentioned, he clammed up entirely. Within minutes, Junina was extracting him from the situation.

'I don't like your fishing methods,' she said to Hudson. 'If you are going to caution or charge my client, I will require full official time to consider those matters with him before we proceed.'

Edwards rolled his eyes at Sara. Before Dom and Junina could leave, she knocked on the interview room door and went in.

'I'm sorry to interrupt,' Sara said, after identifying herself on the recording. 'I do have one question for you, Miss Kaur Nagra.'

'*Ms* Kaur Nagra,' said the lawyer. 'Why would you have a question for me?'

'During the investigation for the accident involving Lily Kerr, I noticed that you were never officially interviewed. Why was that?'

Junina frowned. 'I don't have to answer that.'

'I know,' said Sara. 'I just wanted to be sure. It appears that you were not actually in the vehicle when the accident occurred.'

'That's true,' said Dom. 'Junina stayed at home that night. She was revising for her exams.'

When Sara looked at the lawyer for confirmation, the woman wouldn't meet her eye.

* * *

Aggie had made good progress tracing Lily Kerr when they got back to the office. She had the gift of the gab when it came to speaking to people with similar roles in other organisations.

'The Stoke Mandeville Hospital administrator was most helpful. Their historical files are fully automated now, and she sent over the records.'

'She went to live with her grandmother,' said Sara.

'Poor thing was in the specialist unit for months,' continued Aggie. 'They made some advances, but there was no way to restore any activity to her legs. She was paralysed from the waist down and would always be in a wheelchair.'

'Could she still have painted?'

'Apparently, the head injuries left her with both cognition and coordination issues. They seem to have done some art therapy with Lily at first. It didn't help, they said. How did they put it?' Aggie searched through the reports on her screen. 'Art therapy would be "a diminishing return" was the phrase I noticed.'

'Poor lass,' said Edwards. 'Not just robbed of her mobility, her talent taken from her as well.'

'Anyway, she went to stay with her grandmother. I traced the name and address. Social Services provided some support until five years ago when, unfortunately, the grandmother passed away. After which, I can't trace Lily's movements. I've been calling assisted living places in the Leicester area without luck. There are loads of them.'

'What about her parents?' asked Sara. She opened the NUA file. 'We were told her father was disabled. Should I look into that, ma'am? Try to trace them?'

DCI Hudson had been hovering by the whiteboards, contemplating their lists. 'Yes, as a matter of urgency, I would say. We need to know what happened to them and how they feel about all this now. Perhaps Lily is living with them these days.'

Sara pulled the NUA file towards her and began to flick through the pages. There were attendance reports and critiques for Lily's work over her eighteen months at the Art School. A form at the front recorded her grades for the various assignments, most of which were practical. It was clear that Lily was smashing the course. There was an unmistakable air of excitement among the comments.

She could hear Hudson and Edwards talking quietly in the corner office about the interview with Dom Wilkins while Aggie patiently rang Leicestershire care homes. Sara's stomach rumbled, and as she contemplated heading to the canteen, Bowen pushed open the office door, looking excited.

'The van hire company are really pissed,' said Bowen without preamble. 'The burned-out van was theirs. It was brand new. They'd only had it a few weeks.'

'Mike,' said Edwards, the frustration clear in his voice, 'who hired the bloody thing?'

'A woman called Anne Neville. She hired it for eight weeks, starting three weeks ago.'

'ID?'

Bowen brandished a photocopy of a driving licence. 'It's a copy of a copy, so the image is crap.'

Edwards grabbed the piece of paper and examined it. With a grunt, he passed it to Hudson, who seemed similarly unimpressed. Sara was next in line, and she studied the image more closely. The face was grainy and hard to see. Even so, there was something about the picture.

'Doesn't this woman look familiar?' she asked Edwards.

He took the copy back and starred harder. 'Maybe,' he conceded.

'Is that Anne with an "e"?' Aggie asked.

Edwards nodded. Aggie tapped away at her keyboard.

'Do you know what?' said Edwards. 'I'm not sure that's a legitimate driving licence.'

Sara looked where he was pointing. 'If it's a fake, it's a good one.'

'Bugger,' said Aggie.

They all looked up at this. Their admin never swore.

'Problem?' asked Bowen.

'There's loads of information about Anne Neville.' She said with a wry twist of her lips.

'How come?'

'She was the first wife of King Richard the Third. It's going to be difficult to cut through all this historical stuff to find the lady on the licence.'

'Richard the Third?' Sara remembered a play that Chris had been in at the Maddermarket. 'The one who killed the princes in the tower?'

'That's strongly debated,' replied Aggie. 'One thing is for sure. He was the King in the Car Park.'

'Come again?'

'After the Battle of Bosworth, he was hastily buried in the nearest cathedral. An archaeological dig in a city-centre car park in 2012 rediscovered his body, and it was reinterred with a full ceremony in the current cathedral. Leicester Cathedral, to be precise.'

CHAPTER 52

DC Adebayo and his partner worked methodically through the available staff, taking official statements from anyone who knew or worked with Taryn Deacon. Rose's turn came just before the professor finished his teaching session.

'Are you sure you're up to this?' The DC seemed genuinely concerned.

'I don't want to hold you up,' she said. 'Poor Taryn.'

She described how Taryn had been upset at the lack of contact from Joe Summerhill, and that they had been in a relationship together, which they had kept hidden from Dom Wilkins because they were afraid of his temper.

'You mentioned this to DI Edwards?' asked DC Adebayo.

'On Friday when they came to do the initial interviews.'

The DC scribbled on his notepad. The blonde woman was typing on a notebook computer.

'Taryn came into work while Joe was still missing,' continued Rose. 'It was rather a mistake, I felt. She was very upset. The professor agreed with me, so I took her home.'

'And looked after her?'

'I'm not sure I did any good. I just kept making endless cups of tea, which she didn't want to drink. Apart from the last one. I did manage to get Taryn to drink that one, which was lucky.'

'Why?'

'I put a little calmer in it.'

'A what?'

'Just some valerian and hops.' Rose waved vaguely in the direction of her office. 'I keep some in my handbag in case I have a bad day myself. They calm you down.'

DC Adebayo nodded. 'Did you stay all afternoon?'

'I stayed until she received a phone call from Summerhill's parents about teatime. It was bad news, and she got hysterical. The only thing I could think to do was call the young man who had been staying with her the night before. Rhys Davies.'

'Not Dom Wilkins? They were best buddies, weren't they?'

'She told me that she was afraid of him. It made no difference anyway. It was Wilkins who turned up. The two men must have called each other.'

'You left Taryn with him?'

'He insisted,' said Rose. She frowned as a burst of pain ran up her arm. She laid it carefully on the arm of her chair. 'I could hardly argue without betraying Taryn's confidence. Luckily, as I was leaving, your sergeant turned up. I felt better leaving after that.'

'Did Taryn seem worried by Wilkins's presence?'

'She was beside herself.'

'Your "little calmer" hadn't helped?'

'After that phone call, no. She became quite aggressive towards me once Wilkins turned up, poor thing. It was all too much for her.'

'Then what did you do?'

'It was too late to go back to work, so I went home.'

'Can anyone vouch for that?'

'No, I live alone.' The words snapped out angrily. 'Am I a suspect, then?'

The two detectives looked at each other in surprise. DC Adebayo shook his head. 'Just a routine question. We ask everybody.'

'Seems rude to me,' Rose continued quickly. The pain in her arm was getting worse. She felt dizzy with it. 'I did a kind act, and now you suspect me of something.'

'I'm sorry you feel like that,' said the DC. 'I can understand that you might not be feeling well. Perhaps you should go home. We can sign this statement another day.'

'Let's get it done.' Rose was itching to get out of the room to take more painkillers.

The blonde woman read out the statement she had written on the notepad. 'If you are happy that this represents our conversation, you can sign it off on here. Or I can bring a printed copy for you to read again and sign tomorrow.'

'Sounds fine.' Rose held out her hand, and the woman gave her a stylus pen. Holding it in her left hand, she grimaced. 'I'm right-handed. It won't really look like my signature.'

'We can both witness it if you are happy with that,' explained the woman.

Rose pressed the stylus on a soft pad which was part of the keyboard. Her signature looked like a child's first attempt at writing their name. She was in too much pain to care. Struggling to push back the chair she was sitting on, DC Adebayo came round the table to help her.

'Can I fetch you a drink?'

'Thank you.'

He guided Rose back to her own office.

'Won't be a minute.' He returned with a cup and saucer that Rose recognised from catering. He was also holding a box.

He put the drink on her desk, looking a little sheepish. 'I'm sorry. I was asked to do this by DS Hirst. It slipped my mind. Would you mind giving us a DNA sample?'

'No problem. But why?' She would do anything now to get the man out of her room. The plastic bottle of painkillers was waiting in her handbag. She desperately needed to take some.

Adebayo unpacked the box, pulled on the plastic gloves inside and brandished the long swab stick. 'If you could just open your mouth.'

Rose did as he asked.

'It's because we know you were at Doctor Deacon's house. We need to eliminate you from the samples that Forensics took there. We might need to take some fingerprints as well, at some point.' He dropped the swab into a tube. 'Thank you. Perhaps you should consider going home after your drink. I don't think your boss will mind, under the circumstances.'

Rose was sure that he wouldn't, but that didn't suit her plans. At the very least, she had to deal with Don Wilkins today. The London bitch would have to wait.

Swigging the tea, she shovelled down more of Lily's tablets. In a matter of moments, the effect was both calming and pain-reducing. Taking her padded coat, Rose went back to the storeroom. Hardly anyone ever came in here except her. There were no windows in either the walls or the door. Carefully stored in a box at the back of the bottom shelf were some dust sheets. Maintenance had left them with her for exhibition changes last year, then forgotten all about them.

She locked the door behind her and left the key in the lock. She set her mobile phone alarm for 4.30 p.m. Then she arranged the pile of sheets into a makeshift bed, wrapped herself up in her coat and closed her eyes.

CHAPTER 53

Before Sara could decide who the grainy photo reminded her of, her phone rang. It was Tracey Mills.

'I'm at the airport, waiting to pick up Taryn Deacon's mother,' she said. 'We're going straight down to the mortuary. I wondered if you wanted to join us?'

DCI Hudson was sure that Sara should. 'See if she knows anything about this old accident.'

'She may be too upset to talk,' said Sara. 'She's coming to identify the dead body of her only daughter.'

'Best time to tackle her then. More likely to tell the truth.'

Sara winced. Hudson was nothing if not direct.

She still had serious misgivings when she reached Dr Taylor's room. He was waiting for them, as ever, with one of his special cases.

'Tracey is on her way,' she said. A text had pinged onto her phone as she reached the hospital. 'Shouldn't be long. Can I ask you something?'

'Sure.'

'What did Hudson say to you that made you angry with her?'

Taylor looked at her guardedly. 'Rude.'

'I just want to understand,' said Sara. 'I get it that the boss was put out. The force has lost a lot of staff in the last few years, allowing him to do his own thing and reporting more or less directly to ACC Miller. Suddenly we're gifted with this new hierarchy. He's no longer the boss.'

'No, I meant she was rude, not you.'

Sara looked at him expectantly.

'The evening you were all told, Edwards came round to my place. I thought he was going to trash my living room, he was so angry. Ranting and raving about being passed over, being shown up in front of his own team. I couldn't get him to sit down for ages.'

'I can imagine. A full-on northern tantrum, I'll bet.'

'That's about it. I managed to calm him down, but he still wanted to hand in his notice. You know what happens then.'

They all did. Cuts to your pension if you hadn't completed the minimum time, difficulty finding another job, lack of friends because you'd sacrificed all of that for your career. Loneliness.

'In the end, he slept in my spare room because he'd drunk most of my good whiskey. When I got up in the morning, he was gone. I was very worried. When I got in here, that bloody woman rang me and pretty much went through my CV as if she were interviewing me for a job. Then she demanded to know where the reports were — asked if I was working at full capacity, for God's sake.'

'Jeez.' Sara sighed. 'Not the best start, I agree. Edwards seems to be over it now.'

'So I gather.' Taylor still sounded cross. 'I, on the other hand, am not. If DCI Hudson speaks to me like that again, I shall register a formal complaint.'

Sara wasn't about to make excuses for the new DCI. She realised that Hudson was feeling challenged by her new responsibilities, but if she didn't want them, why had she applied for the post in the first place? This wasn't her fight to resolve.

246

The visitors' room door clicked open. Mrs Deacon was a tall, slim, tanned woman. She was dressed immaculately in designer clothing. Her make-up was flawless, and her hair looked as perfect as if she had just walked out of the salon. The look on her face told a different story. Her lips were pressed so tightly shut that they formed a small thin line of bright red between her nose and chin. Her eyes looked haunted.

Tracey made the necessary introduction before escorting the woman into the viewing room. When Dr Taylor gently folded the sheet from Taryn's face, Mrs Deacon took a tee-tering step backwards on her Jimmy Choos. She stared for a long time, standing so motionless that Sara glanced at her ribs to check the woman was still breathing.

'Does she have a snake-and-dagger tattoo on her left arm?' Mrs Deacon asked.

'She does,' said Taylor. 'Do you need to see it to be sure?'

'No. This is my Taryn. I just wondered if she still had it.' Mrs Deacon nodded. 'Thank you. Now, I need to get out of here. Is there a café somewhere?'

Despite the height of her heels, Taryn's mother fled at speed along the corridor to the main hospital building. Sara almost ran to keep up while Tracey floundered along behind. When they reached the first atrium, Mrs Deacon halted. 'Café?'

'This way.' There were several on the site. Sara took them to the smallest and most out-of-the-way one on the first floor. They managed to find an unoccupied sofa and, while Tracy bustled off to find drinks, Sara tried to get Mrs Deacon to sit down. The woman stood looking out of the long window. Her back was rigid, her hands gripping a Gucci handbag.

Suddenly she turned to Sara. 'You will catch him, won't you?'

'We'll do everything in our power,' Sara assured her. 'What makes you think it was a man?'

'I know who it will be,' said Mrs Deacon. 'There's no doubt in my mind. You should find and arrest a man called Dom Wilkins.'

'We're aware of Mr Wilkins.' Sara kept her voice low. 'Why do you think it was him in particular?'

She waited for Mrs Deacon to talk about the anger management issues or jealousy at Taryn's new relationship. Instead, she sat on the sofa next to her and spoke confidentially. 'You'll have found out about the accident?'

'The art student? Lily Kerr?'

'Yes, poor soul.' Mrs Deacon smoothed an imaginary crease from her silk trousers. 'You know the girl died about a year ago?'

Sara remained silent. It seemed her misgivings at DCI Hudson's tactics had been misplaced. Mrs Deacon had something to say. Sara prayed silently that Tracey would be enough time in the café queue not to interrupt them.

'They said it was suicide, that she could no longer cope with the level of her disability and the pain she was in. Taryn found out about it. I don't know how. Maybe it was in the paper. She was surprised because it seemed that the girl had changed her name.'

If what the hospital had said was true, Lily Kerr was in no way capable of changing her name for herself. Or of killing herself, for that matter.

'When Taryn came down to stay with me in the summer break, she told me about it.' Mrs Deacon was white with tension under her perfect foundation. 'Of course, I remember what happened at the time, but Taryn had never spoken of it since. Now she wanted to confess something to me.'

There was a clatter of a plastic tray on the table beyond them. Mrs Deacon started and turned round. A café worker in a red tabard was clearing up and wiping down.

She moved in closer to Sara. 'Taryn told me categorically that they had all lied to the police. That Dom Wilkins had been driving and was completely pissed. They all lied to cover it up. Joe Summerhill didn't drink, and as they waited on the roadside, Dom bullied them all into saying Joe had been at the wheel. I think they were afraid of him, even back then.'

Sara glanced over to the queue. Tracey was putting take-away cups onto her tray.

'Taryn felt so guilty. She had worked out who the girl's mother was too, although she had also changed her name. Claimed she worked with her. Taryn decided to confront Dom Wilkins and make him confess.'

Sara could barely breathe. 'Mrs Deacon, this is a really important question. What was Lily Kerr's new name?'

Mrs Deacon chewed her bright red lips furiously. 'I'm sorry. I can't remember.'

CHAPTER 54

When DCI Hudson had brought up the old accident, Dom had fallen silent, and Junina had soon cancelled the interview. The subsequent appearance of the DS had rattled him. Afterwards, Junina had insisted on driving them both to a quiet country pub for a late lunch.

'If they were any good at their jobs, they were going to find the old reports,' said Junina.

They were sitting at a table near the window. Outside, it had started to rain again. One of those sharp, drenching showers that were common in April.

Dom nodded, his eyes focused on the placemats, which depicted an old-fashioned hunting scene, faded with prolonged use.

'What really happened that night?' she asked.

'If I tell you, it can't be unsaid. You'll know, and that will make a difference.'

'I'm your lawyer,' said Junina. 'You can tell me things we don't have to divulge to the police unless it helps your case. The onus of proof is with them.'

'You'll think of me differently.'

'Possibly. Shall I say what I think happened, and you can agree or disagree?'

'All right.'

'I know you finished a bottle of vodka before you went out because I had a couple of shots too.' Junina began to tick things off on her fingers. 'I heard you all arguing outside the house and you insisting that you were all right to drive. I didn't look to see who was at the wheel, but given your nature, I suspect you got your own way as usual.'

'My nature?' Dom finally looked at Junina. Defensive anger surged through his body.

Junina sighed. 'Let's be clear, Dom. You've always been a bully.'

'In your opinion.' His voice was tight with emotion.

'In the opinion of all of us. We all drank a lot in those days, except Joe. He was never fond of it, was he? When you drank, you became even more aggressive. So off you all went. It was dark and raining. There were no cameras where you hit that poor girl. No street lights either.'

'She had no bike lights on.'

'That's not what Taryn told me last year.'

'What?'

'Taryn found out that the girl had died. After years of pain and disability, she overdosed on sleeping tablets. Taryn came to see me in London, wanting to go to the police and confess.'

'Confess what?'

'That you'd been driving and were drunk. That after you ran her over, you climbed out and pulled the lights off her bike. Taryn saw you as she was trying to help the girl, and Joe was ringing for the ambulance. You walked down the road, then threw the lights over the hedge into a farmer's field. She said she was going to confront you about it.'

'She never did,' Dom insisted. 'I didn't do that. I didn't remove any lights.'

'If you say so.' Junina sounded weary. 'I do think she told Joe, however. At least, that's what she said to me at the reunion dinner.'

'Why would she say all these things?'

'I can tell you that too. It has to do with both accidents. You'd only been in the hospital a few days when Taryn took up her new post at the Sainsbury Centre. We'd all been to see you, of course. But I lived in London, and Joe was busy with his PhD work, which was taking him away a lot. Even five years ago, Taryn felt so guilty about lying after the first accident that she took it upon herself to be the one who supported you through your recovery. When she visited me last summer, Taryn confessed that she thought you were getting sweet on her again, and it was the last thing that she wanted.'

'She often relied on me afterwards,' said Dom. 'It was quid pro quo.'

'Taryn was always prone to being nervous about things,' agreed Junina. 'The new job was challenging, she fretted about her exhibitions not making money, all sorts of things. Then she worried about the accident more and more. You had a poor opinion of what she did and of her emotional capabilities. To be frank, you made that obvious. It was Joe she confided in, not you.'

'If that's what you all thought of me, why did you put up with me? If I'm such a horrible person, why did you claim to be my friend?'

'We were your friends,' said Junina. 'We always have been. I still am. But I have to ask you this, Dom. Did you kill Joe and Taryn?'

'No!' Dom shot out of his seat. 'No, I didn't. How dare you?'

'Sit down, Dom. Don't make a bloody scene.' Junina sounded stern, and Dom obeyed.

'I'm your legal counsel. I need to know the truth. You must be able to see how this all looks to the police. You knew both victims well, and had access to both their houses. If they get to the bottom of the old accident, if they find out half the things we know, then it's a short step to believing that you killed both of them to keep them quiet.'

'And shoved one in a crappy sculpture and posed the other like in a Dracula movie. Why would I do that?'

'That's up to them to prove. Revenge? Jealousy? Your terrible temper when crossed? From here on in, you don't say anything voluntarily. Let them caution you first, and even then, it's up to you what you say. My advice is that you say nothing, at least for now.'

'I took your advice once before — we all did — and look where that got us.'

Junina scowled. 'I wish I'd never got involved, but it was Joe facing the charges and I had to do what I could for him. It's the biggest regret of my life.'

Dom glanced over Junina's shoulder. The landlady was approaching with two plates of pie, chips and peas. His stomach revolted. Spearing chips and pie with her fork, Junina began to eat hungrily. Dom didn't even unwrap his cutlery from its paper napkin.

'Do I think differently of you, Dom?' asked Junina once her plate was half empty, and she was slowing down. 'I have ever since Taryn told me what she knew. I think you're a coward.'

Dom looked at her aghast.

'When the police have got to the bottom of this, you'll have a choice to make about that old accident.'

'Meaning?'

'If it were me, I would finally go to the police and confess. You put that girl through hell for years. Her family too. I couldn't live with that on my conscience.'

Dom looked horrified.

'You could finally be a man.' The sarcasm ran through every word. 'You could finally give that family some peace. Are you brave enough? Bullies aren't often brave, are they?'

'I'm not a bully,' said Dom. 'Why are you turning on me like this?'

'Honestly? I've waited months to ask you about it. Now it's on behalf of Joe and Taryn, who are probably dead due to your selfishness. Now eat your food, and I'll take you home.'

'Jesus! What a bitch you've turned out to be.'

'For being the one to confront you with the truth? I don't think so.'

'I can't eat this.' Dom pushed the plate away. His emotions were overwhelming him. He didn't know which to react to first. His head was full of noise, of the pain caused by his friend's words.

Junina stood to pay for the food. 'I'll take you back to your parents.'

'I need to go to the university first.'

'Why?'

'I promised I would pick up some of Taryn's stuff. It won't take long.'

Junina sighed. 'I don't understand you, Dom. But if it still seems important to you after all this, we'll go there first. Then I'll take you home.'

CHAPTER 55

Sara had spoken to Aggie before she returned to the office. Now, the entire team was standing at their administrator's desk. Her fingers were flying, and she had the phone cradled in her neck.

'Good work with Mrs Deacon,' murmured Edwards. 'As always.'

DCI Hudson looked at the pair with bad grace. She began to ask Sara why she hadn't spoken to her as SIO, when Aggie put the phone down.

'I found the account of Joe's court case,' she said. 'Lily Kerr was called Lily Crawford back then, and the description fits. Given that the easiest way to change your name is by deed poll, that was their office I was speaking to. Lily Kerr was changed to Lily Crawford five years ago.'

There was a moment of stunned silence.

'Lily was Rose Crawford's daughter?' asked Sara. 'Is that right?'

'Hang on,' said Hudson. 'Was Lily's name changed about the same time that her grandmother died?'

'I've sent for a copy of the death certificate. The name change happens a few weeks after that.'

'Who applied for the change?'

'Her mother. Rose.'

'And what was her grandmother's name?'

'Linda Crawford.'

'Rose reverted to her maiden name. Then changed Lily's to that too.'

'Maybe it was a tribute to her grandmother's care,' suggested Aggie.

'So, Rose took Lily back home?' asked Hudson.

'I had more information from Social Services in Leicester,' said Aggie. 'They emailed me to say that Lily went home to her mother in Norfolk. She's listed in the handover documents as . . .'

They looked at Aggie, who looked embarrassed. 'As Rose Crawford.'

'Where's that NUA file?' Edwards flicked through the forms.

Hudson turned to Aggie. Sara braced herself to hear the administrator get a telling-off. One of the detectives should have spotted this. It was their fault. It was their job to put these things together, not Aggie's.

'Here it is.' Edwards folded the file open at Lily's application form. 'Parents: Rose and David Kerr. Sara?'

Without a glance at the DCI, Sara hurried over to his desk. He pointed to Lily's home address rather than where she was staying during the week.

'That's it!' She opened the Social Services report that Aggie had sent everyone. The release form was the next to last on the file. 'Look. Lily definitely goes back to the same address that was her home when she was at the Art School.'

'Isn't that on the way to Old Buckenham?'

Sara pulled up local maps on her computer to feed in the address. It zoomed in to show a pair of cottages off a minor road. 'No, boss, it's the other side of the A11. Near the Rocklands.'

Bowen was looking intently at the map. 'Can you get that thing to do street view?'

'Sure.' Her cursor scooted them along the rural lane.

'Hold on,' said Bowen. He tapped at the screen. 'Can you go down there?'

Sara tried to clink on the rough track that went between high hedges. 'Too far off-road. Hang on.' She pulled back to satellite view and brought the magnification up as high as it would go.

'That's definitely the same place you took me yesterday evening,' said Bowen. 'You wanted to get Rose Crawford's swab on the way back from the burn site.'

The office door opened. DC Adebayo and his partner had returned from taking statements. The pair joined the cluster around Sara's desk.

'This is the same woman who looked after Taryn?' Hudson was now hanging on their every word. 'She left Taryn's house that night when you got there, didn't she?'

'Doesn't mean she didn't go back,' said Sara. 'We thought Dom Wilkins might have done the same.'

'I've got her DNA swab now,' said Adebayo. 'Like you asked me. I dropped it off with Forensics on the way in.'

'Did we check the CCTV around Taryn's house on the night of her murder?' asked Hudson.

'We got it in,' said Noble.

'And then what?' she demanded.

No one replied. Hudson turned to Edwards, pouting with anger. 'Why wasn't this followed up?'

Edwards slammed his hands on his desk. 'No more benefit of the doubt!'

Sara flinched. The fury in his face was enough to make Hudson take a step backwards.

'Don't you dare try to throw the blame onto my team! It wasn't followed up because of you. You got here and decided moving the bloody desks about was more important than finding out about your new team and the work we'd already done. Your instructions took precedence over properly assessing what was already in hand. Sara, have you still got that envelope?'

'No, boss,' she lied. 'Threw it away.'

Edwards glared at her, then turned back to Hudson. To Sara's admiration, the DCI didn't flinch again or lose her temper.

'My office, now.' She prodded Edwards in the chest. 'Just you.'

'Ma'am?' Sara picked up the photocopied driving licence and pointed to the picture. 'Isn't this also Rose Crawford? A younger picture, perhaps.'

Hudson turned away from Edwards and snatched at the copy. 'Could be. Why Anne Neville?'

'The Leicester connection. Where her own mother lived and nursed Lily, while Rose nursed her husband. Perhaps she saw it as some kind of historical pun or joke.'

'Easy enough to buy a fake driving licence,' said Edwards. 'Even round here. I said it didn't look right.'

'My God,' said Hudson, apparently forgetting her feud with Edwards for a moment. 'What happened in the last five years to cause all this?'

'Accidents,' said Sara. 'This all has to do with car accidents. Lily was run down twelve years ago. Five years ago, someone ran down Dom Wilkins, giving him life-changing injuries.'

'Not as life-changing as Lily's, though,' said Bowen. 'If that was Rose Crawford taking her revenge, perhaps she was trying to leave him paralysed like Lily.'

'Or kill him,' said Edwards. 'Maybe she failed to do what she set out to achieve.'

'In which case, surely this is her finishing the job.' Sara's anxiety levels ratcheted up another notch. 'She's already killed Summerhill and Deacon, but the other two are still alive. Kaur Nagra and Wilkins must be her final targets. Revenge on the Famous Four.'

'Why would she wait so long?' asked Hudson. 'Why didn't she do something sooner?'

'Can I chase up something, ma'am?' asked Aggie. The phone was already in her hand.

'Of course.' Hudson nodded. 'The quickest way is to ask the woman herself, isn't it? Let's get her in pronto. Where are we most likely to find her?'

'We just left the Sainsbury Centre,' said Adebayo. 'I think she'd already gone home before we left. She wasn't well.'

'Worried that we were catching up with her?' suggested Edwards.

'No, sir. Said she'd had an accident in the garden yesterday. There was a bad burn on her arm, and her face looked a bit raw.'

'Burns?' Hudson almost yelled. 'The van, she must have been injured burning the van. I'd put money on it. Right, Edwards, you're with me. We'll take the house. Sara, you and Bowen take the Sainsbury Centre, just in case. Noble, get those CCTV videos searched.'

'Can we help?' asked Adebayo.

Hudson glanced at him. 'All right. The more, the merrier. You two split up, and one of you get to Wilkins's house. Make sure no one touches him. The other one, find Kaur Nagra and do the same.'

'Ma'am,' said Aggie. She carefully put her phone down. 'I think I know why it all kicked off five years ago. David Kerr had suffered from MS for years, then he developed cancer. He died six weeks before Dom Wilkins was run down.'

CHAPTER 56

Professor Chandler spotted Rose as soon as she got back to her office.

'I thought you'd gone home,' he said. 'Where have you been?'

'Looking after those two police officers,' she replied. Sleeping all afternoon had made her feel stronger, though she needed more painkillers. 'Then I went down to the storeroom to sort some stuff out for Friday.'

'I insist that you go home now, then,' said Chandler, his tone an exaggerated concerned-boss effort. 'It's the end of the day, after all. Nor do I expect to see you tomorrow.'

'Thank you,' said Rose. 'I'll just turn things off.'

With a nod, Chandler went back to his own office. He collected a couple of files and headed to Emilia Thornton's office on the mezzanine floor.

Rose swallowed several painkillers, enough to make her feel woozy. Then she carefully dripped three drops of the clear liquid from one of her little glass bottles onto her tongue. Seconds later, she was flying, heart racing, confidence bursting and grinning like the Cheshire cat. The pain had vanished too. She slipped the bottle into her cardigan pocket and headed up to the café in the gallery to buy two fresh cappuccinos. Back in her office, she doctored one of the takeaway cups with a careful dose of her liquid.

There was a tap on her office door. It stood propped open, and in the reflection of the glass, to her delight, Rose could see Dominic Wilkins and Junina Kaur Nagra. Her heart fluttered with pleasure.

'Do come in,' she called. 'I might be a minute or two. I just need to get this email finished.'

Rose waved a casual hand towards some empty chairs, and Wilkins and the lawyer came into her office to sit down.

'Would you like a cappuccino?' she asked Dom. Her mind was racing at the glorious opportunity that now sat before her. 'I brought one for you when I got my own.'

She took a sip from her own cup. The psychology worked. Wilkins picked up his cup and selected a couple of little bags of sugar to tip into the drink. Her action had caused his action. It was so bloody simple.

'I didn't realise Dom would have company.' Rose smiled at Kaur Nagra. 'Would you like me to fetch one for you too?'

'No thanks,' said Junina. 'The sooner we can get this sorted, the better.'

'Oh, sure.' Rose made a show of typing as quickly as she could with one hand. On the screen, it was partly gibberish and partly triumph. *GOT HER, GOT THEM BOTH*, she typed. *FIND A WAY. TIME TO FINISH THE JOB.* She carried on until Wilkins had reached the bottom of his cup. Then she drained her own. 'All done.'

She stood. 'The box is downstairs in the bunker. Ever been down there?'

Both of her visitors looked surprised. It was known among the university staff that there were spaces under the Sainsbury Centre, but they were never open to the public, and few students or staff were allowed down there.

Rose lifted up her bandaged arm. 'It would be easier if you came down with me. It's difficult for me to carry.' Mercifully they didn't question why it was down there in the

261

first place. Rose didn't care. She had come this far — nothing was going to stop her. 'Would you like to see it?'

They would, naturally. The gallery was closing for the evening. Rose didn't even have to show her work pass as the three headed down in the access lift. This moment was preordained. *All shall be well.* Her brain crooned Saint Julian's famous words to her. *All shall be well, and all manner of things shall be well.* Why had she thought of that now? Who cared? She stifled a giggle. Rose was the agency of karma now. She was Nemesis. This was her moment.

The door to the private corridor was shut. It responded to Rose's key card, and she led them out of the public spaces into the secret world. Rose chose the door to one of the conservation workshops. Inside, the conservator looked up from the piece of art she was studying and stretched.

'Hiya, Rose,' she said. 'What you doing down here?'

'Just showing a couple of friends round briefly.' Rose smiled.

'Naughty, naughty,' said the conservator. 'All right, you can bring them in if you can vouch for them.'

'I can,' Rose assured her. Wilkins and Kaur Nagra followed her into the workshop.

The woman slipped off her stool and picked up the small painting she had been working on. 'Just been giving it a clean. It's a loan from the Tate for the Futurist exhibition we're putting on together.'

'That's more my sort of thing,' said Wilkins. He pointed to a life-sized figure of a man in what appeared to be rusting iron that stood in the corner of the room. 'There are several of them around the university.'

They made appropriate appreciative noises about both pieces before the conservator took the painting away. Leaving Wilkins to admire the iron man, Rose followed the conservator as quietly as she could. When the woman let herself into the condition-controlled storage suite, the door slammed behind her. Rose hit the keypad with random numbers.

After a few seconds, the green light that flickered at the top of the display began to blink red. It was the sign that someone unauthorised had tried to get at the collection. The door would remain locked until an authorised pass-holder came to unlock it.

If Rose was lucky, the security guards wouldn't cotton on too quickly. But at best, she only had a few minutes now. She hurried back to the workshop, delighted to find Wilkins collapsed on the floor by the iron man sculpture. His friend was kneeling beside him, shaking his shoulder.

Without stopping, Rose grabbed a weight bag from the worktable, where the conservators used it to hold down paper artefacts without damage. Lifting it above her head with both hands, she swung it downwards onto the back of Kaur Nagra's head.

The woman slumped forward onto Wilkins's prone shape. To be sure, Rose lifted the bag and swung it again. It connected with a fleshy thump to the woman's skull. Neither of her tormentors moved.

Rose almost crowed with delight. The alarms were starting to sound as she ran to the departmental storeroom, where she extracted the small washbag and the llama she'd hidden earlier in the day. As she scurried back to the workshop, she could hear the conservator knocking on the door of the secure store. Rose laughed as she ran. She slammed the workshop door behind her, seconds before the automatic lockdown clicked into place.

There were cable ties scattered about the workbenches. She grabbed a handful and fastened the woman's hands behind her back. Kaur Nagra groaned but didn't wake up while Rose tied her ankles together for good measure. The pain in Rose's arm began to pop through her barriers of pain-killers and liquid ecstasy as she rolled Kaur Nagra under the workbench.

Dom was too heavy to lift. Rose had planned to display him like a sculpture in the gallery upstairs. Now she couldn't actually manoeuvre him into the position she wanted. She needed to find a compromise.

'My Lily would have been more famous than any of that lot upstairs,' she said to the comatose man. 'You drunken bastards robbed her of that. You killed her, day after day, until I had to finish the job for you.'

She aimed a spiteful kick into Wilkins's ribs. The movement jarred her leg and spiked the pain in her arm again. Rose reached into her cardigan pocket and pulled out her little bottle. Her mind had disconnected from her actions now. She lost count of the drops on her tongue, but it didn't matter. Looking at the iron man in the corner, she had found her compromise.

Rose tugged at the sculpture until it rocked over onto the floor and fell on its face with a huge crash. She dragged and pulled at the unconscious man until she got him on top of the iron one, then attached them together with cable ties. Pulling Wilkins at the knees, she tucked his legs under himself so that he looked like he was riding the iron man below him. His prosthetic leg clanked against the metal of the statue. Rose giggled. It was as near as she could get to the lifelike modern sculpture in the gallery above that showed one young male giving another a piggyback ride.

The world began to spin. Rose heard Kaur Nagra moaning from under the workbench. She would deal with her in a minute. Unpacking the toy llama from its plastic bag, Rose tucked it under Wilkins's arm, the one she had damaged on that dark evening so long ago.

She tipped the contents of the washbag onto the workbench with a clatter. A small selection of antique shaving implements scattered themselves under her avid eyes. She chose her favourite cut-throat razor with the mother-of-pearl handle and flicked it open.

The whiteness of Wilkins's throat gleamed invitingly. Rose lifted his neck to her. The woman under the bench began to scream and shout.

Someone banged at the door. 'Rose! Rose!'

Rose glanced up and lost her grip. Wilkins's face slapped down into the back of the iron man's head with a satisfying crack.

Without warning, her stomach heaved. Spinning away, she vomited on the floor.

The knocking was growing louder. Two voices were shouting outside now. The woman under the table was yelling something incomprehensible.

Head reeling, Rose dropped to her knees, and the razor fell from her limp hand.

The world went black.

CHAPTER 57

Bowen was inclined to grumble at the best of times. For once, Sara felt inclined to join in.

'At least we didn't get left in the office,' she said, trying to look on the bright side as she locked the car in the Sainsbury Centre car park.

'We're never going to get to do the fun stuff anymore,' said Bowen. He shoved his hands in his pockets gloomily. 'I can see that coming a mile off.'

'Speak for yourself.'

They headed for the middle set of doors in the gallery wall, which slid open as they approached. It was quiet inside. The hum of the building was louder than the few distant voices. To their right, the restaurant was in darkness, presumably closed for the day. The lights in the upstairs gallery were being turned off. The main gallery was almost silent.

'Must be home time,' she said. 'Let's check her office.'

There were lights on in Rose's office and Professor Chandler's room next door. Sara knocked and walked in. A large, floppy fabric bag lay on the floor behind the desk, and a smaller handbag was poking out of a desk drawer.

'Her stuff is still here,' she said to Bowen, who was waiting outside in the open-plan area. 'Maybe she didn't go home after all.'

'Can I help you?' Chandler's voice echoed down from above their heads. Looking up, Sara saw him leaning over a metal barrier from the mezzanine floor. She pulled out her warrant card.

'I know who you are. I remember from last week. What do you want?'

'We're looking for Rose Crawford,' she called. Her voice echoed noisily in the roof space. 'Do you know where she is?'

'I thought she'd gone home.' Chandler turned and spoke to someone behind him. 'Are you sure?' The voice spoke again. 'It seems that she took a couple of visitors downstairs.' He turned away again, but they could hear him complaining to whoever was with him. 'I'll have to have a word with her about that. She knows it's not allowed.'

'What visitors?' shouted Sara. 'Did you know them? Professor? This is important.'

Emilia Thornton leaned over the rail. 'I know one of them. Works in the disability care office.'

Sara swore. This conversation was ridiculous. Why didn't the damn man come downstairs to talk to them? 'Was it Dom Wilkins?'

The two academics consulted, then Chandler called down. 'Yes, that's him. Don't know the woman.'

Somewhere in the mezzanine office, an alarm started to buzz. Thornton swore and vanished, dragging Chandler in her wake. Around them, lights began to pulse in the same rhythm. Doors automatically closed, and metal barriers began to grind down over the external glass doors and windows. Chandler appeared at a run down the corridor, Emilia Thornton inches behind him.

'Good job you lot are here,' he said. He was out of breath.

'What's going on?'

'Could be a drill—'

'Nothing booked, I'd have been notified,' said Emilia.

'Well?' demanded Bowen.

'Our emergency system has been activated. Someone has tried to take an object from a case or a picture off the wall in the gallery,' she explained.

'Or someone is trying to break into the store in the bunker,' Chandler added.

'Where is Rose Crawford?' asked Sara. 'Still in this bunker? Where is it anyway?'

'Underneath us.' Chandler pointed to the floor. 'She might be trapped down there.'

Sara grabbed Chandler's arm. 'Take us down there. Now.'

The urgency in her voice added speed to Chandler's run as he and Sara outpaced the other two across the carpeted gallery. It was empty, apart from a bemused-looking barista cleaning tables in the café. By the reception desk, a spiral staircase was shaking with the heavy-footed descent of two uniformed security guards.

Sara pushed in front of Chandler and pounded down after them. 'Wait for me,' she yelled. She held up her warrant card as the two men reached a door in a blank wall. 'Police, I'm here to help.'

One of the guards held open the door. The other ran down the underground corridor. A muffled voice and hammering was coming from behind one of the doors. The guard had already reached it and was speaking on a radio. Sara and the other guard skidded to a halt behind them.

'Security override passcode,' he demanded. 'Someone is locked in Secure Store One.'

He punched the numbers into the keypad. The red light, which was blinking, paused. There was a click, and the green light came on.

The guard wrenched the door open, and a wild-eyed woman fell against him. Chandler, Bowen and Thornton caught up with them.

'Lou? What the hell is going on?' Chandler asked.

The woman recovered her balance but not her composure. 'Rose Crawford. Bloody woman locked me in there, I swear it.'

'Why is she down here?'

'Said she was showing a couple of guests round.' Lou rubbed her face as if to wake herself up. 'I should have thrown them out. I trusted her. Left them to have a look in the work-shop while I took a painting back to the secure store.'

'Which workshop?' demanded Sara.

'Number One,' said Lou. 'That one.' She ran down the corridor and grabbed a door handle. It wouldn't move. Sara tried too, rattling it angrily.

'How the hell has she managed that?' asked Sara. 'It's locked from the inside.'

'Security system will have sealed it,' said the guard who had joined them. 'If the system goes off, it locks down any area that might have valuable objects in it.'

'Isn't that dangerous if there's a fire?' asked Bowen.

Emilia Thornton looked at him, shamefaced.

'Don't tell me. The art is worth more than someone's bloody life.'

Thornton nodded.

Behind the door, they heard a woman scream. Sara pounded on the door. 'Rose! Rose! Let us in. We understand, Rose. Just let us in.'

The security guard was on his radio again, requesting that the door be unlocked.

Emilia Thornton joined Sara's shouting and pounding. There was no reply. Then they heard a thump, followed by a click. The door was unlocked.

Sara swung it open, inwardly praying, *Please don't let us be too late.*

CHAPTER 58

The sight and smell that greeted Sara was one she would find it hard to ever forget. The stench of vomit, warmed in the enclosed air and mixed with the smell of the chemicals the workshop used was an unusually disgusting scent. Three people were on the floor. Junina Kaur Nagra was lying under the workbench, screaming for help.

'I wasn't in the car! I wasn't responsible. I'm sorry. I'm sorry! Help — help me.' Her voice petered out, and she lay panting.

Behind the bench, Rose Crawford was face down on the floor. In the far corner, Dom Wilkins was strapped to the back a life-sized rusting statue of a man, his knees drawn up. His eyes were closed and his face covered in blood, which was running freely from his nose.

Sara turned to Bowen. 'Get one of those security guards to keep people out of here and away from the downstairs door. Call for an ambulance. Call for three ambulances. Call for backup. Move, Mike!'

She ducked under the workbench, where the lawyer was poised to scream again. 'It's all right, I'm a police sergeant. Help is on the way. How are you tied up?'

The woman began to cry with relief. 'Cable ties on my wrists.'

'I'll be back,' Sara assured her.

Stepping around Rose Crawford, she squatted down by Dom Wilkins. He was out cold. His nose was still bleeding. If Sara was any judge, it was broken. Luckily, his face was turned sideways, and the blood was running onto the floor. The unconscious man's natural reflexes had activated. He was breathing cleanly through his mouth. Sara assessed he was okay for a minute or two.

Turning her attention to Rose, Sara found where the stink was coming from. The woman was apparently asleep, lying in a pool of vomit, and Sara rearranged the woman into the recovery position. Outside, she could hear Bowen dealing with the people in the corridor with ruthless efficiency. She and Bowen may not always get on, but there was no one she would rather have at her back in a genuine emergency.

Under the table, the lawyer whimpered.

'Shan't be long,' Sara soothed her. 'Just looking for some scissors.'

As she searched the workbenches for something to cut the cable ties, she pulled her mobile from her pocket. They would need pictures, and these people would need help as soon as possible. She quickly snapped shots of the two unconscious people before she ducked back under the workbench, scissors in hand.

'Try to keep still,' she said. 'These are tight. I don't want to cut you. Can you roll over?'

'I'll try.' The lawyer tried to rock herself while Sara tugged at her shoulder. After a couple of goes, she wobbled onto her front with a grunt.

'Help is on its way,' Bowen called from the door. 'Dear God. Look at this. What do you want me to do next?'

Sara had managed to wiggle the lower blade of the scissors under the ties on Junina's wrists. She compressed the blades with little effect. Sawing at the edges, the white plastic began to respond.

'See if one of those people outside can assist,' she shouted. 'We could do with getting this woman out of here.'

The cable ties parted with a twang. Junina's hands flopped to her sides, where she immediately tried to lever herself up.

'Just another minute,' said Sara. She transferred to the ankles, where the cable ties were less taut. They fell to the floor and she began to help the woman out from underneath the workbench.

There was a shuffling at the door and voices outside. Bowen started to bark orders to the security guards as more of them arrived.

Emilia Thornton came in the room. 'I'm okay with this,' she said. 'What do you want?'

Practical and efficient, just what Sara needed right now. Between them, they managed to get Junina on her feet.

'Let's get her out of the way,' said Sara. Thornton nodded. With Junina's arm draped across her shoulders, Thornton edged her past the workbench and into the corridor, where Chandler was retching at the sights and smells in the workshop. Sara watched them begin their slow progress along the corridor before turning to Bowen. 'Ambulances?'

'On their way,' he said. 'There are security guards upstairs, watching the entrance and doing a check of the building. Anything we can do in there?'

Sara looked at Chandler, leaning with one hand against the corridor wall, wiping his chin with a tissue. 'Professor?'

Chandler nodded.

'What's happening upstairs? Is there somewhere we can interview people if necessary? Can you scope it out for me?' She doubted they would want an interview room tonight. She just wanted the man out of their way.

He waved a limp hand, pushed up from the wall and tottered after Thornton.

'Mike, come and help me.'

They went back into the workshop. Rose Crawford was still unconscious. Her breathing seemed ragged. In the corner, Dom Wilkins also appeared out of it, though he began to stir as if he was having a nightmare. Perhaps he was.

Sara handed Bowen the scissors. She pointed to the cable ties. 'Bastard things to cut off. You have a go. Do his legs first, or he'll have terrible cramp.'

Bowen began to saw with the blades. 'You taken pictures? No one will believe us without.'

'Yes.' Sara flicked through the icons on her screen. The pictures were clear. They wouldn't win any awards, but they were good enough for evidence.

'Ever the copper.' Bowen snorted a quiet laugh. 'Good for you.'

From Bowen, this was the highest of praise. Sara wasn't going to let it go to her head. 'Did you ring the boss?' she asked.

'Which one?'

'Either. They were going together, weren't they?'

'No, I haven't called them yet. Too busy.' Bowen got through the first cable tie, and it pinged across the floor. 'Help me.'

They eased Wilkins's leg straight. She could feel the coldness of his prosthetic limb under his trousers. Bowen moved on to the other leg. Wilkins muttered unintelligibly as they freed that one and stretched it out. A damp patch grew on the front of his trousers.

The effect of the position was vaguely sexual when they stood back.

'Let's not tell anyone, eh?' Bowen suggested. 'Leave the lad his dignity.'

Sara nodded. It took more time to free his hands. 'I don't know what to do for the best. Should we move him?'

They were saved by the sound of help approaching at speed. Two paramedics bustled through the door. It took them seconds to assess the situation and split up to attend to one victim each.

Sara stood up, feeling momentarily weak. Her adrenaline had been pumping since the alarms had started going off. Now it drained from her body. Bowen glanced at her.

'Do you mind phoning Hudson?' he asked. 'I expect she'll go off on one when she realises we had all the fun.'

They could hear more people arriving outside. A second paramedic crew flew into the room. Just in time, it seemed. Behind the workbench, Rose Crawford went into a fit. Her feet pattered on the floor and her back arched. Sara shuddered. Rose's eyes were still firmly shut, and the movements looked like something from a horror film.

'Does anyone know what she's taken?' asked one of the paramedics.

'Not for sure,' said Sara. 'Possibly GHB.'

The medic swore vociferously as he and his partner began to help the woman.

The two detectives moved out into the corridor. There wasn't much they could do now. Bowen said he would wait there in case someone was needed. Sara trudged up the spiral staircase to the gallery reception.

There were lights on in the café. Sara could hear voices there and headed towards them. Chandler and Thornton had Kaur Nagra sitting at one of the tables. The lights were on in the serving area, and there was a smell of fresh coffee.

When she approached, Thornton looked up. 'Mitch was trapped inside when the alarms went off.' She indicated a bearded youth in a barista's apron. 'He's agreed to stay to do refreshments if anyone wants them.'

'Mine's a cappuccino,' said Sara. 'I've just got to make a couple of calls.'

It was raining outside. Sheltering under the awning over the entrance, Sara selected DCI Hudson's number.

CHAPTER 59

DCI Hudson had been rather grumpy on the phone. It took her and Edwards nearly forty-five minutes to reach the SCVA, by which time the ambulances had taken Rose Crawford and Dom Wilkins to hospital. Junina Kaur Nagra had gone back to her hotel after a once-over. The team had then disbanded for the night. It was late when Sara reached her cottage.

An envelope was waiting for her on the doormat. It contained a card with a woodcut of a hovering kestrel done by a local artist. Inside were several pages of closely handwritten text. She read it over a mug of comforting tea. It was from Chris, and Sara went through it carefully. He offered all the usual excuses, which generally amounted to the fact that he blamed her for living so far out of the city when she could have been living with him. Despite that, he wanted her back and needed her to know that he still loved her. It was gaslighting of the first water. The apology that wasn't an apology, laying the blame with the victim.

She threw it into the fireplace and put a match to it, watching contentedly as the flames consumed it. Then Sara sent Chris a text saying she had received his letter, considered it carefully, and he should go fuck himself. If he contacted her again, she would report him for stalking.

There was no reply.

Somehow, she managed a good night's sleep, and when the team gathered the next day for morning orders, Sara felt bright and alert. Aggie was helping them celebrate with three sorts of cakes, which the expanded team was munching when Hudson called them to order. Before she could start the meeting, Aggie held out a small plastic container for the DCI.

'Gluten-free,' she said.

Hudson accepted it with a smile, peeled off the lid and sniffed. 'Smells great. Thank you.'

They settled in.

'It seems clear that Rose Crawford was the person behind our murders,' Hudson began. There was a general nodding of heads and murmurs of agreement. 'Do we have a twenty-four-hour guard on her at the hospital?'

Edwards rolled his eyes. 'I don't think she's likely to escape,' he muttered, then said, speaking up, 'Yes, ma'am. In case of a dying confession, although that seems unlikely at the moment as she's unconscious.'

'You never know,' said Hudson. 'Now comes the really hard work. We need to search her house for anything to help us prove the case. Aggie is doing the search warrant, although technically, we don't need it. Best to go by the book.'

'Do we know how she is?' asked Bowen through a mouthful of red velvet cake.

'Not good,' Hudson told them. 'She is in intensive care. The medical staff seem to think Crawford had taken a cocktail of stuff, and their interaction is making it dicey. She may or may not recover. They're keeping her sedated for now to help her system clear itself.'

'And Dom Wilkins?' Sara asked, scraping up crumbs from her desk and dropping them in her waste bin.

'Awake, apparently. We can go and interview him later this morning. His legal eagle is recovered, so she will be there. Meanwhile, let's get organised.'

Thanking them for their help, Hudson asked the seconded detectives to finish putting their reports into the system. 'You are released back to your team once that's done.'

Edwards was to go with the forensic team as soon as the search warrant was obtained. 'I don't think anyone will disturb things at the house, unless the woman has a cleaner.'

'I doubt it,' agreed Hudson. 'Let's get things underway as soon as we can. I'm sure it will be a treasure trove. If the woman recovers, we're going to need all the evidence we can get.'

If she recovers, thought Sara.

Bowen and Noble were to start the paper trail, speak to the van hire people to see if they could identify Rose Crawford, push for any outstanding DNA results and watch the remaining CCTV footage. Sara watched Bowen frown in disgust. It was his least favourite kind of work.

'Hirst, you'll be with me,' said Hudson. 'I don't think I'll be Wilkins's favourite person, given that I led the search at his house. He might remember you from before. Besides, you saved his life, for which he should be grateful.'

They began the dull stuff. Edwards went to get the search warrant signed while Aggie notified the forensic team. Bowen extricated himself, taking a picture of Crawford up to the airport van hire place to get an ID. By eleven, Hudson was ready to go to the hospital.

Dom Wilkins lay in a separate room on the men's ward. He was plugged into drips and still seemed sleepy. Otherwise, he agreed he was ready to talk to them. Junina Kaur Nagra sat on a chair on the opposite side of the bed, notepad at the ready. Sara set the small mobile recorder running and Hudson began.

'Are you aware of what happened last night?'

Wilkins said that he was. He pointed at Sara. 'Is this the one who saved me?' When she nodded, he grabbed her hands. 'Thank you so much. I can't begin to explain how grateful I am.'

'Can you tell us what you remember?' asked Hudson.

With a shaking voice, Wilkins described their visit to Crawford's office. Periodically, his lawyer spoke up to confirm some detail or other. His story petered out when he fainted in the workshop in the bunker.

'Do you have any idea why Rose Crawford would want to do this to either of you?'

Neither of them replied.

'Ms Kaur Nagra, when I got into the workshop last night, you were shouting something about not being in the car. That you weren't responsible. What did you mean by that?' Sara asked.

The lawyer put her notepad on Wilkins's bed and folded her hands primly in her lap. 'You've worked out who Rose Crawford really is, haven't you?'

'Lily Kerr's mother?' suggested Hudson. 'The mother of the art student that was knocked off her bicycle by a car twelve years ago.'

'Exactly so,' agreed Kaur Nagra. 'The matter was, of course, investigated by your estimable force at the time. The driver of the car was held to be only partly responsible, as the cyclist had no lights on.'

Wilkins shifted in his bed.

'Are you aware how bad Lily Kerr's injuries were?'

'We knew she had ended up in Stoke Mandeville. One of your investigating officers made sure to tell us that.'

'Lily died about a year ago,' said Sara. 'After many years of pain and distress. Crawford nursed her in her final years.'

'I can't imagine anything worse,' said the lawyer. 'I have two children myself.'

They all waited for one of the others to speak. A strained silence filled the room. Sara watched Kaur Nagra struggling against all her barrister's instincts not to fill the gap.

'It was my fault.' Wilkins burst out. 'I'd been drinking, but I insisted on driving. After it happened, I was terrified, so I forced the others to say Joe had been driving because I knew he hadn't had any booze.'

He sank back into his pillows, tears trickling down his face.

'Are you prepared to make that an official statement?' asked Hudson. Wilkins muttered that he would.

'There you have it,' said Kaur Nagra. 'I don't know what you will do about my client and this historic case. Given my connection to the group, I will have to pass any necessary defence to a colleague. I'll advise you who in a couple of days. I would also like to make a statement regarding the accident myself, which may provide you with further information.'

Wilkins looked at her with a horrified expression. 'You promised!'

'I know,' said Kaur Nagra. 'Legally, I can't represent you now. Not to mention the trouble I'm going to be in, when the Law Society find out that I kept quiet about my prior knowledge. Besides, Dominic, as far as I can see, your actions that night caused this poor mother to slowly go mad with grief. Two of our friends have paid the price of your secrecy. You should have owned up years ago. You disgust me.'

'We'll arrange for DS Hirst to take your statement later this morning,' said Hudson. Sara handed Kaur Nagra her card, which she tucked into her handbag with her notepad and pen. Collecting her coat from the back of her chair, the lawyer stood.

'I'll book a time later this week if you will still be here,' said Sara.

'I will be. Let me know when is convenient. You should be aware—' Kaur Nagra turned to Hudson — 'that whatever you decide to do in terms of charging Rose Crawford, I will be arranging her defence throughout. Pro bono.'

Then she walked swiftly out of the room, leaving Wilkins sobbing into his pillow.

CHAPTER 60

Rose had no idea where she was or what the time might have been when her eyes fluttered open. Somewhere down a long tunnel, she could hear a woman's voice calling her name. It took effort to focus on the sound. Her mind crept towards it as the light shaped the figure leaning over her.

'Rose?' asked the woman. 'Can you hear me?'

She could. She tried to speak. Her mouth was dry, her lips cracked and painful. Something was lying across her face. Rose didn't feel up to the effort. *Why bother?* said a voice in her head. Wishing she could slip back into unconsciousness, Rose felt the woman pat her hand softly.

'That's right,' the nurse said. 'Come back to us.'

Then it all came crashing in. The workshop. Dom Wilkins tied to the sculpture, the razor in her hand. The bonus of that woman under the table, just waiting for the sweet caress of the blade. Had she managed it?

No, her mind jeered. *You failed. They escaped.*

With a cry of anguish that sounded like a frog croaking, she tried to sit up. There was little energy in her limbs, no matter how hard she bent her will to them.

Underneath her back, the bed began to rise. 'Let's sit you up,' said the nurse. Her view of the ward changed. 'Is that better?'

A female police officer in uniform stood just outside the cubicle door, watching her. Letting her unburned arm wander over her body, Rose felt tubes and cannulas. She tried to tug at one.

The nurse grabbed her wandering fingers. 'It's there to help, my lovely,' she said. 'Leave it be.'

Rose drifted. Someone brought her a cup of tea. She tried to drink it. Later a doctor came to inspect her, chatted to her, made notes on a chart on a clipboard. She grunted in reply. Then she slept.

There were several more times like these. Were they days or hours? She couldn't tell. All she knew was that everyone seemed pleased with her progress except herself. Rose simply had no reason to live and resented the effort these people were putting into keeping her from the ultimate oblivion.

Her voice returned. The cups of tea were joined by bowls of soup, then sandwiches, then an actual meal. She toyed with the mashed potato, swallowing a few mouthfuls to please the pretty nurse. Her memory was returning and with it the full force of her failure.

Finally, there came a morning when she woke to find three women and a man waiting to talk to her. A different uniformed officer stood outside the room. The first woman Rose recognised as the detective sergeant who had been looking into Taryn's death. Had she figured it out now? There was the lawyer, the London bitch, who somehow seemed to be on her side now. Why? Kaur Nagra introduced the man, explaining that he would be representing Rose. The third woman seemed to be in charge of them all. She had a hard face.

'Are you happy to talk to us?' this woman asked. They had all given Rose their names, but she couldn't hold them in her memory. The woman produced a mobile recorder, which she placed on the bed and turned on. Then she said something about being under caution which Rose couldn't comprehend.

'Happy? Not really. Why is there a policeman out there?'

The London lawyer leaned forward and explained that she was under guard as a suspect in a murder inquiry.

Rose would have laughed if she could. 'All right. What do you want?'

The DS pulled up her chair closely to speak with Rose more softly. 'Rose, we've been to your house. We've found the llamas and the computer, the drugs and the information on the boards. We know what you've done. Do you understand?'

'Not my Lily's bedroom.' She struggled to sit up, anxious that the bedroom might have been ripped apart.

'It's okay, Rose,' said the DS. 'We were respectful.'

Rose subsided. 'Well?'

'We know what you've done. We even think we know why you did this. Can you fill in the gaps?'

'What gaps?'

'Was it you that ran down Dominic Wilkins five years ago?'

Rose nodded. The memory of that dark evening slammed into her mind. Of having to turn the car around and drive at him a second time because she had failed the first time. She shifted on the bed.

'Why?'

'He ran down my Lily.' They didn't need to know any more than that.

'How did you know?'

'You don't know grief, do you?' Rose glared at the DS, who waited. 'We went through all that hideousness when she was injured. Visits by you lot, endless questions and investigations . . . and for what? They got away with it. I've been watching the lot of them ever since.'

'Why then? It was just after your husband passed away.'

Rose grunted. 'Yes. Cancer officially, but it was a broken heart. My mother was also dying and Lily came back to live with me. I thought it was my only chance to get at one of them.'

'But it wasn't?'

'Four years, I nursed my baby. While they got prizes and jobs and medals. And jobs where I worked. Karma opened the door for me.'

DS Hirst nodded. 'How did you get Joe Summerhill into that urn at Barnham Parva Hall?'

Rose smiled at the memory of her cunning. 'People don't suspect you when you reach my age. They'll give you a hand because they think you're helpless. I got chatty with Joe during the lunch breaks. Asked him to come to help me in the garden.'

'And he did?'

'Oh, yes. It was easy. I gave him a cup of tea.'

'With the GHB in it?'

'Yes. Then I locked him in the shed. Kept him drugged for two days when I knew the Hall would be empty at night.'

'The evening of the exhibition party?'

'I helped them get it started, then left early. After that, it was just a case of persuading Joe that I was trying to help him.'

'You drove him to the Hall and got him to climb those museum steps?'

'I bought an extra set. Kept them in my shed until I needed them.'

'Why now?'

'I'd been waiting for my chance for years. Then my neighbours went away for five months, and the opportunities all lined up. Perfect.'

'And Taryn? How did you do that?'

'I put the drops in the bottle of wine in the kitchen. It was already open. I thought she might drink it. Or the others might.'

'It was your suggestion the others should call the doctor?' Sara was keeping her voice steady and low.

'Yes. In case she didn't drink the wine. I stole a set of keys before I left and went back in the middle of the night. I didn't even have to persuade her to come downstairs. She heard me, came down to see who it was, though she was confused by whatever she had taken. I tied her to the chair.'

'How did you know that Dom was actually driving the car?'

Rose sneered. 'I saw them at the court. The day Joe Summerhill was being prosecuted. Dom was so worried that Joe might break down and tell the truth, he didn't notice me. Had him pinned up against the wall, snarling at him.'

Kaur Nagra let out a gasp.

'And then there you were.' Rose's eyes fixed on the lawyer. 'Telling Joe what to say, sending Dom out of the building to clear the air. Coaching them so they could get away with it.'

'I was only trying to help my friends,' said Kaur Nagra.

'One hundred and fifty pounds,' Rose screamed, sitting up in the bed. 'They fined him one hundred and fifty pounds. That was all my daughter's future was worth—'

Rose slumped back against her pillows, panting to catch her breath. The effort of it all was getting too much for her now. Besides, she thought bitterly, who cared anyway?

'Thank you, Rose,' said the DS. 'There's a couple of other things I still don't understand. Why go to all the trouble of collecting and posing those toy llamas?'

'Collecting the toys was easy. I knew Joe was alone in the house that weekend. I just took his keys and went there after I'd knocked him out. Turned the place upside down to find the stupid thing. Taryn left hers on the mantelpiece when I took her home that afternoon.'

'And the poses? Leaving the new toys?'

'That was a message from Lily. They sacrificed her life, her talent, with their arrogance and lies. I sacrificed them in return, each one looking like an artwork that Lily could have bettered if she had been allowed. It was easy enough to choose. I walk past them every day.'

'It was Lily's death that sparked all this?'

'Lily's death set me free to get justice for her.' Rose became agitated. She grabbed the DS's hand to pull her closer. 'I had to do it. Had to help her. She kept asking me with her eyes.'

284

On the edge of her vision, Rose saw the nurse step in to intervene. The DS and the hard-faced woman moved away, but the lawyer leaned over her.

'Don't worry, Rose,' Kaur Nagra whispered. 'We're going to look after you now. We'll fight them all the way.'

When the room went quiet, Rose dozed for a while. She was woken by a commotion of doctors and nurses with an injured patient newly brought in. He was yelling and struggling as they tried to get him into a bed at the far end of the ward. The uniformed officer that had been standing outside her door had gone to help them. There were six cubicles, and Rose was nearest the door on one side. No one was watching.

With a sweep, Rose ripped all the tubes and cannulas out of her body. Grunting with the pain and effort, she swung out of bed, placing her bare feet on the cold floor. Her numbed legs could hardly support her weight. Gasping in short agonising breaths and shuffling as quickly as she could, Rose made it into the corridor outside the ward. Blood ran from her arms and nose where she had ripped out the needles and tubes.

She looked left and right, checking the signs. *Café and East Atrium*, an arrow pointed. Rose worked her way along the corridor, clinging to a handrail. She was exhausted but determined. There was no point anymore. It was over. She had confessed, done all she could to bring an end to her own grief and revenge Lily's years of agony.

The corridor opened out into the atrium. She was three storeys up. That should do it.

Frantic voices were calling her name. People were running towards her, their shoes clattering on the vinyl floor tiles.

There was nothing else left. Rose put her hands on the metal barrier and leaned out over the atrium space beneath.

CHAPTER 61

Rose Crawford's house had indeed been a treasure trove. They had found all the evidence they needed to get a conviction, even without DNA results. The team also had those. With Rose's voluntary swab, they could place her at the scene of the burned-out van. The black hat Noble had spotted was covered in her blood. They also found it at Joe Summerhill's house, where she had ransacked his room. They had gone through her things in the office at work and found the painkillers she had been taking. This information had helped the doctors save Rose's life. There was also a fourth new llama, still in its packaging. Presumably, this had been for Junina Kaur Nagra.

Not that any of it mattered in the end. They had waited a week for Rose to recover enough for them to talk to her. If the rest of the team was surprised at Rose's confession, Sara wasn't. She had sat closest to the woman and felt the sense from her that there was nothing left to lose. Rose had wanted someone to know why.

By some miracle or twist of karma, Rose didn't die when she had launched herself off the top floor onto the marble pavement of the atrium beneath. Her injuries were severe, and this time she remained in her coma, unresponsive and indifferent. Junina Kaur Nagra's colleague had been appointed as Rose's legal guardian. Now it would be up to him when the machines would be turned off. Sara strongly suspected that Kaur Nagra would have some sway with him, albeit unofficially.

'I doubt we will ever be able to charge Crawford with anything,' said Hudson on Friday morning, two weeks later.

'Would you want to?' asked Sara. 'I think Kaur Nagra was right about her being mad with grief.'

'That's true. She'd end up in Broadmoor or somewhere like it. But the other two didn't deserve to die like that, did they?'

Sara knew her sense of justice was offended on behalf of the parents now mourning the loss of their children. She was grateful that it wasn't her job to sit in moral judgement.

'Have you decided about Dom Wilkins?' Sara asked. They were hefting the desks back into their original informal pattern. Maintenance were measuring up for a second glass office next to Hudson's room to keep DI Edwards happy.

'I added the confessions to the file and sent it to the CPS,' replied Hudson. 'It's up to them now. Shall we leave the coffee station where it is? What about Aggie's desk?'

'Maybe we should put her opposite Bowen,' suggested Sara.

Aggie and Bowen had been missing from the office on several occasions recently. They were no longer hiding their relationship. Sara was waiting to see how that played out with the senior management.

'Has Aggie spoken to you recently?' she asked Hudson.

'What about?' The DCI looked puzzled. 'Has she got a problem?'

'No. Far from it.' Sara smiled. 'She's applied to start an Open University degree. In art history, apparently. Did you know?'

Hudson looked impressed. 'She didn't say. That's great news. Good for her.'

They finished moving the desks, and Sara organised drinks for them both. As she put Hudson's camomile tea on the desk, her boss pointed at the chair.

'Sit for a minute,' she said. 'And close the door before you do.'

Sara did what she was told, wondering what was coming. Since they had solved the worst case they'd tackled in years, the team had been rubbing along nicely. Hudson was learning to trust their strengths and idiosyncrasies.

'What you say about Aggie makes me think about exams.' Hudson sipped at the urine-coloured liquid with every sign of enjoyment. 'Are you happy as you are?'

'Very much so.' Sara tried to keep the wariness out of her voice.

'I've been very impressed by your work and the intelligence that you bring to it. I wondered if you've ever thought about going for your inspector exams?'

Sara didn't answer. Was this the DCI trying to get rid of her?

Hudson was watching her carefully. 'When I did the shake-down briefing with DC Bowen, he was very impressed with the way you took charge that night at the gallery.'

'Bowen said that, did he?' There had been another thawing of attitude since Sara had called him Mike in the crisis. He had subsequently told her that she could call him by his Christian name if she liked. Bowen had taken to calling her Saz, which she was less keen on. She knew he only did it to annoy her.

'Of course, if you were successful, you might have to move department or even forces to get a posting.'

That would mean leaving her cottage. Sara didn't fancy that. She was just getting used to the pace of life here. She'd be damned before she let Hudson drive her out.

'I'll think about it.'

'No pressure,' said Hudson. 'I'd hate to lose such a good officer, but I certainly don't want to stand in your way.'

Sara returned to her desk, now back in its old position by the draughty window. Just when she had been getting used to Hudson, now she was beginning to doubt her motives again. Which was a pain in the arse, to say the least.

Bowen and Aggie appeared from another of their mysterious trips, coming through the office door holding hands.

'We've got an announcement to make,' said Bowen. He was swinging his hand, and Aggie's with it. 'Aggie and I have some news.'

The team turned to look at them. Even Hudson stepped to her office door and leaned on the jamb.

'We've been in conversation with personnel for a few days,' said Aggie. 'You know that we were worried that people would find out that Mike and I were in a relationship?'

She stopped, a blush spreading across her face.

Bowen smiled and pecked her on the cheek. 'We took your advice, Sara,' he said. 'We spoke to them about it, and they've finally said that it's fine. It doesn't contravene any rules.'

'So, we are officially moving in together at the weekend.' Aggie went to pull away from Bowen, but he held tightly onto her hand. 'I've got the celebration cake.'

'Before you get that out, there's something I want to ask you.' Bowen fumbled in his pocket, then dropped down on one knee. 'Well? Will you make it truly official?'

They all held their breath.

'Oh, yes,' said Aggie. Her grin could have run a power station. 'Of course.'

The team exploded with cheers.

* * *

It was neither dark nor cold when Sara reached her cottage. She still felt the need to light the fire. For comfort, she supposed.

I'm the odd one out now, Sara thought as she sorted out the grate. Bowen and Aggie were officially engaged. So were her mother and Javed. That made two weddings to go to where she wouldn't have a plus-one. She knew that DC Noble had a long-term girlfriend despite his shy nature. Even Edwards appeared to be taking the magenta-haired art tutor out for dinner.

'Just me and Hudson, then,' she said. Not that she knew Hudson's personal status. She didn't know her well enough to ask yet, and the DCI never spoke about her home life.

A knock at her front door brought her out of her musings.

Please don't let it be Chris. She hadn't heard from him since she had sent him that text telling him to go fuck himself.

It was her neighbour, Gilly, with her two grandkids in tow. They were laden with boxes and a pet carrier. 'Can we come in?'

They crowded into the small living room, the girl and boy giggling conspiratorially.

'You can say no, but I really hope you won't.' Gilly put the pet carrier on the floor, from which sounded a small mew. 'Unless you're allergic. Oh goodness, I didn't think of that. Look, my daughter's cat has had a litter, and I know you've been feeling a bit lonely lately.'

She had. She didn't realise it had been so obvious. Sara had also forgotten that Gilly's daughter bred Siamese cats and put them into shows.

'I thought you might like some company that wasn't too demanding. Not like that boyfriend of yours. Her name is Linthwaite Pearl Princess, better known as Tilly. She's a seal point Siamese, is five months old and in need of a home.'

'Isn't she worth money?'

Gilly shook her head. 'Your well-being is worth more than her breed fee. Show Sara what you've got.'

The two grandchildren ripped open the boxes they had been carrying. It was a complete cat-care kit, right down to the litter for the litter box.

'I can see you're not taken with the idea,' said Gilly. She gathered up the two youngsters. 'Why not just give it a night or two. Don't let her out yet. She won't know where to come back to. Feed her, and she'll love you.'

She hustled the little ones outside. The mew in the pet carrier got stronger and sounded a bit irritated. Sara lifted the carrier onto the sofa and peered in.

A pale face with a dark brown mask and ears peered back at her. The eyes were cerulean blue.

The kitten spoke again. It definitely sounded like swearing. It tried to stand up in the carrier, revealing chocolate-brown paws.

'All right, all right.' Sara opened the carrier and let it out. 'Let's see how this goes.'

Later, after tidying up the mess of boxes, putting down the litter tray and water bowl, then feeding both of them, Sara settled on the sofa to watch Tilly explore the house.

'Is this what I've become then?' she asked Tilly. 'Am I a hopeless case? The eternal singleton? A mad cat lady?'

The kitten jumped up beside her and nestled on Sara's lap. Her purr was ridiculously loud for such a small creature. Her eyes began to close trustingly.

'Perhaps I am,' she said, stroking the silky fur. 'Maybe life will be simpler this way.'

THE END

ACKNOWLEDGEMENTS

I would like to thank Antony Dunford for his beta readings and notes. Our year cohort on the MA Creative Writing course are still together as a support group, and without the Crime Gang 17 I wouldn't be here today. My special thanks to Clive Forbes, a former DI, for his police procedural advice and thoughts on whodunnit. Any incorrect procedures are there because I made an executive author's decision (or mistake!).

My gratitude goes to Jasper Joffe for welcoming me to Joffe Books. It means more than I can say to belong to this fantastic publishing house. I am grateful to all the other authors and the staff who are so supportive and generous with their time. I am proud to be a member of this wonderful band. My special thanks to Emma Grundy Haigh, Cat Phipps, and Matthew Grundy Haigh all of whom have helped me improve the novel with their wonderful suggestions, edits and weeding out of random punctuation. My grateful thanks to the rest of the Joffe Books team for all your work, from organising blog tours to spending time on reviews.

Last but not least, my family. My husband, Rhett, and my daughters, Gwyn and Ellie. We have had some scary moments during the pandemic, especially on the health front. Without your support and love I could not have kept writing.

Thank you for reading this book.

If you enjoyed it please leave feedback on Amazon or Goodreads, and if there is anything we missed or you have a question about, then please get in touch. We appreciate you choosing our book.

Founded in 2014 in Shoreditch, London, we at Joffe Books pride ourselves on our history of innovative publishing. We were thrilled to be shortlisted for Independent Publisher of the Year at the British Book Awards.

www.joffebooks.com

We're very grateful to eagle-eyed readers who take the time to contact us. Please send any errors you find to corrections@joffebooks.com. We'll get them fixed ASAP.

Ingram Content Group UK Ltd.
Milton Keynes UK
UKHW040717280623
424179UK00004B/265

9 781804 054000